GOTHIC NOVELS

GOTHIC NOVELS

Advisory Editor:
Dr. Sir Devendra P. Varma

THE

RECESS

OR

A TALE OF OTHER TIMES

Volume 3

SOPHIA LEE

Foreword by J. M. S. Tompkins

Introduction by Devendra P. Varma

ARNO PRESS

A New York Times Company

in cooperation with

McGRATH PUBLISHING COMPANY

New York—1972

Reprint Edition 1972 by Arno Press Inc.

Special Contents Copyright © 1972 by Devendra P. Varma

LC#   77-131325
ISBN 0-405-00806-6

Gothic Novels
ISBN for complete set: 0-405-00800-7
See last page of this volume for titles.

Manufactured in the United States of America

THE

RECESS;

OR, A

TALE OF OTHER TIMES.

THE

RECESS;

OR, A

TALE OF OTHER TIMES.

BY THE AUTHOR

OF THE

CHAPTER OF ACCIDENTS.

———————

" Are not thefe Woods
" More free from peril than the envious Court?
" Here feel we but the penalty of Adam
" The feafons' difference."

———————

VOL. III.

———————

LONDON:
Printed for T. CADELL, in the Strand.
M.DCC.LXXXV.

ERRATA of the FIRST VOLUME.

Page 124, l. 19, *for* reproached, *read* reproach.
196, l. 3, *for* pair, *read* plain.
227, l. 21, *for* Sydney, *read* Sydney's.

ERRATA of the SECOND VOLUME.

Page 22, l. 8, *for* out, *read* our.
94, l. 16, *for* was, *read* were.
113, l. 2, *after* each other *add* a comma.
121, l. 5, *for* as, *read* a.
159, l. 8, *for* perusing, *read* preserving.
186, *for* this embryo rival that, *read* that this embryo rival.
213, l. 4, *for* no, *read* not.
286, l. 21, *for* obliterated, *read* obliterate.

THE

RECESS, &c.

WHEN the sick languor of the faintings gave place to reflection, I found myself in my own bed; whither I understood I had been conveyed by the orders of Lord Arlington, as soon as the wound was staunched:---his proved so slight that it left him no pretence for apprehension. Eagerly I enquired for Lady Pembroke, when to my inexpressible rage and astonishment I was informed, she had been turned from my door, whither friendship led her to venture a re-

　　　　pulse.

pulfe. The immaculate character of that admirable woman I thought even Lord Arlington would have refpected; but without deigning to inform himfelf of the real circumftances of the unforefeen interview he had fo dreadfully interrupted, by this rude implication he treated two of the moft eftimable and diftinguifhed perfons in the kingdom as abettors, if not contrivers, of his difhonor.----The little blood left in my veins turned to gall at the idea. I watched an opportunity to tear away the bandages; and difdainfully refigning myfelf to a premature fate, endeavoured to forget the generous hearts this rafh action would pierce.----The awful God whofe juftice I thus queftioned, ftill extended to me his mercy----my dangerous fituation was difcovered in time by my careful attendants, who infinitely more attached to me than their Lord, ufed every means to prolong the life he, perhaps, wifhed at its period.

In the cruel ftate of mind which dictated this defperate refolution, it proved
a me-

a melancholy advantage; as the injury now fell on my conftitution only, and my intellects efcaped. It was many months ere I had ftrength to crofs a room, or fpirits to venture a queftion----during this memorable interval I called together every enfeebled power, and placing my confci-ence as umpire between myfelf and Lord Arlington, fixed and afcertained the rights of either. Convicted even by my own heart of imprudence, I wondered not he conftrued error into guilt; and while thus cool offered him every vindication of my innocence he could reafonably de-fire: but Lord Arlington was the flave of paffion and caprice, and not having firmnefs of foul to form, or fix, a judg-ment, followed through years with in-vincible obftinacy the impreffion of the firft moment.----From this period he ever treated me as an artful woman, whofe licentious conduct had obliged him to rifque his life in vain defence of that honor already fullied, and loft in my

perfon;

person; nor did he affect to assert his legal rights from any other reason than to separate me from Lord Essex. This conduct, and the misrepresentations of Lady Essex, blazed the fatal incident throughout the Court, and fixed a stain on my character, time could never erase.---happily that stain reached not my person or my heart, and an injustice so aggravating on the part of Lord Arlington, entitled me to forgive the little error in myself which occasioned it.

In this conjuncture I once more turned my tearful eyes every way around in search of a protector to interfere between me, and a fate alike unmerited and severe.---Alas! there was not a human being virtue allowed me to call to my aid; and I exercised the faculties Heaven had so unexpectedly blessed me with, by resolving to suffer with patience.

Elizabeth Vernon (our old companion) the fair and gentle cousin of Lord Essex, resolved if possible to see me---she addressed

dreffed Lord Arlington, and demanded
that privilege; the favor fhe held with
the Queen hindered him from denying
a requeft he granted with the utmoft reluctance. That fweet girl bathed me in the
tears of innocence and affection---fhe told
me the fear left his prefence fhould incenfe
Lord Arlington to further brutality, had
induced Effex, when I loft my fenfes, to
withdraw from a fcene which rent his
very heart---the fame reafon ftill obliged
him to remain at a diftance.---That during the long and dire uncertainty attending my illnefs; he had fcarcely breathed---
his own foul continually told him how
pure mine was. Fancy prefented me to
him forever, pale, fpeechlefs, expiring,
my fad eyes rivetted on his with a tendernefs death itfelf could not extinguifh:
however guiltlefs of my blood, every
drop which oozed from my veins feemed
to congeal on his heart; in fine, that almoft deified by my fufferings, and his
fenfe of them, I reigned alone in his affections, which were from this moment

con-

confecrated to me by a moft convincing
proof. Having ufed the utmoft art and
diligence to difcover how Lord Arlington
fo foon became apprized of his fecret return to England, and a meeting fo un-
planned, and fudden, as to interrupt it
almoft immediately, though fuppofed to
be as far off as Greenwich ; Lord Effex
learnt that his Mafter of the Horfe being
among the domeftics he brought with
him to Pembroke Houfe, had quitted it
as foon as he alighted, and haftened to
Greenwich in fearch of a girl attending
on Lady Effex, of whom he was enamor-
ed; through her means her Lady became
likewife acquainted with his fecret arrival without knowing its motive. That
fufpicious woman had already remarked
Lord Arlington was among the bridal
train, and in his hearing publifhed the
return of her Lord, with all her own injurious furmifes.---ill fortune for once had
given them the colour of truth, and Lord
Arlington needed no more than the hint
to make him mount the fwifteft horfe and

fly

fly to satisfy himself.---Lady Essex was quickly informed of an incident she ought to have foreseen, and giving way to another extravagance, passionately conjured every friend she met to follow, and prevent the conflict to which her Lord now stood exposed---but when could friendship keep pace with love and vengeance? The straggling mediators arrived only time enough to witness the event no human power could guard against. Incensed beyond all bounds at the conduct of his Lady, the rash Essex took the only step wanting to my ruin. Determined to make her share the misery she had occasioned, he parted with her at once and forever---in vain were all her subsequent vows of sorrow and repentance---in vain had she from that moment indulged hopes of his cooling and conciliating ---his temper till this fatal period, no less yielding than fiery, now assumed a cold and philosophic sternness; in fine, that the grief and disappointment to which Lady Essex resigned herself would severely punish her

                                    unjust

unjuſt ſuſpicions, and ere long releaſe
her Lord from the ill-judged bondage
he had hitherto groaned ſo impatiently
under."

The fair Elizabeth thus ended her recital, which was ſo clear, conciſe, and
affecting, that I could not avoid taxing
her with being the emiſſary of her couſin;
her bluſhes acquitted her, and beſpoke a
ſecret, time ſoon explained. She was
ſecretly beloved by the gallant Southampton, that heroic friend who was only
leſs attached to Eſſex than myſelf, and
from him had learnt the various particulars public report could not appriſe her
of.---I held myſelf infinitely indebted to
her friendſhip, and through her means
ſent that farewell to Lady Pembroke I
was not allowed to pronounce.

It had been but too obvious through
her whole recital, that I was totally the
victim of calumny, nor could any human
power now juſtify me.---I had been found
in the arms of Eſſex---the fact was indubitable, the true cauſe of that fatal impulſe
not likely to be credited, even when re-
peated.

peated. My youth, my wound, and
my paſt conduct, blended the raſh judgment of the many with compaſſion, but
the moſt liberal-minded ventured not to
acquit me. Thoſe impaſſioned vindica-
tions the conſcious ſoul of Eſſex offered,
were always conſidered as a mere point of
honor in him, and no leſs neceſſary to
his own juſtification than mine, and thus
only ſerved to ſtamp guilt on both.---Oh,
misjudging world, how ſeverely on the
moſt ſuperficial obſervation doſt thou
venture to decide!---let the barbed arrow of misfortune reſt in the boſom it
has wounded, nor by inhumanly tearing
it out to diſcover whence it came, rack
the heart already broken.

Defamed, dejected, and forgotten by
all but the generous ſiſters of the Sydney
family, I followed, once more, my fate in
Lord Arlington; and reached again that
Abbey deſtined alike to entomb me in
playful childhood, and in blaſted youth---
the ſame imperious will which had deſtroyed me, had deprived that venerable
manſion of its ſweet, its ſolitary charms---
the

the hallowed ſpot where once the ivied
trophies of time bound up the defaced
ones of religion, preſented nothing now
but a bare and barren level; and the
lofty woods which ſo long protected alike
the living and the dead, had wholly given
place to infant plantations, through the
thinneſs of which the weary eye every
where pierced: I turned with diſguſt
from the deſolated ſcene, and locking
myſelf up in the remoteſt, and moſt
gloomy chamber of the Abbey, ſpent my
life in meditating on my every loſs.

Lord Arlington now valuing me only
as the appendage of his pride, conſoled
himſelf for my undiſſembled averſion,
and cared not what employed me, provided I was yet his legal priſoner.---
Alas, I had no longer reſolution to reſt
my hopes on any object---to form any
ſubordinate deſign, or to reap any ſubordinate pleaſure. The poor children
ſtill ſupported by my bounty, no more
touched the lute in my preſence---that
over which my own fingers once wandered
with the wild elegance of untried youth,
now

now ufelefs and unftrung, hung up, an emblem of the difcordant foul of its owner. Tafte, genius, and fcience, thofe rich columes with which enthufiaftic fancy erects in peaceful minds a thoufand light aerial ftructures, deep funk, and broken in my heart, prefented to the mental eye a ruin more terrible than the nobleft fpeculation ever paufed over.----Mifan-thropy, black-vifaged mifanthropy, reign-ed there like a folitary favage, uncon-fcious of the value of thofe treafures his rude hand every day more and more de-faced.

I was roufed one night with the infor-mation that a favorite fervant of Lord Ar-lington's, who had long languifhed in a confumption, now found himfelf at the point of death, and importunately de-manded to fpeak with me---but ill-dif-pofed at this feafon even to the gentle offices of humanity, and convinced he could have nothing to impart I fhould think of confequence, I rejected the re-queft; but finding his Lord was inebri-ated beyond the power of comprehend-
ing

ing him, on being again follicited, I rofe,
and accompanied by a maid who loved
me, entered the fick man's chamber.---
I caſt a harſh and cold glance round, and
hardly heard the thanks he gave me---
having diſmiſſed all the ſervants except
the maid I mentioned, I prepared to liſten
to him, imagining ſome matter relative to
his office of chief bailiff and ſurveyor,
alone, could thus diſturb his laſt hours.---
" Lady, ſaid he, in the hollow broken
voice of approaching diſſolution, I could
not have departed in peace had you not
beſtowed this indulgence---pardon me, I
beſeech you, for propoſing to myLord the
deſtruction of thoſe ruins I have ſince
ſeen too plainly your heart was ever wrapt
in---alas, that propoſal coſts me my life.
---Condeſcend too to liſten to a ſecret
which continually drags back my ſoul
when ſtriving to quit her dungeon---my
crime perhaps brings with it a ſufficient
puniſhment.——In removing the rubbiſh
of the artificial hermit's cell, in compliance with the directions of my Lord, I
one day ſaw a common laborer turn up
ſomething

fomething which tried his whole ftrength,
when cafting a quick and fearful glance
around, he covered it with earth.   I
difpatched the men in hearing to another
part, and feizing the arm of him I had
watched, I infifted on feeing what he had
endeavoured to conceal---it proved to be
a fmall iron cheft ftrongly faftened---I
agreed with him to convey it away till
the evening, when he might rejoin me, and
we would open it and divide the contents
together.   He yielded rather to neceffity
than choice, and I took the cafket with
a purpofe God has feverely punifhed---
the many keys intrufted to my care fupplied one which immediately opened it;
under a number of papers and trifles of
no value, I found a large fum in gold,
and a few jewels---as I knew my partner in the difcovery had remarked that
the cheft was heavy; in the room of the
gold and jewels, I fubftituted an iron
crucifix, and many rufty keys; then locking the cafket, waited anxioufly for the
evening.   The poor laborer feeing me
return, wiftfully examined my features,
but

but not daring to exprefs the doubt vifible in his own, expected in filence the
deciding hour. I fuffered him to take
infinite pains to break open a cheft I was
confcious would not repay the labor---
great was the poor wretch's difappoint-
ment when he emptied it---I affected the
fame chagrin; but turning over the papers, I offered to give him twenty nobles;
a fure proof, had he reflected a fingle
moment, that I muft have wronged him:
he readily accepted this propofal, and at
my defire, promifed never to mention
the incident; then with much apparent
gratitude departed. Eagerly I replaced
my guilty gains, and fecretly refolved to
take an early opportunity of quitting my
Lord to commence builder in London;
but fear did not fuffer me for a time to
venture this meafure; alas, I have wanted
health fince to do any thing---from this
moment, peace, appetite, and reft, have
fled me---if worn out with watching, I
dropt into a flumber, the idea that my
treafure was ftolen, has made me often
ftart up, and regardlefs of the cold fweat

the

the mere apprehenfion has produced, I have
flown in the dead of night to convince
myfelf it was fafe—imaginary whifpers
have ever been near my bed, and uncertain
forms have glided through my chamber—
the dawn of day never gave me relief,
every eye feemed to dive into my fecret,
and every hand to be intent on impo-
verifhing me—in a word, Lady, to this
fad moment it has prematurely brought
me; for many months doubtful whether
I fhould furvive, I have been confidering
how to beftow that wealth I could no
longer hope to enjoy---the poor man I
fo bafely defrauded of it, perifhed a fhort
time after by the fall of a pillar, and
reftitution to him can never be made.
It came into my head this evening, that
you were faid to have been brought up
in thefe ruins; certainly I had often feen
you walk and weep on the very fpot
where this cheft was found; perhaps in
giving it to you I only reftore it to the
right owner; accept it, Madam, and
fwear you will never difcover the gift to
my Lord."——This requeft appeared a
needlefs

needleſs injunction, if the treaſure had
not been obtained by defrauding Lord
Arlington; and though perhaps I ſhould
have been ſilent through choice, I thought
it beneath me to engage to be ſo—finding me pauſe, he continued, " fear not
any ill deſign in this requeſt, Madam,
you will one day be glad you complied
with it, and for your own ſake alone is it
propoſed; the hand of my Lord is grudg-
ing—yours bounteous as that of heaven.—
Do not rob yourſelf of the means to be
liberal which now are offered to you—yet
on no other condition than the vow of
ſilence will I give it up." A ſtrange deſire to examine the papers, more than any
I felt for the money, made me at laſt ac-
quieſce. My maid by his direction, drew
the iron cheſt from an obſcure corner, and
emptied it of both gold, jewels, and papers,
which ſhe and I divided, and with ſome
difficulty concealed till we reached my
apartment---he ſeemed only to have lived
to make this diſcovery, a..d a few hours
after expiated his ſin with his life.

While

While he ſtrove to impreſs my mind
with the neceſſity of concealing the ad-
venture, I pondered deeply over it; not
eaſily diſcerning how I ſhould interpret
this ſtrange ordination of providence;
it at laſt occurred to me the treaſure
might be put into my hands for the aſſiſtance and comfort of my ſiſter---how
did I know whether ſhe was not even then
haſtening towards me, perhaps impoveriſhed, certainly diſtreſſed ?---Oh, how
conſolatory ſhould I find it to miniſter
to her external wants, though thoſe of her
heart ſhould be beyond my power of com-
forting! The contempt I felt for Lord
Arlington was rooted too deep to admit
of my thus applying his fortune, had I
been the unlimited miſtreſs of it; I
therefore ſaw a degree of wiſdom and
propriety in receiving and ſecreting a
gift heaven ſeemed ſo ſtrangely to put
into my hands, as if it were to forerun
ſome yet unknown incident.

The papers conſiſted chiefly of the
correſpondence between Mrs. Marlow and

Father Anthony, while yet they were lovers, and after the cruel difcovery which
annulled the nominal union---I perufed
thefe invaluable epiftles with pulfations
of tendernefs I lately thought myfelf incapable of; they recalled me to life and
fenfibility, and I gathered fortitude from
thofe who now were duft; I raifed my
eyes to heaven in fearch of their pure
tranflated fouls, and wandering from planet to planet, fancied there muft be one
peculiarly allotted to lovers now no longer unhappy---A thoufand trifles whofe
value muft ever be ideal and local, were
preferved with thefe letters: cyphers,
hair, fonnets, dear perpetuators of thofe
bright hours of youth we look back on
with pleafure to the lateft moment of
decaying life. I kiffed the innocent re-
liques of fuch an unhappy attachment
with devout regard, and held them not
the leaft part of my legacy.

Time diffipated the flattering illufion
which led me to expect my fifter---my
mind funk into its ufual inertitude,
                                    and

nnd the acquisition remained, if not forgotten, at least neglected.

From this profound stupor I was at
last roused as by an earthquake---Lord
Arlington in hunting fell from his horse,
and breaking some blood-vessel, was
brought home to appearance lifeless---
conscience and humanity called on me to
forget my injuries; I made every effort
to save him, and for a time he appeared
to mend; but the incurable habit of
inebriety he even at this period indulged,
defeated both care and medicine; and
after enduring a series of sufferings which
annihilated my sense of wrong, he expired
in the prime of his days.

Good heaven, what a transition did
this event make in my life!---habituated
to slavery---accustomed to suppose Lord
Arlington destined to survive me, I beheld this incredible revolution with mute
surprise---the horror of his sufferings gave
way, when they ceased, to the sweet idea
of liberty---liberty, sighed out my weary
heart, ah! to what purpose is mine now

reftored? I beheld myfelf in the fituation
of a criminal, whofe fhackles are ftruck off
only to launch him into the immenfe
ocean in a little boat, without rudder,
oars, or fuftenance—where could I find a
hope to reft on? alone in the vaft uni-
verfe, I turned around in vain in fearch
of one generous hand, whofe aid I might
receive without fear or fhame.

The relation of Lord Arlington who
fucceeded to his title and eftate was an
illiterate rude fea officer, whom his illnefs alone had detained in England. He
came on the news of his deceafe; efcort-
ing the late Lord's two fifters, to whom
the perfonals were all devifed. I waited
only the reading of the will to quit the
melancholy manfion I meant to abjure
for the future.——Gracious heaven! how
deep was my indignation and rage to
find myfelf mentioned in it as an infane
wretch to whom he bequeathed a mere
maintenance, and left to be confined under the charge of his fifters in St. Vincent's
Abbey, which as a purchafe of his own,
                                    def-

defcended to them! Never, in all the
trials I had hitherto experienced, had I
felt a tranfport like that this ufage exci-
ted---to extend his tyranny beyond the
grave!---Mean, execrable wretch! even
at the moment I was exhaufting the little
conftitution his cruelty had left me in unwearied attendance, deliberately to condemn me to an imprifonment fo fhocking, and render it perpetual!—human
nature could not refift fo pungent a pang
—it *made* the mifery it punifhed; and I
funk into the dreary gulph once more
from which I was lately emerging—my
brain ftill fires but to remember it.——
Oh, my fifter! whatever the inflictions
of your myfterious fate, thofe of mine
may furely difpute the woeful pre-emi-
nence.

The overjoyed Effex difpatched an exprefs, as foon as the news of Lord Ar-
lingtons death reached the Court, conjuring me to quit the melancholy prifon
I had fo long inhabited, and retire to a

feat of Lord Southampton, in Here-
fordfhire; whither that nobleman's bride
would immediately repair to meet and comfort me.   Lady Southampton was the fair
coufin of Lord Effex, I formerly mentioned,
who by marrying privately had wholly loft
the favor of the Queen.   The declining
ftate of Lady Effex's health, he added,
daily promifed him that freedom, made
doubly defirable now I had recovered
mine.   It had always been the intention
of Lady Southampton to follow her Lord
to Ireland; and he befought me to
give him the fweet fatisfaction of knowing I was fafe in the company and protection of his coufin, folemnly promifing
not to obtrude himfelf on me ere the laws
of fociety authorized the avowal of thofe
fentiments which had fo long lived in his
heart.

The relations of Lord Arlington, poffeffing by his will an abfolute power, intercepted, and opened this Letter---far from
pouring the balm it contained into my
bleeding heart, they kept the dear tefti-
mouy

mony of an unequalled attachment; and
sent back the messenger with the melancholy news of my insanity and confine-
ment : but Lord Essex had been already
duped, and could not easily credit this information.   He deputed Henry Tracey,
a young officer, much in his confidence,
to ascertain my real situation; command-
ing him not to be dismissed by any other
mode of conviction than being admitted
into my presence.—Alas! ere this was
resolved on, resentment had again fired
my bewildered brain, and Lord Arlington had little to apprehend in allowing
Tracey to enter my apartment. Buried in a
profound stupor, I replied not to his questi-
ons, but drawing my mourning veil over
my eyes, sat like a self-devoted Persian,
the voluntary victim of despair.   The
faithful Tracey, still fearful of being imposed on, insisted on having my picture,
and a lock of my hair, to prove to his
Lord it was indeed *myself* he had beheld
in this deplorable state: he obtained this
request and departed.

C 4   But

But what became of Eſſex when Tracey returned with this melancholy confirmation?---the teſtimonials his confidante had brought, added force to the eternal paſſion of his ſoul: a thouſand times he made Tracey deſcribe the apartment---my dreſs---my looks---and ſometimes fancying even that cautious friend had been deceived; at others, that the wretches in whoſe power I was left, had, for the ſhort period Tracey was permitted to behold me, ſtupified my ſenſes; he created a thouſand deluſions to counteract the fearful impreſſion of the truth.

Diſtracted with theſe ideas, Lord Eſſex ſet out for Ireland, inveſted with abſolute powers, and heading an army attached to him alike by gratitude and expectation---he had not marched far ere he formed the bold reſolution of committing the conduct of the troops to Lord Southampton, and turning off, he poſted to St. Vincent's Abbey, determined to judge from his own ſenſes of the ſtate of mine: he arrived there at midnight, and requiring the

the unwilling owners to produce me, in
a tone which admitted neither denial
or delay, they conducted him to my
chamber-----a dim lamp alone glim-
mered in it, and closing my eyes as
the stronger lights approached, I waved
my hand in stupid silence to have them
removed. The transports of grief and
surprise which overcame the generous
Essex at this terrible conviction, threatened his own intellects--- by some wonderful ordination of providence my cold and
apparently uninformed heart waked at
that well known voice---day broke once
more upon my soul, and my eyes once
more opened to behold their darling object. This surprizing effect of his presence would have persuaded him that reason had never deserted me, had not my
poor maids expressed a joy at this unexpected revolution too unfeigned to be mis-
construed; they intreated him to leave
me time to strengthen my faculties ere he
again absorbed them, and he confined to
                                    stifled

ftifled exclamations, and filent homage,
all the paffion and the projects with which
his bofom fwelled.

Alithea, who had for years been my
favorite attendant, informed him (as foon
as he could be perfuaded to withdraw,
and leave me to repofe) of the cruel and
unjuft will, which, by rendering me a
prifoner for life, had occafioned this
dreadful relapfe. His haughty foul, negligent at all times of prudence, and now
perhaps of propriety, induced him to tell
the Arlington family, that he would perifh ere I fhould again be left in their
power: having planted fome of his moft
faithful domeftics to guard my chamber
door from every one but my own maids,
he retired to the apartment allotted him,
to meditate on the mode of proceeding
leaft likely to endanger my newly recovered intellects.

Alithea very prudently had me bled,
and I funk into a fweet and found fleep,
the comfort I had long moft wanted.
I waked late the next morning with intellects

tellects entirely clear, though weak; I
remembered I had seen, or fancied I had
seen Effex; Alithea imparted to me the
truth, and shed tears of joy to find I answered her rationally---I yielded to her
intreaties in delaying till the afternoon a
meeting so dear and affecting, and took
the medicinal cordials and other nourishment she offered me; a few hours strengthened me surprizingly, and I was at last
allowed to receive the generous lover my
soul so much desired. While he poured
forth the most ardent vows of unremitting
affection, and surveyed in tender sorrow,
the ravages grief and disappointment had
thus early made in my wan countenance,
and emaciated form, I beheld with surprize the advantages he had acquired in
both instances; his graceful flower of
youth was settled into firmer manhood;
his fair and florid complexion, sunned
over by his military exploits, had gained
strength without losing delicacy, and his
eye, now no less accustomed to command
than charm, seemed to employ its first
power on all the rest of the world, while
its

its laft was folely referved for me. Ah
man, happy man! how fuperior are you in
the indulgence of nature! bleft with fcientific refources, with boldnefs, and an activity unknown to more perfecuted woman;
from your various difappointments in life
ever fpring forth fome vigorous and
blooming hope, infenfibly ftaunching
thofe wounds in the heart through which
the vital powers of the feebler fex bleed
helplefsly away; and when relenting
fortune grants your wifhes, with un-
blighted powers of enjoyment you em-
brace the dear bought happinefs; fcarce
confcious of the cold dew-drops your
cheeks imbibe from thofe of her, permitted
too late to participate your fate.

It was fome days ere I dared truft myfelf to converfe long with Effex, who employed that fweet interval in amufing my
mind with lighter topics, while he ar-
ranged his future plans; but finding I
ftill appeared calm, he ventured at laft
to unfold to me the mighty defigns which
floated in his imagination. " Inexorably
oppofing choice to fate, my deareft Ellinor,

nor, said he, never from the moment I
first beheld you, have I formed a project
in which you were not a sharer; this I am
about to unfold has been for years the
child of my dotage---collect yourself,
listen without wonder, and, if possible, ap-
prove it: from the moment I knew the
base arts that must have been made use
of to separate us, I clearly comprehended
we should never unite with the consent of
Elizabeth; but, however indebted to her
partial distinction, it was a point in which
even she could not controul me; it is
not the posts or advantages I derive from
her favor, on which my soul values itself;
elevated on a more solid foundation, it
has taken every road to glory, and I may
proudly say, given a grace to dotage; yet
as that dotage, however unbecoming her
years and her rank, has been uniform
and generous, I have sworn to yield Elizabeth, to the latest moment of her life,
every homage but that of the heart;
and sacrifice to my fealty all but my
happiness.---It is hard to reconcile duties
and

and inclinations fo entirely oppofite, yet I think you will own I have done fo.

To a blind partiality for me, and her own egregious felf-love, the Queen ignobly facrificed your youth, your hopes, your happinefs; but alas, fhe forgot in fo doing, that fhe would only make them more perfectly mine---without any confideration for the hufband fhe had given you, a wretch I could at any time look into infignificance, I ftudied folely how to extricate you from a bondage not more infupportable to you than myfelf.--- Among a thoufand other projects, I refolved to apprize the King of Scots of your exiftence and fituation, foliciting from his fraternal regard a fafe afylum, and that peace and protection my youth and circumftances would not allow me to offer you. I found means to convey to his knowledge your whole melancholy ftory---but how fhall I declare to you his ungenerous conduct? Fool that I was to think the man who could tamely fubmit to the murder of his mother, would be interefted by any other tye! Far from ex-

exerting himself to rescue the dear unhappy sister I conjured him to compas-
sionate, he affected to disbelieve the story
of his mother's marriage with the Duke
of Norfolk; though the Countess of
Shrewsbury solemnly assured me he had,
through her hands, received from the
Royal Mary the most authentic proofs of
it, as soon as he escaped from the power
of the Regent, and was allowed to act as an
independent Sovereign. Anxious without doubt to center in himself every
right of his mother, he voluntarily renounced all regard for either her ashes
or her offspring, ignominiously submit-
ting to kiss the hand which had shortened
her days.——What after this is to be
hoped from the King of Scots? and why
should you sacrifice to a brother who dis-
owns you, those bright prospects which
now dawn before you? Born of the first
English Peer, and the Princess immediate in succession to the Throne---a native
of this kingdom; there is only one thing
wanting to establish rights from whence
you may justly form the highest hopes---
authentic

authentic teſtimonials of theſe facts : and
that ſuch ſtill exiſt, I have certain in-
formation---it is true they are diſperſed
among the Catholick relations and friends
of Mary, yet do I not deſpair of obtaining them.——The Engliſh ever diſpoſed
to be jealous of their national rights,
dread the remoteſt chance of their annihilation, and already turn their eyes toward the family of Suffolk in preference
to receiving a foreign Monarch.---That
unhappy branch of the royal line, by turns
the martyrs of fear and policy, have bled
through ſucceeding generations, till reduced wholly to females; among whom
there is not one endued with courage or
talents to venture a conteſt, had they even
the priority of birth which reſts with you.
Let us then adopt the views of Lord Leiceſter, who certainly meant by the moſt
watchful policy, to pave the way for
your ſiſter's ſucceſſion, whenever Elizabeth ſhould expire. Your fate is bound
up with that of a man much more capable
of effecting whatever views he ſhall adopt.
Eli-

Elizabeth daily totters on the verge of
the grave---difpofed to hate the Prince
fhe has irretrievably injured in the perfon
of his mother, fhe ftill refufes to acknowledge the King of Scots for her heir; and
has fully invefted me with every power
that may enable me to profit by the popularity I have honorably acquired.   My
own birth, though it does not give me a
lineal claim to the Crown of England, is
yet noble in many generations, and
princely in fome. Circumftances and merit
thus entitle me to match with you---
doubt not the fuccefs of this project.---
Born as you are for empire, endued with
beauty to adorn, and majefty to dig-
nify it----with inconteftable evidence of
your birth (which I will employ every
art to procure) I will boldly prefent to
the people of England another blooming
Queen---they will with joy adopt you;
nor can the feeble attempts of the boyifh
Scotch pedant againft an army won by
my munificence, endeared to my command, and relying on my valor, affect a

claim fo ftrongly fupported. How many
inftances does our own hiftory fupply
where courage and popularity have de-
throned monarchs in full poffeffion of
every other advantage?—You now are informed of what has long been the ul-
timate object of my life; every action and
view has had a fecret reference to it,
and far from idling away my youth in the
various pleafures the gay Court of Elizabeth offered to her favorite, I have continually ranged the feas, watched in
camps, difciplined armies, and by every
poffible means ftudied to increafe my military fame, knowledge, and popularity,
as what muft one day decide more than
my own fate. It is this that has made
me eager to conduct the Irifh war—In
that country I fhall be at the head of an
army, which will eafily enable me to profit
by the lofs of the Queen, without alarming
her declining years with the appearance
of cabal, myftery, or rebellion.—Boldly
refolve the   my love, to accompany me
thither, as the only place on earth where

3   you

you can be entirely safe; I will lodge
you in some impregnable fortress with
Lady Southampton; I will remain in the
camp, and never approach it but by
your permission---I demand this instance
of your confidence, of your love; and
swear in return inviolable honor and obe-
dience---Oh! answer me not rashly sweet
Ellinor---rather recall the fatal moment
of obstinate prudence which once before
brought on both so tedious a period of
suffering, and remember you again have
the power of deciding my fate and your
own.

Essex rose from my feet, and left me absorbed in the deepest reflection; my mind
however instantaneously adopted the aspir-
ing project he had presented to it. Through
the dark and heavy cloud which had long
hung over my soul, the sun of love now
pierced at once, and turned it all to am-
bient gold.—To mount a throne; to
share it with the choice of my heart; to
give to him that sovereignty I owed to
his valor---I was astonished the idea had

so long escaped me: yet such a train of
misfortunes had succeeded my birth, as
might well obliterate my sense of its
rights. "Base and unworthy son! sighed
I, ungenerous, cruel brother! why should
I sacrifice to thee my only chance on this
side the grave?" The mean acquiescence
of James, under a blow which almost
nerved my arm against the royal mur-
derer, had already sufficiently shocked my
feelings, and shut him out of all my
plans; alas, I could only excuse his mis-
conduct by supposing he was yet subjected
to his mother's enemies; though even
then, a generous soul would resolutely
have protested against the evil it could
not prevent; but to learn he sacrificed an
inviolable duty, and every social feeling,
at the shrine of that bloated idol, *self*,
robbed him of all claim to the feelings,
the duties, he renounced. The determined plan of the generous Essex had
every thing in its favor, nor was my
concurrence so necessary to his success
as happiness---but wherefore should I he-
sitate,

ſtate, when not to unite in it was to
deliver myſelf up to an implacable enemy? yet as avowedly to depart with Eſſex,
or even after him, would awaken dangerous ſuſpicions in the mind of Elizabeth,
and confirm all the ſlanders of the world;
I pondered much on a ſingular idea that
aroſe in my mind, by which both might
be obviated; indeed the ſituation of my
health would have ſufficiently oppoſed my
going with him, had no other objection occurred.—I perceived an air of ſtifled anger in Eſſex when he returned, which I conjured him to expound:—" It is a matter
of no conſequence, ſaid he, with his uſual
frankneſs; fortunately the few friends I
have brought with me are tried and valiant,
and we have the power in our own hands:
the wretches, my love, who ſurround you,
pretend an authority from the Queen, as
well as from the late Lord Arlington, for
your detention; this will oblige us to
uſe a violence I had rather have avoided,
but that is a trifle." Oh! call not any
thing a trifle which affects your ſafety,

how

however remotely cried I ; in yielding to
the bold project you have ventured to form,
beware I do not become its ruin—yes,
look not on me with so marked a wonder;
my soul accords to, adopts at once all
your views. I will at last indulge my
heart, and thus affiance it to yours—born
to pursue your fortune, I will joyfully consent to partake it, so you, in return, swear
the confidence will render you but more
guarded ; in considering my own honor,
I am only watching over yours; pledge
then your word that you will not interfere with my plan, and I in return will
vow, that all I henceforward form, shall
have the same tendency with your own."

The generous Essex scarce credited his
senses, and gave with readiness the assur-
ance I desired.—Resolved to guard my
sister's prior rights, and unable to judge
of the motives which might bury her
for a time in oblivion, I insisted on his
supporting her claim in preference to
mine, if ever she should appear ; and he
perhaps the more readily acquiesced in
this request, from a conviction she no
longer

longer exifted, as all my opinions on that head appeared to him entirely vifionary.

Refufing to confide in this dear rafh lover the means by which I meant to rejoin him, I obliged him to affume an air of grief and defpair, which perfuaded the Arlington family I had relapfed into infanity. In the interim a maid of mine had been feized with an epidemic fever of the moft dangerous kind; I impatiently haftened the departure of Effex, left the cruel malady fhould infect him, and conjured him to wait with Lady Southampton at the Port, from whence the troops had already embarked, till I fhould rejoin him. The air of fatisfaction he perceived in me, made him comply againft his better judgment, and the Arlington race no lefs overjoyed at his departure than my fuppofed relapfe, and fearful of the epidemic fever, fhut up thofe who immediately attended on me, in the quarter of the Abbey I inhabited, avoiding it themfelves as though the plague were enclofed there.

In this folitude I executed a furprizing project I had long meditated: from the moment I was informed of the mock interment of Lord Leicefter, my mind had dwelt on the idea; I faw it was only to methodize the moft wild and romantic plan, and however unfeafible it at firft appeared, time might form and bring it to effect.—The treafure of the furveyor now became a treafure indeed; reflection convinced me the bequeft originated in that wretch's having been the confidante as well as witnefs of his Lord's ungenerous will, and by thus difpofing of it, he enabled me to efcape from the defpicable bondage it entailed upon me, without betraying his truft —The maid, who alone witneffed the myfterious legacy, had, by her inviolable filence on fo fingular an event, fufficiently proved that fhe could merit my whole confidence; fortunately, fhe was no lefs favored by thofe in whofe power I was left, and became of courfe the propereft, and only affiftant I could fix on:—by thus turning the artifice of the Queen upon herfelf, I might at once efcape from
her

her power; and that of the guardians under whofe care fhe had placed me ; and
gratify the firft wifh of Effex without
endangering his fafety.

Alithea embraced the plan with joy,
and engaged her parents, who were la-
borers in the neighbourhood, to aid the
delufion.—I affected to be feized with the
fame fatal fever as foon as the maid's
fymptoms became mortal, and when fhe
foon after died, refigned my bed to her
corpfe: her hair, height, complexion, and
age, fo far agreed with mine as to fecure
me from common obfervation, and dread
of the contagion faved us from a very
ftrict fcrutiny; as it was believed the
maid expired at the fame time with myfelf, by Alithea's judicious management
her fuppofed body was to be delivered to
the parents of that faithful domeftic; when
placing myfelf and treafure in the homely
coffin, I was boldly conveyed like the
Emprefs Maud through the midft of
my enemies, and lodged in their humble
cot till enough recovered to purfue the
route of Effex.

Alithea

Alithea now published the news of my death through the family, who heard of it with joy; the unguarded conduct of the generous Essex had suggested to them, that to have acted under the authority of the Queen, might one day be a very insufficient vindication :—this idea added fear to that hatred they always entertained for me, and with pleasure they buried both those passions in my grave.—Having surveyed my wardrobe, jewels, and papers, without finding the least deficiency, they prepared for my interment, and discharged my immediate attendants; among them the favored one who had aided my scheme, and her return to her parents restored peace to my bosom.

From the humble cot of that honest creature's parents do I close this period of my memoirs—here, as from an invisible world, have I surveyed the gloomy pageant, with which the erroneous judgments of those from whom I escaped have dignified a low-born female, and by placing her pompously at the side of Lord Arlington, they perhaps have blundered uncon-

unconfcioufly on propriety.—As the fable
train wound by my window, my foul
paufed on the folemn vanity——Oh !
that in thy tomb, thou quiet fleeper, fighed
I, may be interred with my name all
the painful part of my exiftence ! that
renovated to a new and happier being, I
may emerge again into that world which
ftill opens a flowery path before me,
with corrected fpirits, unfaltering reafon,
and a temper fuperior to the fhocks of
misfortune !———

* * * * * *

The foul, ever capricious and uncertain, fully enjoys only the pleafures it
makes for itfelf.—Often do I feem even in
this ruftic afylum, concealed in the coarfe
garments of the other fex, and looking towards a diftant kingdom as my home, to
have hoards of hope and happinefs to build
on, my youthful, healthful days were never bleft with.———

* * * * * *

My

My own fate has once more recalled to
my mind that of Matilda—I have meditated much on a fifter fo dear—alas, too
certainly Effex is in the right, and there
exifts not a being I can call by that name.
—Long years have fucceeded each other,
and ftill that incomprehenfible myftery,
that dreadful filence continues; there is
no circumftance but death that could
occafion it.----Farewell then, oh name
ever fo pleafant to my lips, fink deep
into my heart, and remain eternally en-
graved there—farewell, thou pure fpirit!
too etherial for a world fo grofs, I will
no more look for thee on its furface, I
will no more imagine thee beneath it—
no, I will now raife my ftedfaft eye to
that heaven "where the wicked ceafe from
troubling," and in fome yet undifcovered
ftar fancy I behold thee! Ah deign, if
fo, to guide the uncertain fteps of a wanderer, and if my cruel fate conduct them
ftill toward precipices, irradiate the fcene,
and deliver me from the danger!—My
fpirits are high wrought, and a folemnity
too exquifite for defcription poffeffes
every

every faculty—I muſt ſteep them all in
a lethargy ere I recover my equanimi‐
ty.————

*   *   *   *   *   *

Happineſs! undefinable good, in what
ſhall I comprize you? no, I will not
ſuppoſe it can be done in gold, and yet
how pure was the tranſport a little of that
vile metal called into the care-furrowed
countenances of Alithea's venerable pa‐
rents!   To the earth which gave, I have
reſtored the remainder; it is buried eaſt‐
ward under the ſpreading cheſnut planted
by Edward IV.——that popular tree, pro‐
tected alike from the caprice of its owner,
and the ſpade of the laborer, will hide it
ſafely: but, oh! if ever one noble heart
ſighs under its ſhade, oppreſſed with the
ſting of penury, may ſome good angel
whiſper, "you reſt on that which can
fully relieve you."

All is now prepared for my flight; I
have refuſed the attendance of Alithea;
it will be well ſupplied in the remem‐
brance

brance that she is happy---indulgent heaven has given to *her*, parents who grow
old in peace and virtue, a lover who
knows not falsehood or ambition, and a
soul justly grateful for blessings beyond
all valuation—the faithful creature delays
the happiness of him she loves till he shall
have conveyed this broken narrative into
the hands of Lady Pembroke; nor do I
fear to trust him with it.—Dear, noble
friend, once more my soul fondly salutes
you; bestow on my flight those pious
prayers with which virtue consecrates our
purposes, and believe mine rise ever for
you. If we meet again, remember it
must be with pleasure.

LADY PEMBROKE WRITES.

Scarce had I recovered from the surprize and grief occasioned by the publication
of this sweet creature's supposititious death,
ere a rustic demanded permission to see me,
and mysteriously delivered the wonderful
packet---alas, how affecting did I find it !

far,

far, however, from drying up my tears at·
learning she yet lived, I looked with terror on the future, left every following day
should multiply, or terribly finish her miseries. Ah, dear Matilda! I cannot agree
with this fair visionary, who so easily adopts
the romance of her lover.—Something
seems to assure me thou art still alive, and
suffering; and for thy sake I will preserve
these melancholy memorials: alas! perhaps it were truer kindness to destroy
them.

L E T T E R   I.

Dated Drogheda.

FROM the safe shores of another king-
dom once more do I greet my friend.---
Alas! ill can we judge for ourselves, dear
Lady Pembroke.

Provided with a fleet horse, I set out to
follow Essex, but scarce had I travelled a
single day, ere my shattered constitution
(no longer able to sustain the least toil)
claimed two, to recover the fatigue of the
first. During my stay at the inn, my
youth,

youth, the delicacy of my perſon and manners, with the air of reſerve I found it necef-
ſary to aſſume, excited a curioſity my liberality alone was able to bound; though even
that gave riſe to ſuſpicions almoſt equally
dangerous. I began to fear my ſcheme
would wholly fail in the execution; I
hired, however, two ruſtics well recommended, as a guide, and an eſcort; yet in
travelling on the ſolitary mountains of
Wales, often dared not turn my head
over my ſhoulder, leſt in my guards I
ſhould behold my murderers. My impaired health rendered the journey very
tedious; during its progreſs, I paſſed for
a poor youth following the ſteps of my
father, and far gone in a conſumption.—
After immenſe fatigue, I arrived at length
at the port; where I underſtood with in-
expreſſible chagrin that Eſſex had embarked for Ireland a week before.—Alas!
a moment's recollection enabled me to
account for this, apparently, ſtrange de-
ſertion:—in my eagerneſs to conceal my
favorite ſcheme, I had forgot to guard
                                                  againſt

against the chance of my Lord's being informed of my suppofed death ere I reached him. On enquiry, I plainly perceived he had left fpies in the neighbourhood of St. Vincent's Abbey when he quitted it, who, mifled by report, had haftened after him with news of the melancholy event. I learnt he had delayed crofling from time to time without giving any reafon for it, but on being roufed by the arrival of two officers, he ordered the feamen to be called in the dead of night, and embarked the moment the tide favored his departure.

Though this information left me only myfelf to reproach, it did not leffen my chagrin. I wandered toward the fhore to meditate at leifure: it was ftill littered with foldiers and their appendages; they were indulging with ungoverned licence, in drinking and riot.—Every thing I beheld, increafed my fears of the voyage: it was indeed a tremendous thought; to embark with a numerous body of licentious men for an unknown country, while wrapt in myf-

tery myself, and without a protector.---
How, if actuated by curiosity, or a less
excusable motive, they should guess at my
sex, and pry into my story? perhaps
even the name of their general would
want influence to guard me. I turned
woman again, and trembled at the bare
idea. While irresolute in what manner
to dispose of my unfortunate self, I observed a body of travellers approaching,
and understood with joy it was Lady
Southampton and her train, escorted by
a chosen troop, for whom those I had
already seen waited—I blest indulgent
heaven, which thus relieved me from the
effects of my own indiscretion, and demanded to see her—to see her was enough,
for with the penetration natural to her sex,
she instantly knew me, and throwing her
arms round my neck, reproached me
with a generous freedom for having re-
tarded her journey, by obliging her to
wait in vain for my arrival; and finally,
for shocking her with the fictitious story
of my death.—I explained to her my unguarded conduct, and its motives.—She
assured

affured me fhe dreaded the effect it might
have on my lover, as her Lord had not
time to write more than that Effex was
in defpair for my lofs, nor dared he venture to leave him ; therefore conjured her
to confide herfelf to the care of the officers he mentioned, and follow with all
expedition.——This information doubled
the regret which had already feized on
me; but to guard againft all fufpicion
and enquiry, I refolved to retain my mafculine habit, and pafs for one of Lady
Southampton's pages, till fafely lodged
in Ireland.

We arrived here laft night, and found
a letter from Lord Southampton, lament-
ing the impoffibility of waiting for his
Lady, without abandoning Effex to a grief
which urged him to rafhnefs and defpair;
he ended with conjuring her to remain
in this town till he had confidered how
to difpofe of her fafely.----Oh, fortune, fortune, how unfairly do we accufe thee, when
folly alone has led us into error!---I am
more miferable than it is poffible to ex-

prefs.

prefs. Lady Southampton would fain perfuade me this overfight may eventually
prove lucky, as it will prevent my again
feeing Effex ere the death of his Lady.---
Ah! what alteration can her lofs make in
my fate?—" I tell you, my watchful friend,
you cannot love my honor more than I
do his fafety---between him and me there
is another bar not lefs infurmountable.---
Did not my fifter's marriage with a favorite of Elizabeth coft him his life?
Alas, perhaps hers too was facrificed !"---
over her myfterious fate a dark veil early
fell, dipt perhaps in the blood of her be-
loved---rather may I fee my own veins
opened, than furvive fuch a calamity; nay,
even at this moment it has perhaps fallen
on me, and I may be dying in Effex while
yet unconfcious of my fate---oh, what
horrors take poffeffion of my foul at the
bare idea !————Lady Southampton has
fealed her Englifh difpatches, and I can
only fay adieu.

LET-

LETTER II.

Dated Drogheda.

BOUND to this fpot, my generous friend, and dreading all which paffes beyond it, hardly can my heart feel the congratulation you beftow. Environed by enemies, and rendered rafh by defpair, Effex now renounces the glorious vifions he poffeffed my imagination with, and refigns himfelf wholly up to his command.---Oh, that the arrow which ftabs me fhould have been fharpened by my own hand!---All here is alarm, uncertainty, and confufion---we get and lofe in the courfe of every day a paffage to our friends, nor dare we truft to that channel aught of importance. Sir Coniers Clifford with a chofen body of troops was yefterday furrounded, himfelf and half his men cut off immediately---among the officers was a relation of Lady Southampton's; fhe has been weeping the whole day for him.---For my own part, confcious I have not a tear to beftow on common inflictions, I

E 3   gather

gather mine into my heart, which feels ready to pour forth a deluge the moment one of my many fears shall be confirmed---you can form no conception of the wants, the woes, the horrible scenes we witness.---Born and bred in the arms of luxury and prosperity, a distant war but faintly affects our minds; but oh, how tremendous does it appear when once we are driven into its tempestuous seat!---death, ghastly death, assumes a bloody variety of forms; while rapine, famine, sickness, and poverty, fearfully forerun him.

I have hitherto thought my sister's fate more consummately wretched than even my own, but how is every evil lightened by comparison!---Beloved Matilda, born as you were to woe, you saw but one bounded prospect of the infinitude the globe presents to us; the horrors of this were unknown to you---uncomforting is the pillow of her who sleeps within the sound of a drum, and fancies its every stroke is fate.---Is this to live? Ah no! it is to be continually dying.

This

This country fo nearly allied to our own, yet offers to our view a kind of new world; divided into petty ftates, inveterately hating each other, it knows not the benefit of fociety, except when neceffity combines the various parties againft a common enemy; yet, though neceffity unites, it cannot blend them; the leaft ceffation of general danger awakens all their narrow partialities and prejudices, which continually break out with bloody violence. The advantages of commerce, the charms of literature, all the graces of civilization, which at once enrich the mind and form the manners, are almoft unknown to this people; with a favage pride they fancy their very wants virtue, and owe to their poverty an unregulated valor, which often enables them to contend with well-difciplined troops, whom they fometimes defeat by mere want of knowledge; at others, on the contrary, they obftinately purfue an unequal conteft, while fpeculating reafon turns away from the bloody fcene, vainly confcious that their mangled bodies ftrew the earth, only becaufe no bene-

E 4   volent

volent being has yet deigned to attempt the conqueſt of their minds.

How deeply muſt ſuch reflections operate on a heart bound up in the life of the accompliſhed leader! endued but with the common powers of humanity, expoſed with the reſt, alike to the ſword and to the elements, he, even he, muſt one day periſh; and while I weep the wretches every hour deprives of their beloved protectors, I know not but I may at the ſame moment be added to the number.---Ah, if deſpair ſhould impel Eſſex,---his natural heroiſm needs no ſuch incentive,---ſhould he fall, unconſcious of my yet ſurviving, to that fatal though well deſigned artifice I ſhould forever impute his loſs, and die for having feigned to do ſo.

A wild fancy has taken ſtrange poſſeſſion of my mind---Lady Southampton ſays it is madneſs; perhaps it really is ſo, but I can think of nothing elſe; ſhe, however, is too timid to judge---ſhe will paſs her whole life here I really believe.

Were

Were I but for a moment to behold that expreſſive countenance,---were I by a kind of reſurrection again to appear before him!------

Something irreſiſtible impels me---a choſen troop are now ſetting out---I ſhall be ſafe under their protection.---Ah, if this ungovernable impulſe ſhould be but a preſentiment of his danger---never, never ſhould I forgive myſelf were I to leave him wounded and dying, to the care of perſons comparatively indifferent.

"Argue no longer, my dear importunate friend, I will go, but depend on my haſtening back."----Lady Southampton would have made a wretched love for Eſſex; ſhe is the moſt apprehenſive of women; but ſhe was not born to mate with that aſpiring hero.

THE.

THE

RECESS, &c.

PART V.

A Silence so tedious will make you
number me among the dead; recover
yourself, my beloved friend---born to a
perpetual contest with ill fortune, I sink
not even yet under the oppression.--I have
been collecting all my thoughts to pursue
my strange recital, more strange indeed
every day.

In

In our way toward Ulster, we were intercepted by a body of the rebellious Irish, and a desperate skirmish ensued---how shall I own it, and call myself the the love of Essex; yet so it was---I, who had been so valiant in imagination, and remote from the field of action---I, who had in fancy lifted a sword with the strength of Goliah, and interposed a shield before Essex, heavier perhaps than myself, shrunk into annihilation at the bare sight of the conflict; and the faintings which laid me among the slain, perhaps alone saved me from being added to their number. I revived in the hands of some ferocious women, who in stripping the dead, had discovered at one moment that I yet lived, and was of their own sex. Induced either by a sentiment of humanity, or the hope of a reward, they listened to my eager supplications for life, and conveyed me to a neighbouring cabin; whither they soon summoned a priest, who opened a vein in my arm. On feebly

re-

reviving once more, I cast my eyes round
in speechless astonishment, scarce knowing whether I should think my escape a
blessing. I was environed by a set of
beings who in complexion alone bore any
resemblance to myself, their language,
manners, and lives, seeming no more ana-
logous, than those of the inhabitants of the
Torrid Zone. I laboured in vain to comprehend them, or to make myself understood, and was, in despair giving up the
attempt, when the priest already mentioned came to my relief. Through his
means I informed them that the Lord Deputy would redeem me at any ransom,
provided they secured me from danger
and insult. I should, I believe, have en-
sured my own safety, had not the victo-
rious party learnt, by some straggler, that
an English woman of distinguished rank
had been discovered among the slain.
They eagerly turned back to demand me,
and the hope of reward alike influencing
my preservers to keep me in their hands,
a dispute no less fierce, though not so
bloody,

bloody, as that I had before witnessed,
followed; it was too violent to be com-
promised, and at length, as the only way
to prevent murder, both parties agreed I
should be put into the hands of their
General Tiroen; or, as some called him,
O'Neal. Intreaties or resistance would
have been equally vain, and I was obliged
to rejoice they thought me of consequence
enough to act so honorably by me.

During this interval, one of the servants deputed by Lady Southampton immediately to attend on me, having lingered a few minutes behind the English
troop, followed to rejoin them at the moment of the onset; the sound of the
firing reached him ere he fell in with
the scouts, and clapping spurs to his horse,
he flew back to the village we all had
lately quitted, there to wait in safety the
event of the contest: at this place he
was informed, a band of rebels had issued
out from an ambuscade formed in the
neighbouring mountain; and while he
was wavering what step to take, the
news

news of my sex and capture suddenly
reached him; struck with the idea of
some important mystery, as well from my
disguise as the cautions of his Lady, he
hastened back to her with the strange intelligence. The generous but timid Lady
Southampton, impressed solely with the
idea of my danger, wrote instantaneously
to Essex, briefly reciting all he did not
know of my story, and strongly conjuring
him to exert his utmost influence to preserve me from insult.

But who shall paint the feelings of
Essex, when the surprizing intelligence
first reached him! intelligence which,
in one moment, opened all those sources
of tenderness in his soul, grief and despair had well nigh congealed. To think I
still lived would have been consummate
happiness, had I not been thus unaccountably snatched away, even at the very moment of my miraculous renovation: so
singular a complication of events almost
deprived him of his senses, and wrought
impulse up to agony. Perhaps the last
un-

untoward incident of my life was neceffary to fave his brain from partaking the
diftractions of his mind---fick at the
heart of an incurable forrow---fatigued
with the cares of government, and the
flavery of command, the news of my
exiftence and capture made him find in
diftinctions hitherto fo oppreffive, the fole
profpect of recovering a treafure, which
alone could give value to his future
life.

From the knowledge acquired in his military command, Effex was enabled to decide
on the character of Tiroen---he juftly believed it unprincipled and ungovernable ;
how muft he tremble then to recollect my
fate was in his hands !   In a conjuncture
fo dangerous, he refigned himfelf entirely
up to the guidance of an impaffioned
heart, and difpatched an officer of rank,
charging the arch-rebel by the blood of
thoufands yet unfpilt, not to exafperate the
Englifh, and himfelf in particular, by
maltreating the lady fortune had thrown
into his power ; for whofe ranfom any
                                    fum

sum was tendered her captors should demand.

This rash and impetuous address had
consequences only less dangerous than
those it guarded against. Tiroen unfor-
tunately discovered at once that he had
the happiness of the Lord Deputy in his
keeping, and though he flattered him
from time to time with promises of noble
treatment, he secretly determined no
doubt, that if he ever parted with me,
it should be upon his own terms.

It was not till several of these messages
had passed, that Tiroen's curiosity led
him to visit me: the attention excited
by my masculine habit had led me immediately to request one more suited to
my sex; and the delicate situation I stood
in, obliging me to conduct myself with
the utmost caution, I had thought it peculiarly fortunate to escape the notice of
the General.

The continual repetition of his tedious
visits, when once he had seen me; the
lavish supply of such accommodations as
that

that ravaged country then afforded---an obstinate silence on the state of my affairs, and the most wearisome discussions of his own, all too soon convinced me, that neither his pride, his ambition, or his ferocity, had been able to guard the heart of Tiroen from that powerful passion which invigorated the being of his distinguished rival---I trembled at the recollection that I was wholly in his power---already misjudged as the voluntary mistress of Essex, unwilling to announce myself, and unable, had I done so, to prove my right to any name or distinction, mine was indeed a fearful situation. I was not allowed to hold any correspondence with the English, and only knew by the watch kept over me, that a human being was anxious for my release.

Whatever consequences might follow my appearing pleased with the distinctions lavished on me by Tiroen, I felt every day more sensibly that I had no other means of avoiding the licentious insolence of his officers; who fancied their services so important to the cause they had espoused, as to secure their conduct from too strict a scrutiny.

Tiroen sought occasions to break off, renew, and prolong, the secret intercourse in which he had now engaged with Essex; but a lingering treaty agreed not with the fiery impatience of that unfortunate hero. His divided soul no longer could attend to the duties of his command---the business of the war was at an end---Essex was no longer a cool and prudent General, watchful to seize every advantage, and harrass the enemy---alas, he was now only a mad and extravagant lover, ready to sacrifice every thing to the recovery of one adored individual.---Delivered up to passion, to terror, to agony, to every torturing excess of overstrained sensibility, at this fatal period the generous Essex was gradually sacrificing the whole renown of a life hitherto so glorious. The news of Tiroen's love crowned his misfortunes; and that execrable traitor, determined to bring the Lord Deputy to his terms, by various

emis-

emiffaries had him informed of plots he
never laid againft me, and repulfes he
never fuftained; fpecioufly difowning
fuch defigns in terms calculated only to
redouble the fufpicions of his rival.

By artifices like thefe the warlike talents
and dignified mind of Effex were kept in
abfolute fubjection; he no longer dared
to exert the valour which burned proudly
at his heart, but ftifling every emotion
love did not excite, he eagerly engaged
in a fecret and dangerous treaty.---The
rafh propofal of Effex to confer with
Tiroen from the oppofite banks of a rivu-
let, I imputed to the paffionate defire a
lover ever has to judge of the perfon and
talents of the man who dares to rival him---
this interview could not be kept a fecret---
alas, perhaps it decided the fortune of
the Lord Deputy!---Misjudged from that
moment by a bufy world which fees only
the furface of things, to timidity, to avarice, to indolence, to ambition, by turns,
has been afcribed an incident, of which
love had all the merit or the fhame.---Ah!
had the erroneous multitude confidered

F 2   but

but a moment, furely they had difcerned a mvftery in his conduct ---What could ambition, glory, pride, require, he did not poffefs already? If to hold the moft abfolute fway over the moft abfolute of Sovereigns conld gratify thofe wifhes, they were gratified.----Rather, ye bufy Many, learn to pity than condemn the generous frenzy of a bleeding heart which boldly facrificed every thing to an over-ruling, an irrefiftible paffion---a paffion mine muft break to anfwer---and it *will* break.----Oh! my fhook brain, how wild it wanders!———

*   *   *   *   *   *

Gay vifions of a higher, happier fphere, where are ye? ah! deign to gild awhile this gloomy world!---how inexpreffibly fweet are at intervals the trances of my mind!———care, forrow, fuffering, mortality itfelf is forgotten; abforbed in a bright obfcure, every high-wrought faculty hovers proudly on the verge of a long eternity---fye on this
earthy

earthy covering, how it drags down my foul, my foaring foul.

* * * * * *

I wake from thefe day dreams, and return to my fubject--in fruitlefs and tedious negociations were thus confuming thofe days we would in vain recall, thofe important days fraught with the very fate of the noblest of mankind.

The long delays, the eternal difappointments, exhaufted my patience; agitated by a thoufand apprehenfions, which no lefs concerned my lover than myfelf, mifery once more ftruck her iron fangs through my quivering heart. Compelled to ftruggle with a foul juftly confcious of purity; to fupport an apparent tranquillity; to adopt an artificial character; to fuffer Tiroen to delude himfelt into a perfuafion the tye between me and Effex was difhonorable, left an uncertain one fhould want power to reftrain him, how many implicated indignities did I patiently endure!---Perfecuted with

F 3   his

his bafe folicitations; overwhelmed with
bribes as fplendid as they were contemptible, I could ward off his expectations
only by a feint my nature difdained.　In
anfwer to his unbounded offers, and tender proteftations, I one day bad him remember that in thofe inftances he could not
furpafs the generous lover he fought to
rival; for that it was in the power of Effex
to give me every thing but his *title*.---Ti-
roen paufed indignantly for a moment, and
my heart exulting in its artifice, fondly
hoped the fpectres of his whole line of royal
anceftors would fweep before him, pre-
cluding every idea of a union fo difhonorable.　His whole eftimation, and the fuccefs of the war depended, I well knew,
on his retaining the affections of the people, and how could he hope for thofe if
he difgraced the blood of the O'Neal's?
He fcarce credited the boldnefs of idea
which appeared in this hint of mine, and
ftruck with a perfuafion I muft be of fome
fuperior rank to dare thus to elevate my
eyes to him, he once more attempted to
dive

dive into a myſtery ſo carefully and obſtinately concealed. I was however on
my guard, and ſunk again into my original obſcurity. Still· eager to poſſeſs
a woman he could not eſteem, he at laſt
aſſured me (after having obſerved that an
engagement to a lady of his own family alone held his party together)
that he would bind himſelf in ſecret by
every tye I ſhould dictate. I unwarily
replied, the conduct and love of Eſſex
had been ſo unqueſtionably noble, that
nothing but a ſuperior and public marriage could vindicate me even to myſelf,
in breaking with him.----Tiroen's look and
anſwer made me ſenſible of the danger of this ſpeech, and that in leaving him without hope, I had left myſelf without ſafety. I felt from this
moment like a wretch entirely devoted; and under the name of indiſpo-
ſition (of which indeed I had ſufficient
reaſon to complain) I procured from a
ſurgeon who bled me, a quantity of li-
quid laudanum, ſome portion of which

F 4

I pre-

I pretended to take every night, but in reality reserved the whole of it for that fatal one which should confirm my fears.

Such were the sufferings of Essex and myself, while the two camps were in sight of each other, and nothing but the most guarded vigilance could prevent the incensed English from coming to action.---I was one evening alone in the tent allotted to me (for Tiroen would never trust me in any neighbouring fort or town) which, from the ascent it was pitched on, commanded the whole valley, and looking with tearful eyes towards the increasing fires in the English camp, when Tiroen approached me unawares---his complexion was flushed with wine, and his eyes and air shewed a determination at which my nature shuddered---no longer regarding decorum or respect, his manners made me in a moment sensible I had deferred taking my laudanum too long.---An idea, at which I have never ceased to wonder, suggested itself to my mind; and while fluctuating between the possible and im-

impoſſible, I a little ſoothed the boiſterous wretch, at whoſe profligate vows I
trembled---intoxication deprived him of
the guard he had ſo long kept over his
lips---imagining himſelf already poſſeſſed
of the beloved of Eſſex, he could not forbear vaunting of the addreſs which ſecured
her to him.---I learnt with equal horror
and amazement, that the long delay my
capture and the ſubſequent treaties had
occaſioned in the war, were all concerted
ſtrokes of diabolical policy to ruin the
fair fame of the Lord Deputy.---That
during theſe fatal treaties, Tiroen himſelf
had ſent the moſt indubitable proofs
to Elizabeth of the miſconduct of her
General, and had every reaſon to ſuppoſe he would immediately be recalled,
and ignominiouſly puniſhed: nor could
ſhe ever ſelect another equally dear
to the army, on which every thing
in war depended.------I turned with
ineffable diſdain toward the monſter.---
Oh, that an eye-beam could have killed
him!---Engroſſed, however, by his vari-

ous

ous views, inflated with felf-love and ap-
plaufe, and confufed with wine, he faw
not a glance which would inftantaneoufly
have -unfolded my whole heart, to the
execrable, the ungenerous traitor; unworthy the race he fprung from, and the
fword he drew.---He continued to expa-
tiate on his hopes of wholly expelling
the Englifh, and afcending the throne of
Ireland; but what after this unwary and
black difcovery could his views be to me?
A thoufand dangers were prefling upon my
foul, and a thoufand projects floating in my
brain: I had hardly temper or recollection
to methodize any---while he continued to
charm himfelf with the difclofure of all
his vanity and ambition, hatred and horror nerved my heart with courage to execute a ftrange defign, the defperation of
fuch a moment alone could have fuggefted.
Convinced, by the tenor of his difcourfe
and conduct, I that could efcape his licentious purpofes only by feigning an intention of yielding to them, I fmoothed my
agonized features into a fmile which almost

moſt ſtiffened to a convulſion, and complained of thirſt---a glaſs of water ſtood
by, of which I drank---inclination no leſs
than gallantry, made him inſiſt on pledg-
ing me; but refuſing to give him the
water without wine, I mixed it with an offi-
ciouſneſs perhaps too obvious, adding the
whole quantity of laudanum provided for
myſelf. The haſte and tremor attending
ſo dangerous a tranſaction, might well
have excited diſtruſt in him at any time,
much more at ſuch a criſis; but not in a
condition to obſerve very ſtrictly, and delighted with a condeſcenſion on my part
alike new and unexpected, in a tranſport
of gallantry he dropt on his knees, and
uniting my name with his own, cemented
both with that of happineſs: the latter
ſeemed to tremble back into my heart as
he eagerly ſwallowed the beverage. Sleep
had before hovered over his eyelids; it
was now forerun by ſtupefaction. The
hour of reſt arrived; but the women who
uſually ſlept in the outer tent came not near
it—I could not doubt but that their abſence was owing to the previous orders
                                        given

given by the General, and falling on
my knees, intreated him who armed
the Affyrian with courage voluntarily to
dare the fituation into which I was brought
unconfenting, to bear me boldly and
fafely through it. A fortitude equal to
the danger, feemed to fpring from the
addrefs and the occafion.---The regimental cloak Tiroen had thrown off on enter-
ing, ferved to cover my mafculine habit,
which I refumed with expedition: it was
a cloak fo remarkable, and familiar to
every eye in the camp, as almoft to enfure my fafety. I overweighed my throbbing temples with his warlike plume, and
finally, drawing from his finger a fignet to
produce if neceffary, I boldly grafped his
dagger to decide my fate fhould I be difcovered, and iffued forth a fecond Judith.

I had warily marked the progrefs of the
night; the laft watch had now gone by,
and the time was paft when it was probable any officer fhould be ftirring of note
enough to addrefs the General. I had
heard Tiroen fay it was his common prac-
tice to walk the camp at night, and
in

in that confidence ventured to pass for him. Scarce had I gone a hundred paces when the homage of the centinels assured me the counterfeit was undiscovered.

With an agitated heart I passed from one to another, guided only by the distant lights (for Tiroen always pitched his camp on a hill) till near the advanced guard, I then retired behind a large tent, and disrobing myself of their General's accoutrements, put on a common hat I had carried for that purpose---what were my terrors when having reached the confines of the camp, now doubly watched, I presented the signet as a proof I was sent on earnest business.---The guard hesitated, but after tediously debating, while I went through tortures, they judged it prudent to admit a token which alone could have enabled me to reach them, and I was suffered to pass.

I shot like an arrow from a bow when once these dreaded limits were overleaped, scarce daring to address my very soul to
heaven,

heaven, left one loft moment fhould un-
do me.

Whether my eyes had deceived me in the
imagined nearnefs of the Englifh camp, or
my trembling and unguided feet had wandered wide of it, I know not; but forely were
they bliftered ere I approached its limits---
piercing through thickets which tore alike
my garments and my flefh, with fpirits fainting even to death, I fuddenly heard a fcout
give the watch-word in Englifh.   Overjoyed to think myfelf fafe, I unhappily
wanted prefence of mind to pronounce a
fingle fyllable, and the officious foldier
miftaking me for a fpy, levelled his piece,
and inftantly pierced my fide.---My fpirits were no longer equal to contending
with danger or with death, and the fear
of difcovery being the prevailing fentiment of my fex, I feebly conjured the
man, if he hoped for pardon, to bear me
to the tent of the Lord Deputy.   The
delicacy of my complexion and cloaths
had already furprized the inadvertent
foldier- -he quickly called together fome

of

of his companions, who affifted in laying
me on a hurdle, and bearing me toward
the tent of Effex. The morning was
now broke---I faw the early beams of
the fun emblazon the golden ornaments
of the General's tent---fome officers came
out of it as I approached.---My heart,
from which life feemed every moment
ready to iffue, made a courageous effort
to collect into itfelf the fcattered principles of a being I appeared on the
very point of refigning. I fancied ere
he yet fpoke, I heard the voice fo dear
to me---I fancied! ah, I indeed *faw*
him rufh forward on the firft hint;
but, root-bound as it were, he ftopped
before he came to me, and fent his very
foul forth in a groan.---" Yes, Effex, cried
I, extending my feeble hand, the wretch
heaven did not allow to live in thy arms,
receives its next indulgence in being permitted to die there."——But how fhall I
defcribe the tearful tranfports, the touching agonies of his recovered intellects!
I funk under the keen eftafy of the moment;

ment, and long faintings succeeded, occasioned by my loss of blood, which once
more brought me to the very verge of
the grave.

The amiable Lady Southampton came
at the instance of her cousin, and gave
by her presence, a decorum to my situation it had long wanted. Every effort
of art was exerted to soothe my broken
spirits, and strengthen my exhausted
frame. He, who alone could give effi-
cacy to medicine, hovered ever near,
and when speech was interdicted, by affectionate looks sustained me.---Ah, how
pleasant were even these sufferings! how
sweet was it to collect back into my
heart those gentle impulses war and terror
had driven from their home!---To affiance
my soul in silence to its only Lord, and to
fancy whatever fate heaven should hereafter ordain him, mine could no longer be
divided from it.

As soon as my amended health allowed,
I entered into a detail of all that had
passed since Lord Essex left me at St.
Vincent's

Vincent's Abbey. He in return informed me, that the lethargy into which Tiroen was plunged by the laudanum I had fo haftily adminiftered, was very near being fatal to him, as the utmoft effort of care and medicine could only preferve him the faculty of breathing; fince to difturb his deep and unwholefome flumbers always threw him into a dangerous delirium. The courageous effort by which I had recovered my liberty, he added, had formed the whole converfation of both camps while my fate was yet uncertain. I bleffed the awful power who faved me the guilt of murdering even a villain, and did not immediately remark that Effex gave me no farther information.

I foon learnt from Lady Southampton the painful truths my Lord fought to hide from me---that Elizabeth had inceffantly urged him to profecute a war which his fears for me had hitherto fufpended; but finding at length that both intreaties and commands were loft upon him, fhe grew cold and

difgufted. His friends in England had given
him but too much reafon to believe that
his enemies were gradually acquiring the
afcendancy in her heart, he as gradually
loft; fince all her favours were now lavifhed on Sir Walter Raleigh, the houfe
of Cecil, and the Earl of Nottingham, a
party who had long meditated the down-
fall of Effex and Southampton, of which
they now fpoke as a certainty; and that
even the common people beheld with
difcontent the flow progrefs of the war
in Ireland, nor could Effex any longer
depend upon popularity.

The unguarded friend who made me
this recital, engroffed by her own fhare
in it, forgot how it interefted me. I
called to mind the information fent by
Tiroen to Elizabeth, which but too well
accounted for the Queen's anger and
difguft, and conceived at once all its
probable confequences. Effex, unlike
all other favorites, could never be brought
to know any claim to fuperiority but
merit-----incapable of thofe little arts
by

by which meaner minds attach the infidious train of fycophants a Court always
abounds with; he had ever fcorned a
partial monopoly, and politic diftribution,
of pofts and places.----The mercenary
wretches who had bowed to him in vain,
paid their court to his enemies with more
fuccefs, and inftructed by them in every
weaknefs of the favorite, were ever ready
to ftrengthen any prejudice the Queen
might conceive againft him. A thoufand
fears incident to age and decaying power,
were thus cherifhed in her, which magnified
by paffions time itfelf could never allay,
might perhaps ftamp the bafe intelligence
of Tiroen with the fatal authority of un-
biaffed truth, and give to the inactivity
of Effex, the appearance of treafon.---
Such a train of circumftances could
hardly fail to ftagger a mind in full
poffeffion of the nobleft and moft im-
partial judgment; what then might we
not fear from a Sovereign always influenced by prejudices each paffing day
ftrengthened, as it infenfibly impaired her
reafon? Fortunately, by an extrava-

gance

gance of dotage which almoſt puniſhed the errors of her youth, thoſe prejudices had hitherto united in his favour :---yet while I perceived but a ſingle chance againſt him, my ſoul ſhrunk from the idea of entruſting his life with her.

To give Lord Eſſex the opportunity of vindicating himſelf to Elizabeth, I re-ſolved to account for her conduct; and divulged to him the inadvertent acknow-ledgment made by Tiroen, during our laſt memorable interview, of his own perfidy and diſſimulation. A generous ſcarlet burnt on the cheek of Eſſex while he execrated the traitor; but ſtruck immediately with a full conviction of the conſequences that might reſult from this baſe intelligence, he formed the extraordinary reſolution of returning to England to juſtify his honor.

This determination no leſs ſhocked than ſurprized me; far from imagining my in-formation would lead to ſo wild a pro-ject, I rather ſuppoſed it would ſuggeſt to him the impoſſibility of ever reviſiting En-gland, unleſs the reduction of Ulſter was fully accompliſhed.---In truth, I dared

not

not confefs my fears that even then to remain with the army alone could enfure
his fafety.---Every reafon I durft urge,
or Southampton enforce, were in his judgment feebler than his own---his honor
was piqued, and nothing could hinder
him from vindicating it.---Perfuaded a
ftep as bold as this, alone would convince
Elizabeth of his innocence, and accuftomed to regain, whenever he appeared,
that influence over her, his enemies had
often encroached on in his abfence, he
perfuaded himfelf he need only be feen to
triumph, and concluded a truce, as the
preliminary to his departure.

The pride of fex, fenfibility, and honor, contended with the leading paffion
of my nature, and taught me to difdain
over-ruling him I could not convince :---
neverthelefs, I almoft funk under the
conflict.---The frightful fituation in which
I had been placed fince my arrival in Ireland, made me obftinately refufe to continue there, whenever Effex fhould leave
it ; and the curiofity I had excited alike
by my bold efcape, and wound, made

it

it hazardous to commit me to the charge
of any officer left behind. Surrounded
with friends, relations, and dependents,
Essex (such is the painful uncertainty
ever attending on elevated rank) knew
not one to whom he could safely intrust so
delicate a care. The generous Southampton, determined to share the fate of his
friend by accompanying him, proposed
to unite that of his Lady with mine, by
shipping us off ere they embarked, with
servants they should mutually select; apparently bound for France, but in fact for
the coast of Cumberland. In the most romantic and solitary part of that remote
county, the Wriothesleys had long owned
a castle, where malice itself would hardly
seek, and certainly never find us; there
he assured Essex we might repose in peace,
till they should return again to Ireland.
I felt all the merit of this project, by
which the amiable Southampton robbed
himself of the dear society of his wife,
merely to do honor to the beloved of
his friend; and adopted it with the utmost

moſt eagerneſs, from the hope that if the
buſy tranſmitters of Lord Eſſex's actions
had ever mentioned me, this total ſepa-
ration would extinguiſh all jealouſy in the
mind of Elizabeth; who I knew would
much ſooner overlook the loſs of an army
than his heart.

Although Eſſex knew not how to place
me happily in Ireland, it was with pain
he conſented to my quitting it; but finding me obſtinately partial to Lord Southampton's deſign, he conſented to my re-
ſuming my maſculine diſguiſe, and ſe-
lected a veſſel whoſe captain was devoted
to him, having ordered a lighter one to
be prepared for himſelf.

So ſad a preſentiment ſhivered my ſoul
on the morn appointed for our embarka-
tion, that it was the utmoſt effort of my
principles to ſuffer Eſſex to act in confor-
mity to his. I had previouſly inſiſted he
ſhould ſail at the ſame moment with myſelf, to end my fears of that formidable
ſavage Tircen; and when he entered my
chamber to conduct me to the ſhip, my heart

qui-

quivered on lips which had no longer
the power to utter a fyllable.---He befought, he conjured me, to fupport my
finking fpirits; "the higheft hopes, he
added, with an air of fincerity, elevated
his own; that it had always been his
pride, his pleafure, to deferve the diftinctions lavifhed on him by the Queen; and
whatever views he had formed when heaven fhould call her hence, he could not
refolve even by ingratitude, much lefs
treafon, to fhorten her days who had
crowned his with glory. Doubt not, concluded he, my love, but I fhall recover
all my influence, and remember when
next we meet it is to part no more "

Ill-omened feemed that fentence to
me---I fancied too his voice founded hol-
low---I fancied!---alas, every dire chi-
mera fenfibility prefents to an impaffioned
heart, took full poffeffion of mine; yet,
as to exert the leaft influence at fo trying
a moment was to render myfelf account-
able for his future fate, I oppofed every
ennobling fentiment to an ungovernable
passion,

paſſion, and heroically reſigned him up to his duty.

We quitted the port at the ſame inſtant: he ſteering for that neareſt the Iriſh coaſt, I for the North of England.---Both by conſent remained on the deck with ſouls fixed on each other, till the beloved individual vaniſhed, and the veſſel ſeemed an object only leſs dear; that at length diminiſhed to a cloud, the cloud ſhrunk to a ſpeck, and the ſpeck became inviſible.--- I threw myſelf on my bed, and giving way to the tears I had hitherto ſtifled, I beſought the Almighty to guard him he had ſo eminently diſtinguiſhed.

Compaſſion had induced Eſſex to conſent to our conveying over an old officer who had been deſperately wounded. The intenſe ſickneſs produced by the element, cauſed his wounds to open, which obliged us to put back and land him, or ſacrifice his life to our convenience; and this unforeſeen delay, expoſed us to a calamity as laſting as it was grievous.

Launched

Launched a fecond time on thofe reft-
lefs furges to which alone I could compare my own perturbed foul, the next
day brought the comparifon ftill nearer—
A dreadful tempeft arofe, nor were we
within reach of any port. The enraged
and howling winds drove the veffel at
pleafure a thoufand times fidelong into
the deep, and the impetuous and foam-
ing waves threw it up again with equal
violence.-------We remained ftupified
with terror; fhut down with our women in the cabin, the rapid motions and
cries of the feamen, the tremendous
cracks and groans of the veffel, united
with the warring elements to make that
fate indifferent every moment brought
nearer. To prepare my mind for the im-
pending event, I, however, recollected,
with due gratitude to heaven, that the
light veffel in which Effex failed, had
doubtlefs made a near port, ere the ftorm
began, and landed him in fafety.

I pondered once more on that wonderful character I had fo often confidered. I
faw, however ftrong the predominant
foible

foible of Lord Effex, it ftill gave way
to rectitude; and fearful the paffion which
led him towards me, might one day affect
his fafety, I bent to the awful God who
thus in thunder called away its weak
and helplefs object :--not without admiring the fingularity of that deftiny, which
by interring me in the ocean, fecured the
forged death and funeral I had publifhed
for myfelf, from ever being difcovered.

Strengthened, if not confoled by thefe
ideas, I fought to chear my no lefs fuffering friend; who, rejecting alike food and
comfort, refigned herfelf wholly up to
ficknefs, faintings, and forrow.----Ah,
who fhall fay we fuffer in vain! the feelings of the foul, like the organs of fight,
gain ftrength by ufe, till we dare to ana-
lyze that fate we once could not have ventured to confider; while the refined and exquifite fenfe of mental anguifh which renders us fuperior to common evils, often
gives an apparent fublimity to efforts which
are little in our own eftimation.---Lady
Southampton, yet diftinguifhed by nature,
fortune, love, clung to thofe rich poffeffions,

fions, and fhrunk from the awful immor-
tality which threatened every moment to
take place of them.----She liftened to me
with wonder, and this inftance of fortitude impreffed her mind with a reverence for my character, time could never
obliterate.

The fudden abatement of the ftorm
contributed little to our fafety; as the
fhip, ill calculated for fuch a conflict,
had bulged upon a rock, and now filled
fo faft with water, that the utmoft diligence of the crew could hardly fave us
from finking.----The fight of land ere the
evening clofed, had fcarce power to
chear for a moment, wretches who no
more hoped to behold the dawning of the
morn.----To the uproar and turbulence of
the ftorm, a filent horror and defolation
had now fucceeded fcarce lefs fhocking.
Midnight was hardly turned ere a difmal univerfal cry informed us the veffel
was finking---Lady Southampton threw
her arms helplefsly round me, and the
unprincipled part of the crew burfting
into

into our cabin, increased the horrors of the moment by opening our coffers, and gathering together their most valuable contents: an officer followed, who taking our hands in silence, led us toward the deck:---two boats were now preparing---the last melancholy hope we had of surviving.---The captain, who happily owed every thing to Essex, informed us, that as the larger boat had the better chance, he had fixed on placing us in that, ere the scattered crew could collect, and by pressing too numerously upon us, rob us of a last hope.---We were conveyed into the boat while he was yet speaking, and the sailors so impetuously followed, regardless of the captain's remonstrances and commands, that our danger seemed hardly diminished by the removal.----A hope nevertheless arose, which encouraged each individual to an exertion from whence the general safety was ascertained. Entirely enveloped in the only watch-coat which had been taken from the wreck, Lady Southamp-

ton

ton and myfelf (who were the only women
faved) knew but by the voices of our
companions whether life or death was to
be expected---the fea ran high, and the
grey dawn prefented to our eager eyes
a coaft, which we were informed was that of
Scotland, at no great diftance; an old
caftle appeared, on a fharp projection of
the land, whofe folid battlements feemed
proof againft every attack of art and nature; but the fhoals, rocks, and furf
which intervened, threatened to make us
ever behold it at a hopelefs diftance, unlefs we could intereft the compaffion of
its owners.

Every fignal of diftrefs was made for
hours apparently in vain, till the turn of
the tide; when two fifhing boats appeared, flowly working their way towards us.
A difcordant fhout of joy on the part of
our companions fplit the ears of my fick
friend and felf, who inly worfhipped the
power that preferved us.----The bene-
volent ftrangers approached, and their
garb no lefs than unknown language pro-

proclaimed them natives of the Scotch coaſt. To the men around us they of-fered biſcuits and whiſky in abundance, and beſtowed on me and Lady South-ampton a draught of cold water, which ſeemed as much more refreſhing as it was innocent.

Revived by this unexpected revolution in our fate, we by joint conſent ſhook off the heavy watch-coat which had a little ſaved us from the inceſſant ſpray of the enraged ſea, and when the boat was at length drawn towards the flight of rude ſteps leading to the caſtle, we both quitted it with no leſs celerity than thankfulneſs.---Our progreſs was for a moment impeded by ſurprize---at the gate of the caſtle ſtood two beings who ſeemed of ſome ſuperior order; ſo ſingular were their dreſs, beauty, and benevolence.------A youth and his ſiſter waved us toward them with graceful courteſy---the latter wore a light veſt and coat of Scots plaid, with a belt of green ſattin claſped with gold; the rude wind had carried off the covering

of

of her hair, and caufed her long auburn
locks to ftream on the bofom of the morning, expofing to view her flight ancles
half booted, and tinging her cheeks with
that pure cold colour, youth, health, innocence, and heaven, alone can give.---
The youth, who in features ftrongly re-
fembled his filter, was habited as a
hunter, with a fpear in his hand, and a
dagger hanging in his belt.---Both with
fmiles of hofpitality ran forward to receive us; and while the young lady took
the arm of my friend, the youth with an
impaffioned pleafure fhook my hand,
cafting a look of mingled wonder and
difdain at the foiled, though rich habili-
ments I had on; which indeed originally
rather agreed with my own fex than that
I intruded upon. The antique hall into
which they conducted us, was hung with
tattered banners, mouldy coats of arms, and
every proud remnant of war and ancientry.
Refrefhments fuitable to our paft diftrefs
were bufily fet before us, nor, with that
intuitive politenefs fuperior minds always
poffefs,

possess, did either venture to express a
curiosity till they had frankly satisfied
ours.---From them we learnt that the spot
fortune had thrown us on, was an island
on the coast of Scotland, and the place
which sheltered us, Dornock Castle, held
by the Laird of that name; that they were
brother and sister to that Laird, who was
now absent on a family concern of no small
moment; in short, that their elder sister
Mabel, famed through the country for
her beauty, having unhappily shewn it
at Court, the King would not suffer her
to return; and their brother, fearful she
should yield to his licentious wishes, had
hastened thither to claim her. The young
people who made this artless recital, were
formed to grace it---when the fair Phœbe
spoke of the charms of her sister, her
own were heighthened by a softer, fuller
bloom; and when she mentioned their
dangerous effect, the proud blush of a
generous shame gave manliness to the
boyish features of her brother Hugh.---
Accustomed as my friend and self had
long been to every worldly charm and

advantage, we faw in this remote fpot, and thefe untutored children of nature, a fimple and noble grace art only refines away.

When it came to my turn to narrate, I ufed every artifice to guard againft the poffibility of danger.------Adopting the name Lady Southampton had lately quitted, I called myfelf Vernon; a youth employed till lately as a page in the train of the Earl of Effex, and now his fecretary---the lady with me, I faid, allied to the Earl of Southampton, was lately wedded to me; and both were following thefe noblemen when overtaken by the tempeft which had thrown us upon their fhore, and rendered us debtors to their humanity. Finding we came from the feat of war, and were converfant with the Court of England, they both afked a thoufand various queftions fuitable to their fex, age, and fimplicity, refpecting the one and the other; and our defcriptions, to their unformed conceptions, comprized every charm of magnificence, glory, and gaiety.

The

The happy device of a pretended marriage enabling me to fhare the chamber of Lady Southampton, we chofe the hour of retirement to confider our prefent fituation, and the mode moft likely to reftore us once more to the country and connections from which the ftorm had feparated us.----My friend juftly remarked, that the failors wrecked with us, and its natives, were all the people likely to vifit this remote and folitary ifle, and that if we failed to take advantage of the departure of the firft, we fhould throw ourfelves wholly upon the generofity of the Laird of Dornock, of whofe character we could not venture to decide from thofe of the amiable young people, who had fo warmly embraced our caufe.----After the application of Effex to my brother in my favour had been rejected, I had every thing to fear if any circumftance fhould betray me into his power, and the ftricteft fecrefy on our names and condition alone could give us a hope of liberty;---how under fuch reftrictions we could clearly

H 2   explain

explain our prefent fituation to the two noblemen whom alone it concerned, neither
of us could difcover; neverthelefs, neceffity obliged us to come to fome refolution; and perfuaded the writing of each
would be known to him to whom the
letter was addreffed, weary as we both
were, a part of the night was fpent in
preparing two epiftles for the failors to
convey.---The morning came, and with
it the mortifying information that we were
a few hours too late; the men faved with
us having hired a fifhing fmack in which
they failed away at the turn of the tide:
nor did the owners know their deftina-
tion till the veffel returned. I was not
without an idea that our youthful protectors had voluntarily concealed fo material
an event, in the hope of detaining us; but
certainly had that really been the cafe, it
was not half fo inexcufable as our own
imprudence and negleft.---We hired a
boat to purfue them with the letters, but
after feveral days fpent in painful expectation, the packets were returned to us
with

with the mortifying information that all enquiry had proved fruitlefs. We had now no refource but in the generofity of the Laird of Dornock, and endeavoured to fortify ourfelves with patience to wait his return.

The youthful brother and fifter ex-preffed a generous concern for our fituati-on; but wholly without power, they could do no more.---Prifoners at large, as we were, effectually bounded by the roar-ing ocean, and depending folely on con-tingencies for freedom, the days to us crept heavily away---I fometimes remem-bred with a figh that I was in Scotland---that kingdom where by inheritance I might claim a rank that would enable me to decide my own fate, had not a com-bination of events, forerunning even my birth, made every advantage of fortune and nature alike ufelefs to me. I en-deavoured to difcover the real character of their King, but even from the report of his friends, to be able to term it good, I was obliged to think it weak; and in

that

that cafe knew he would inevitably be
furrounded with artful politicians ready
to profit by his foible; in fhort, I found
however near he and I were allied in
blood, we were born to be diftinct beings in creation, and to meet would endanger the fafety of the weaker.   When
I turned my anxious foul toward England, it brought me no relief.---As far
from the reach of intelligence as if in the
wilds of Arabia, I in vain fought to difcover the reception Effex had met with
at Court.---That name which in the vanity of my heart I had often thought the
world refounded with, I found, with
checked pride, was fcarcely known in an
adjacent country, till my lips fo often re-
peated it; and even when moft anxious
to oblige me, thofe of others only echoed
the found fo dear, fo beloved! I had
but too much reafon to fear doubts of my
fafety would make him carelefs of his
own, and often would have refigned
every brilliant profpect fancy ever fpread
before me, to afcertain the life of the Earl.

Too

Too late I regretted the pride of heart which had made me refist the defire I felt to detain him in Ireland; and could not but acknowledge it was rather that than principle which reconciled me to his departure; yet, in a fituation fo delicate as ours, to wifh was to command; and the facrifice his own foul did not dictate, mine difdained to receive.

My mind now daily paffed through fuch a chaos of ideas and emotions, as would have prevented the time from appearing tedious, had not its prolongation been the origin of moft of them

Often fitting on the rude battlements of the caftle while the furges beat againft their bafe, have I tuned the lute of Phœbe, and while fhe warbled a few wild airs of inconceivable melody in a language unknown to me, my full foul has wept over the myfterious fate of my fifter.---Ah, how eafy is it to be unknown! - -to be entombed alive!---If I even in a civilized adjacent kingdom, in effect the country of all my anceftors, can be thus

helplefs,

helpleſs, what may the poor Matilda have been?-----Turn buſy imagination from the fatal ſuppoſition.

The overſight we had committed in ſuffering the ſailors to leave us, became every day more and more regretted.---Lady Southampton ſoon found herſelf in a ſituation that required the tendereſt indulgence, and would forbid removal, even if our aſylum ſhould be traced by anxious love. We ſpent our lives in fretting, and had we not poſſeſſed an unlimited intimacy, I know not how we ſhould have endured the inceſſant chagrin. _---deprived even of the uſual reſources; a ſcanty library, a lute, ſome ruſtic airs, and a pedigree as old as the creation, bounded the poſſeſſions, and knowledge of our young friends, and could not add any thing to our own.

The Laird of Dornock, however, returned at laſt.---Ah, how unlike his gentle kindred!----phlegmatic, ſelf-willed, creſted, and imperious, his aſpect preſented a correſpondent harſhneſs; and we inſtantly felt it vain to reſt a hope on his friend-

friendſhip; he no doubt reproved his brother and ſiſter for having lived on ſuch
familiar terms with ſtrangers, avowedly
ſubordinate; and though he often made
us ſenſible our company was a burthen,
he took not a ſingle ſtep to relieve
himſelf from it.   Phœbe had begun
to improve herſelf in muſick ere his arrival; it was his pleaſure ſhe ſhould continue to do ſo; but his preſence threw a
coldneſs and conſtraint over the whole
party, which made what I had once
thought a relief, an inconceivable toil.
The ingenuous noble girl ſaw her brother's
inſolence with a grief which prevented
her from profiting by the leſſons ſo much
deſired---her guſhing tears would often
relax the ſtrings of her lute, while low-
warbling tales of hopeleſs love, and her
ſad eyes fix themſelves on mine with an
expreſſion too ſtrong to be miſunderſtood.
I perceived while unconſcious of the danger, becauſe poſſeſſed with the remembrance of my own diſguiſe, I had won the
gentle heart I only ſought to form.---Cir-
cumſtanced as I was, this could not but
be

be a dangerous acquifition; and by a fatality yet more alarming, her elder brother foon after became enamoured of Lady Southampton; nor did he conceal that inclination---he had from his arrival regarded me with an eye which indicated doubt on the fubject of our marriage; but the increafing fize of my friend, and our habit of living together, appeared to controvert a fufpicion which neverthelefs remained in his mind.

Anxious to profit by the only hour in the day which could favor his views, he was obliged to give the advantage he fought; and permit me to teach his fifter with no other guard than his younger brother Hugh, while he paffed the interval with Lady Southampton.---All equally rejoiced at an incident all had equally defired; as to myfelf, determined from the moment I had been convinced of the paffion of the fair Phœbe, to feize the firft opportunity of intrufting her with my difguife, ere fhame for the miftake fhould difguft her with the object, I was not forry to confide it to

her

her brother: as if it did not more attach him to my intereſt, it would at leaſt
obviate every fear he might entertain on
his ſiſter's account, whom he could then
ſafely leave at any time. This juſt candor produced more conſequences than
one. The ſweet Phœbe ſtarted, bluſhed,
and firſt lifting her ſwimming eyes toward
heaven, then covered them with her
hands----when I ceaſed to ſpeak ſhe timor-
ouſly raiſed them to my face.----"Ah! why
had you not been thus ſincere at firſt?
cried the generous girl, the power was
then in our hands---*now*"-----ſhe ſhook
her head, and in that emphatic geſture
ſtrongly finiſhed her imperfect ſpeech.
Alarmed and anxious, I conjured her to
confide to me thoſe reaſons which made
our ſituations in her opinion ſo hopeleſs.
She could not reſiſt my entreaties; and at
length acknowledged, that from the moment her elder brother returned, Hugh
no leſs than myſelf had obſerved a haugh-
tineſs and ſeverity in his air and language more forbidding than uſual; at
luſt

laſt they had diſcovered that their ſiſter Mabel, far from liſtening to virtue and the Laird of Dornock, had yielded to the King; and to protect herſelf from her family, had been compelled to publiſh her ſhame, by claiming her lover's protection. To reconcile the Laird of Dornock to ſo cutting a diſgrace, a title had been offered him, with any poſt about the Court he ſhould fix on: and that at length the fair Mabel conſoled herſelf for the forfeiture of every rational diſtinction, by the temporary honor of reigning in the heart of her King, and being called a Counteſs." I enquired with ſurprize, how an event ſhould affect us in which we apparently had no concern ? Hugh anſwered, " his brother, far from accepting the ſplendid coverings offered for infamy, had retired from Court in great indignation; that at firſt they had both been compelled to ſcorn and return every letter and preſent ſent by their ſiſter: yet of late ſome view, inexplicable to them, had made a ſingular alteration in the Laird of Dornock's ſentiments.---

ments.---Several couriers had been difpatched by him to the favourite Countefs,
but neither their commiffions, nor the
anfwers, ever tranfpired; yet many circumftances had given them reafon to believe that our pacquets had never been
forwarded as we were taught to believe.---
I changed colour at the idea of this deliberate treachery, thanking heaven I alone
had been informed of it; as Lady Southampton, often unable to govern her feelings, by fome imprudent fpeech would
infallibly have betrayed her knowledge of
it. The young Hugh, obferving my uneafinefs, affured me, though hopelefs of
finding a faithful meffenger, he held himfelf anfwerable for the releafe of thofe he
had contributed to enthrall, and that I
might depend upon his own fervices if I
would deign to confide in him, nor fhould
we be fufpected as the caufes of his dif-
appearance, fince the Laird of Dornock
well knew his fifter Mabel's particular
fondnefs for him, and would naturally
imagine he was determined to profit by
the

the high favour fhe held at Court."——
Is there a charm on earth fo touching as
generofity ?——The noble youth paufed
with an air that indicated his ardent defire of having his offer accepted, left it
fhould be miftaken for a vaunt. I took a
hand of each young friend, and returning
acknowledgments fuitable to the occafion,
declined embroiling them with their fullen brother; who could not want power
to render our fituation much more intolerable, if once he fufpected us of alienat-
ing his family from their duty.---I perfuaded them, as well as myfelf, that our
own friends would with unwearied diligence fearch us out the moment they
difcovered any part of the crew furvived
the wreck ; of which the Captain would
certainly inform them, unlefs he funk with
the fhip.

Yet day after day proved this hope vain
and fallacious.----A dreary winter paffed
away in this remote Caftle, through every
aperture of which the keen and howling
wind poured unreftrained; and the wild
ocean

ocean fwelled with frequent ftorms, while our affrighted fenfes often miftook the roar of the tempeft for the groans of the dying.

I had almoft ceafed to hope, when one day while our hoft was hunting, I wandered to the battlements as ufual, and defcried from thence a fmall veffel approaching, better built, and more clean, than thofe I was accuftomed to fee; as it drew nearer the land, I perceived Englifh dreffes.------My heart took the alarm, I leant impatiently forward, ftraining the keen fenfe whofe imperfection I complained of.---The boat drew near.---I difcerned the regimental of Effex; I gave a groan of exquifite delight, and reeling forward, fhould have plunged into the ocean, had not the young Hugh who ftood behind held me faft.---The officer looked up, and I inftantly perceived him to be Henry Tracey, the favorite aid-de-camp of Lord Effex, once before deputed in fearch of me.---Difappointment mingled with the various and interefting emo-

emotions of the moment.---I pointed to the ſtranger, ſighed, and fainted away.

They bore me to Lady Southampton, who thunderſtruck at ſeeing me lifeleſs, and unable to gueſs the cauſe, ſeemed little better herſelf. Hugh, who clearly comprehended from my impaſſioned geſture, how intereſting the arrival of the ſtranger was to me, haſtened to bring him him to our apartment, while yet his brother was abſent; when inſtantly retiring, he left us full liberty.————" Tracey ?" cried both of us at once, " Eſſex ?" " Southampton ?" echoed each heart, " ſum up all in a word."----" They live, returned he, and need only behold you to be happy."---Ah, gracious heaven ! cried I, lifting my eyes thither, while I preſented my heart with my hand to the faithful meſſenger, receive my tranſport; we now can breathe freely; give us the relief of knowing the events which followed the dangerous voyage of Eſſex and Southampton." " I ſhould hardly dare to do ſo, had I not firſt aſſured you of their ſafety, reſumed Tracey, for

ſorrow

forrow I fee has been preying already
on your bloom; it would not perhaps
have been more fpared had you paffed
this trying interval in London."

Apprehenfive every moment of an in-
terruption from the Laird of Dornock,
I befought the worthy Tracey to difpenfe
with all preface, and haften his recital.

"With terror and anxiety, continued
he, I followed my Lord into the veffel felected to convey him home, nor were
thefe emotions diminifhed when I perceived the Lord Deputy full of fits of doubt
and reflection, which at times were obvious even to himfelf; often would he
affect to drown them in gay fociety and,
wine, and for the firft time in his life, he
affumed a falfe bravery.----At the hours
of retirement, far from indulging that
intimacy fo long eftablifhed between
him and Lord Southampton, of which I
had often been a grateful and humble
partaker, he funk into an abfence of mind,
and total filence, no lefs alarming to his
beloved friend than myfelf; in effect,
that Nobleman faw he had ' fet his for-

tune on a caſt, and he would ſtand the hazard of the die,' as I conjectured by his turning to me one day, and by an expreſſive motion of his head, leading mine towards the ſide of the veſſel, where my Lord leant; his thoughtful countenance apparently fixed on thoſe rolling waves which yet perhaps he ſaw not.——— " All is not well in the heart of thy Lord, Tracey," ſaid his noble friend, then pauſing a moment, he added, in a lower tone, " Ah Eſſex, *aut Cæſar, aut nullus!*" the Lord Deputy happily advanced, and ſaved me the neceſſity of corroborating ſentiments it gave me pain to adopt.

It was not with the cuſtomary greetings we beheld the pleaſant ſhores of our native country---doubt and anxiety threw a gloom over thoſe lively and ſpontaneous emotions which often ſuſpend even the ſenſe of ſuffering. Lord Eſſex loſt not a moment, but poſted toward the Court, with ſuch expedition, that he outwent all information, and was his own harbinger.---We arrived one morning ere
yet

yet the Queen left her chamber; but alas,
it was no longer the Court we had left---
every face around appeared ftrange to us;
and we faw too plainly that the invidious
Cecils reigned there triumphant.---Lord
Grey, a favorite of theirs, whom we had
met on the road, had prefumed to pafs
the Earl of Effex without notice---that
Nobleman gave him only an eye-beam,
and haftened on to decide his fate.---Form
was annihilated by circumftances, and he
rufhed into the prefence of Elizabeth the
moment his arrival was announced---ac-
cuftomed to behold him with complacency, to receive him with kindnefs, fhe
yielded through furprize to the habits of
fo many years, and granted the private audience he requefted.---She liftened
to a vague and weak vindication of his
conduct in Ireland, and the dotage of her
foul was tranfiently gratified with the idea
that he had preferred the recovery of her
affection to that of his reputation in
arms. After a long conference, the Earl
rejoined his friends; pride and pleafure

had

had flushed his cheek, and the idea of reaf-
suming his accustomed influence, diffused
through his mien that benignity and graciousness which are at once its nature and
its charm. Resentment and rage never
constituted any part of his character but
at the moment he suffered by those passions:
such galling sensations were already forgotten.----Overwhelmed with the congra-
tulations of his friends; encircled even
by his overawed enemies, the heroic
Essex rose above the triumph he could not
but desire---every face was instantaneously changed, and those who knew not
an hour before whether they should recollect
him, now with servile adulation hallowed
his very footsteps.----This fatal interval
of short-lived power was, however, the last
heaven allowed him.----The crafty Cecils
and their faction seized the moment he in-
judiciously quitted the Queen, to per-
suade her this indulged favourite had not
only acted contrary to his commission, in
venturing himself to return, but that he
had brought home with him all his chosen
ad-

adherents, as well as every afpiring fpirit likely to ftrengthen his fway, and circum-fcribe hers.----They touched the foul of Elizabeth where it was moft vulnerable, and having thus oppofed to each other the two leading weakneffes of her nature, by throwing the weight of party into the one fcale, it foon preponderated. She was unhappily in that declining age which renders every human being in fome degree capricious and timid.---Already tinctured with fear, fhe foon yielded to the various informations officioufly brought her by factious confederates.---She was told on all hands that Lord Effex was holding a Court even in her Palace, and infolent and daring as this conduct could not but appear, it was of lefs confequence than the unbounded influence he ever main-tained over the people---an influence he would more than recover the moment he was feen in London. "For *themfelves* they heeded not---willing martyrs to their integrity and fealty; but for their Queen, they all trembled at the profpect."---It was

I 3   too

too hazardous to be rifqued by Elizabeth; fear and refentment conquered the tender prepoffeffion which ftill ftruggled faintly at her heart, and fhe determined to afcertain her own fafety, as well as that of her kingdom, by imprifoning her favorite: nor is this refolution to be wondered at, fince even her love conduced to it, when irritated by the imaginary fling of ingratitude. She had fet the Earl up in early youth as an idol for her own heart to worfhip; but he was not born to be fatiffied with unmerited admiration----the more he acquired the more he fought to deferve; till having eftablifhed his favour on innate noblenefs, he rofe above partial diftinction, leaving her to lament at leifure the very elevation fhe had given. From this period fhe had been weak and irrefolute in every inftance where he was concerned; at intervals lavifhing honors to which he had no title; at others, withholding advantages he had fairly won. The motive of this inconfiftency he could not fail to difcern, but perfuaded an at-
tach-

tachment which thus powerfully coped
with her judgment, was unconquerable;
he forgot that she was sinking fast into
the vale of years, when the noblest paffions infenfibly condenfe into felf love.

You who fo well know the heart of
my Lord, Madam, cried Tracey, turning
to me, will better imagine than I can
defcribe, his deep fenfe of an indignity
entirely public, and apparently premedi-
tated. So unexpected a manœuvre maf-
tered his judgment, and giving way to
the moft paffionate extremes, he drew his
fword, and would have returned it by
her meffenger, befeeching her " to reward his fervices by adding a more decifive blow to that fhe once before be-
ftowed on him, fince both feemed to him,
lefs fhocking and ignominious than fuch
open and unmerited contumely."----In
vain his friend fought to moderate his
wrath; in vain his enemies drew near,
eager to catch and treafure the rafh expreffions he fhould unwarily utter, and
convert them to his ruin.---Touched on

I 4   the

the tendereſt point, his honor, the world
combined would have wanted power to
ſilence him---he gave full ſcope to his
indignant and wounded feelings, and
with a ſeverity of truth more galling and
dangerous than the greateſt exaggerati-
ons declared aloud, " the Queen had outlived all her nobler faculties, and that
her ſoul was grown as crooked as her body." This cutting ſarcaſm was too faithfully conveyed to Elizabeth, who regard-
leſs of his pride while her own was thus
wounded, committed him to the charge of
the Lord Keeper, whoſe houſe was in effect
his priſon.

Oh heavens! what wild viciſſitudes,
what tranſports of paſſion took poſſeſſion
of my Lord, at recollecting the imprudent readineſs with which he had delivered himſelf helpleſs and unguarded into
the hands of his enemies! ſtruggling
like a lion in the toils, every vein would
ſometimes ſwell almoſt to madneſs, nor
dared I leave him a moment alone.

I had no other hope of aſſuaging his
irritated paſſions, than by recalling to his
                                    mind

mind the beloved image of the fair voyager, to whom the news of this event, and the fear of what might follow it, would be little lefs than death. I averted one ftorm however only to give free paf-fage to another; the tear of tendernefs proudly trembled on the burning cheek of anger, and a grief it fplit my heart to behold, took poffeffion of his.---" Spare me the killing remembrance, he would cry---difgraced---defamed---imprifoned; how fhall I ever lift my eyes to that fair, that noble fufferer? I tell thee Tracey, rather would I have died than known this fhameful moment"------Impreffed by the unwearied attachment I had ever fhewn him, and overweighed by the fenfe of his own fituation, my Lord at length con-defcended to lighten his own heart by unfolding to me its deareft views; well he knew they would never pafs beyond mine---no, every vein of it fhould crack ere I would wrong fo generous a confi-dence, which I acknowledge but to prove my fate wholly dependent on the Nobleman

man I ferve: I would have it fo, and heaven could afflict me only by feparating them.

The faithful Lord Southampton was his daily vifitant: though not himfelf a prifoner, the confcioufnefs that every action of his life was watched and reported, bound that Nobleman to a moft cautious obfervance. The Cecils had now no wifh ungratified, for the imprudent bitternefs of Lord Effex had fupplied the only fuel to the Queen's refentment which could long keep it alive; nor did time, in cooling the paffions of my Lord, incline him to fubmiffion----convinced in his own mind he was the injured perfon, reflection only fettled rage into difguft and contempt; neverthelefs, his conftitution fuffered feverely by this variety of paffions; when one feized upon it which annihilated all the reft, and completely debilitated his health---a grief more touching than glory or ambition could occafion, fuddenly overcame him.----The time was now elapfed which ought to have brought to him and Lord Southampton the wel-

come

come affurance that the partners of their
fouls were fafe in Cumberland---the time
was come I fay!---alas, it was gone!---
Afraid to communicate to each other a
terror which preyed alike on both, Lord
Southampton difpatched exprefs upon exprefs in vain.---The days that lingered fo
tedioufly away, however, matured doubt
into certainty. Lord Effex no longer
contended with the nervous fever which
obliged him to take to his bed; where
reaching out a languid hand to his over-
powered friend, he broke, at laft, the fearful, heavy filence. "They are gone, forever
gone, my dear Southampton, cried he, in
the low accent of incurable defpair; heaven
has fpared to fouls fo gentle and fufceptible
thofe trials our ftouter minds can perhaps
better contend with.----Oh, thou dear one!
yet do I regret that this bofom did not receive thy laft fighs! that entombed with
thee even in the ocean, death had not
confummated a union fortune ever frown-
ed on---but I haften impatiently to rejoin
thee, oh Ellinor! my firft, my only love!"

The

The killing remembrance which dif-
tracted his mind, foon rendered a malady
flight at firft, defperate; he was even
given over; the Queen for a long time
withftood the accounts given by his
friends of his fituation, fo deeply had
his enemies impreffed her with the idea
that this was only a refined artifice to
tempt her to humiliate herfelf. Neverthelefs, by one of thofe paffionate emotions with which nature fometimes over-
reaches the moft elaborate fineffes of art,
fhe fuddenly determined to afcertain his
real fituation, by fending her own phyfician to vifit him.---The report of that
gentleman convinced her of its danger---
he was ordered to watch over the Earl
with the moft anxious care, and even to
hint to him that every diftinction would
be reftored with his health.---But, alas!
fympathy itfelf had no longer any charms
for him, and the prefence of Lord Southampton feemed the only relief his fate
admitted. That amiable Nobleman, no
lefs fenfible of the mutual calamity than
his

his friend, had not the same reasons to bury his affliction it in silence.---Repeated messengers were sent alike to Cumberland, and the port you embarked from, ladies: those who returned from the latter, only confirmed the fears which had hitherto fluctuated---they informed the lover and the husband, that the wife of the Captain mourned for him as dead, nor was it doubted but that the crew and passengers were alike victims to a storm so sudden and tremendous. The active and enlivened soul frequently exhausts its most acute sensations by anticipation.-- Certainty could not add to the grief occasioned by surmise; and the extinguished hopes of the friends gave them alike up to that cold and sullen despair, which is the worst of all states, because frequently incurable. Those late hopes the Queen was willing to revive her dying favorite with, made not the least impression on him; and the Cecils learnt with astonishment, that, neither their views, their conduct, nor even his own disgrace-

ful

ful imprisonment, any longer touched Lord
Essex; nay, that not even his recovery
was able to revive those habits the world
were taught to think hitherto uncontroulable. His friends, on the contrary, blest
the skilful physician who prolonged a life
so valuable, and saw with the happiest
hopes, that those romantic flights in his
character his enemies had almost wrought
up to his ruin, were at once extinguished; leaving it without any other
distinction than a melancholy sweetness
which rather turned his thoughts toward
philosophy than war. The people, ever
naturally disposed to side with the unfortunate, cried out, that he was the innocent victim of the Cecil party; - who by
some odious strokes of policy, added popularity to their depressed rival in dimi-
nishing their own.------Elizabeth herself
could no longer support the idea that the
man she still loved was obscurely breaking his heart while yet in the flower of
youth, in an unmerited and disgraceful
prison.---She yielded to the information of
the

the phyſician that his amending health required air, and ſent him her permiſſion to retire to any of his ſeats in the country; but forbad him to attempt appearing in her preſence: a reſtriction perhaps more agreeable to him, than herſelf, could ſhe have ſeen the deſolate ſituation of mind in which he departed.

From the country he addreſſed a letter of thanks to the Queen, which diſplayed at once his eloquence, gratitude, and languor: in truth, the latter gained ground daily in his character. Lord Eſſex was born capable of uniting in his preſon every various and generous purſuit had fortune allowed it, but not even he was equal to living without one.---I frequently trembled at beholding his gloom and inanity. Wholly removed from the ſphere in which he had hither moved, and the pleaſures he had once enjoyed, the rude ſociety of his neighbours, and the boiſterous amuſements the country afforded, rather offended than filled an enlightened and ſuſceptible heart. He wandered

dered all day in the woods alone, and
returned every evening spent and unre-
freshed, only to recover animal strength
enough to enable him to pass the morrow
in the same melancholy manner.

In this situation I fancied a false hope
could not add to his danger, and might
perhaps rouse those active faculties every
hour seemed more and more to absorb.
I one day ventured to repeat to him an
imaginary dream, tending to prove you
still existed.---Not even the firmest mind
can resist the subtle attacks of superstition
when labouring under depression.---His
soul so eagerly adopted the fiction of my
brain, that I was a thousand times tempted
to acknowledge it to be such, but dared
not venture to shew him I had played
upon his wounded feelings.   Revived
with the most vague and distant hope, he
impatiently drove me away on a search
my own soul foreboded to be fruitless.
I even debated after I set out, whether
I should not loiter the time away in England till I could decently return from my
im-

imaginary peregrination, when a dream,
more pointed and fingular than that I
had feigned, awakened in myfelf thofe
hopes I had communicated to my Lord:
but I will not call it a dream, fince,
furely the event proves it a vifitation.---
Oh, gracious God! what joy will my
return pour into the hearts that now ach
for either! How pure will be the fatif-
faction derived from their acknowledgments!"

During this long recital, my tumultuous feelings purfued my love through
every defperate fituation.———My woe-
ftruck heart hardly dared to breathe,
till finding him at laft free and well,
it gave a deep figh, and refpired without pain. Effex infulted, endangered,
imprifoned;———I caft my eyes round
thofe gloomy walls, I fo late thought
my prifon, and raifing them to heaven,
adored the power who there confined me,
unconfcious of the confliets I could not
have fupported. Ah, Effex! what were
the warring elements, the midnight

Vol. III.   K   wreck,

wreck, the long, long folitude, the dire
uncertainty I had fo bitterly bewailed, to
the fingle idea of feeing thee one moment
at the mercy of Elizabeth, one moment
in the power of thy enemies! And yet,
for me thy generous foul loft all fenfe of
even thefe inflictions; pride, vanity, and
grandeur, in vain affailed thee: a true
and noble paffion beat unalterably at thy
heart, condenfing in one favourite forrow, thofe mighty powers which once
fulfilled every various and active duty of
humanity.

But this was not a moment for impaffioned reveries. Lady Southampton
recalled my attention to the prefent moment; and we employed it in informing Tracey of the name, character, and
fituation, we had thought it prudent to
affume, as well as of thofe of our hoft.
Scarce was he mafter of thefe important
particulars, ere the Laird of Dornock
returned, and broke in upon us with an
abruptnefs and anger he took no pains
to difguife. The fight of an Englifh
officer

officer a little abated his wrath. Tracey, according to the plan we had agreed on, called Lady Southampton his fifter, and with every teftimony of gratitude for the hofpitable fhelter our hoft had fo long given us, offered a recompence ftill more agreeable; with which happily he had had the forecaft to provide himfelf.---While the Scot ftood irrefolute refpecting his anfwer, the wary Tracey turned to us, and in an authoritative voice, faid, he muft anfwer to the Queen for his ab-fence, did it exceed the appointed time ; and therefore, we muft quickly take leave of our friends, and haften our de-parture for England. This decifive fpeech increafed the perturbation and difap-pointment already obvious in the features of our hoft; neverthelefs, our going was to him fo unforefeen an event, that not being able to find a fufficient reafon for detain-ing us, he tacitly confented to it.

My heart bounded at the unhoped-for liberation, and I would have failed that moment, defpite of wind and tide; but

K 2

as the failors declared this impoffible, our
departure was delayed till the next morning. Whether the various incidents of
the day accelerated the hour appointed by
nature, or, that Lady Southampton, contrary to her own idea, had reached it, I
know not; fhe was feized at midnight,
however, with the pains of labour, and
fuffered fo feverely, that her life was def-
paired of. In the courfe of the enfuing
day fhe was delivered of a dead child,
and I was obliged to confole myfelf for
the long delay this event muft neceffarily
occafion, in the pleafing idea that the
partner of my fate was not prematurely
divided from it---in truth, her vexation
was fo great, that I was reduced to ftifle
my own, left I fhould contribute to her
illnefs.

The fate which hope yet gilds, though
but from the verge of the horizon, is
never quite infupportable. We found,
in the protection of Tracey, and the idea
of rejoining the world to which he feemed
our immediate link, the means of be-
guiling many a tedious hour; nor was
this

this confolation fuperfluous; for the Laird
of Dornock became, from the moment
of Tracey's arrival, more fullen and impenetrable than ever.---Self, was, in him,
the prevailing principle. Early invefted
with that bounded, but abfolute, authority, which oftener produces and fhelters
tyranny, than a more extenfive field of
action, he had hitherto known no oppofition.---How often has a blind paffion
warped the nobleft natures? nor was it perhaps unnatural that he fhould ftretch his
prerogative to retain in his hands a lovely
and beloved woman, over whom he could
claim no right.---Long inured to fear,
fufpicion, and anguifh, they readily returned to their throbbing habitation, my
heart. I often fancied I read murder
written in dark, but legible lines, on the
knit brow of our hoft; and though Tracey
flept only in an outer chamber clofe by us,
fcarce could I perfuade myfelf he was fuffered to reft peaceably there, or yet lived for our
protection: neverthelefs, I ftrove at times
to reject thofe black chimeras a lively
imagination perhaps too readily adopted;

K 3   The

The Laird of Dornock no longer inter-
fered with us, or our fate; neither did
he withhold from us the company of his
sister.---That sweet girl, new to society,
with a romantic happiness peculiar to
youth, gifted every object with her own
graces and virtues; impressed at once
with the merit of Tracey, she transferred
to a heart which could return it the
passion I had unwarily inspired, nor was
her second choice unpropitious. Tracey,
whose soul had expanded in a camp, was
yet to learn the inconceivable charm of
love: it took full possession of him.
With a sweet, though sad pleasure, I
witnessed pure and innocent vows, which
continually reminded me of those days,
when like Phœbe, I looked enraptured
on the varied landscape of life, yet glowing with the early beams of hope; unconscious of the showers which often
would fall, the heavy nights which must
wholly obscure it. Tracey, no less delighted than his mistress, no longer hastened his departure to England, and looked

                                        aftoaſtoniſhed that we did not find every charm of exiſtence in this diſmal exile.

I, however, anxiouſly waited with Lady Southampton, the day when her recovered health ſhould enable us to de-part.---It came at length, and we were eagerly preparing for the voyage, when the Laird of Dornock ſent us an order to read, by which the King of Scots im-powered him to detain us. I know not any ſhock of all fate had impoſed on me, I ever felt more ſenſibly : nevertheleſs, I had preſence of mind enough to ob-ſerve, by the date of this order, that it had been obtained during the confine-ment of my friend. The diſappoint-ment and deſpair this incident occaſi-oned, was only alleviated by the recol-lection that in abuſing the authority of the King, to indulge an unworthy incli-nation, the Laird of Dornock had made himſelf reſponſible to the laws of his country for our ſafety, by admitting that ſuch perſons were in his cuſtody. Tra-cey gave him notice of this immediately ; and though he moderated his rage in

con-

confideration of the fair Phœbe, he warned the Laird of Dornock to treat us nobly, as he would anfwer it to his own King, and the Queen of England, in whofe name we fhould foon be demanded. To this indignant vaunt, for in truth it was no better, the haughty Scot coldly replied, " that he fhould take his chance of incurring an old woman's anger, who perhaps had already refigned all her rights to his mafter." Tracey could no longer controul the feelings of his generous foul, and replied with acrimony. The Laird of Dornock bad him profit by the occafion, and be gone immediately, if he did not mean to be included among the prifoners. There wanted only this ftroke to confummate our wretchednefs, and however reluctantly we loft our ohly friend and protector, Lady Southampton joined me in urging him to go; and over-ruling all his objections, we haftened him alone into a bark, which an hour before we feemed to fee ourfelves in. He comforted us

with

with the affurance of foon returning, being fully perfuaded the King of Scots
would never authorize fo unjuft and illegal
a procedure, when once the whole circumftance was impartially ftated to him.
I fighed, at remembering I knew him better; but as an explanation at that moment was vain, I urged not the unbounded influence of the fair Mabel,
through whofe illicit connection with the
King, this order had doubtlefs been obtained.   How fhould that Monarch be
convinced of a remote act of injuftice,
who even at the moment of committing
it, was wronging every moral and religious duty? The man who once voluntarily errs, muft either be weak or vicious;
in the firft inftance, he refigns himfelf up
to the paffions of others, in the latter to his
own; and in either cafe fcarce ever re-
covers the narrow but even boundary of
virtue.

   It was not by fuch means I hoped for
freedom---ah, no! my views all pointed to
the lover to whom my heart like the nee-

dle

dle ever vibrated, though far divided.——
Let Effex be once informed, fighed I---
let him once know where to find me, and
he would crofs the globe to enfure my
fafety. When the chagrin of this trying
moment abated, I called to mind the
infinite relief the vifit of Tracey had
given our fpirits, and the change it had
made in our fituation, by acquitting us
of thofe petty obligations which always
humiliate a noble mind, unlefs it finds a
congenial one in the beftower.

I foon obferved that the Laird of Dornock had not courage to profit by the
bafe injuftice he had committed. The
fubfervient fituation Tracey placed himfelf in when we were prefent, and the
profound deference with which he obeyed
our every wifh, neither agreeing with
the rank we avowed, nor the regimental he
wore, a vague idea of myftery had taken
poffeffion of our hoft's mind, which wanted
vigor and activity to attempt developing
it. Confcious too late, that he had in
releafing Tracey, fet a fpy on his own
conduct,

conduct, he vainly regretted the timidity which prevented his detaining him.
He neverthelefs, at intervals, ftill talked
of love to Lady Southampton, offering
to buy a return by imaginary worlds of
wealth: for to us, accuftomed to elegance
and luxury, all his poffeffions appeared
but a gaudy poverty. As thefe oftenta-
tious and abfurd offers were one day
made in my prefence, I could not but
take fome notice of them; he filenced me,
however, by replying, I muft be cautious how I exerted a fpirit fo likely to
make him transfer his attachment, and be
fatisfied with protecting one of the two;
fince I could neither think fo ill of his
difcernment, or my own beauty, as to
believe him the dupe of my difguife. As
it was the firft moment a doubt on the
fubject had ever tranfpired, my confufion gave him inftant conviction: I could
not recover myfelf fufficiently to reply for
fome moments: at length I told him
he had gueffed the only part of our fecret
which did not lie too deep for his knowledge;

ledge; neverthelefs, all he had difcovered, was but the leaft part of the myftery,
and finally, that the day which informed
him of our names and rank, would call
him to a fevere account, if his conduct
were in the leaft unworthy either us or himfelf.—I boldly affirmed, that the only
thing wanting to our fafety, was, to have
the Court of England informed of our afy-
fum, and now that was by Tracey's means
afcertained, we were not without noble
friends to claim us. The grandeur of
air natural to me when infult roufed my
pride, aftonifhed and awed him---his
mind laboured with vague and indiftinct
apprehenfions; and as all attempts at
diving into a fecret locked up folely in
the hearts interefted in retaining it, muft
be vain, he half repented having exerted
an unjuftifiable influence, he could no
longer hope to profit by.

Lady Southampton acknowledged her
obligations to my firmer fpirit; and
both having no farther reafon to affect
fubordination, refumed the habits of rank
and

and diftinction; hiring domeftics of our own till the moment of enfranchifement fhould arrive.

Heartily weary of us both, I often thought the Laird of Dornock meditated propofing to releafe us; and while I was one day infenfibly guiding him to that wifhed-for point, an order from Court was delivered into his hand. Convinced it would liberate us, I caft an eye of triumph on him, while he opened it; and faw his countenance confefs the fame idea; but a moment caufed a vifible change in it. He read the order aloud, and we found with inexpreffible aftonifhment that it contained the ftricteft charge to guard his Englifh prifoners, as he would anfwer it to his King: yet with all due deference.—I eagerly caught at this article without feeming to notice the firft, which neverthelefs funk deep into my heart; nor was his infenfible to the latter.—The wearinefs and difguft he had begun to indulge, increafed; and his pride revolting at the idea that his caftle was become a ftate prifon, and himfelf only a jailer,

a jailer, he felt every way irritated, hu-
miliated, and offended.   No human being submits to power with so ill a grace as
him who has unjustifiably exerted it, and
when its restrictions fall heavily on such,
mere retribution becomes in effect a severe revenge.

A tedious interval had again elapsed
without any news from England.   The
tender, timid, Phœbe, often persuaded
herself her lover had never reached it; and
the singularity of finding ourselves apparently forgotten, sometimes inclined my
friend and self to unite with her in that
opinion---yet, how many other causes
might we reasonably assign for it!---
causes, so much more afflicting, that we
recalled our thoughts to the isle for con-
solation.

Whether the infinite variety, the eternal transitions my own life had already
afforded, inclined me to hope on; or,
whether the incessant prayers I addressed
to him who alone could relieve me, endued my mind with fortitude, I knew
not; but, I certainly found in it resources
3   hi-

hitherto unknown. Every paffing day feemed to refine and fettle its powers and perceptions, till thofe turbulent paffions which of late rufhed like a catara&t through my frame; now, with a gentle, healthful, current, gave motion to my pulfes.

We learnt from Phœbe, that many letters came from Mabel to her elder brother, the contents of which he fo cautioufly concealed, as made it obvious we were their fubject. This news only confirmed us in the belief that Tracey had reached England fafely; and afforded us at the fame time the flattering idea, that our friends were anxioufly labouring to recover us; however their progrefs might be impeded by obitacles, we could neither guefs at, nor decide upon: nor were thefe fuppofitions vain. An order at length arrived, that we fhould be delivered to the officer who fhould prefent its counter-part. Oh, what joy, what gratitude, what anxiety, did this profpect of a deliverance afford us! From the dawn of the morning, till night blackened the ocean, did one or the other

watch

watch with eager expectation the promifed veffel.----We beheld it at laft, and
hardly could Effex himfelf have been
more welcome to my eyes.

Tracey once more landed, and glad
was the greeting on all fides.----He prefented each of us letters----dear and
precious characters! my foul poured
through my eyes when I again beheld them!
With lavifh tendernefs Effex hailed my
fecond refurrection, and vowed to fhew
his fenfe of the bleffing by an implicit
fubmiffion to my will.----" You fhall no
more complain of the terrors of a camp,
my love, continued he, I turn for ever
from the bloody fcene.----A court no longer has any charms for me: infpired
with jufter fentiments, alive to purer
pleafures, in your heart and my own will I
henceforth look for the wayward ftraggler,
happinefs. I am no longer, my fweet Ellinor, the Effex you have known! I am
become an abfolute ruftic, a mere philo-
fopher. With you I will abjure the
world, and in fome folitary fpot, devote
myfelf to love and the fciences. Oh!
shut

shut your heart, like me, my love, to the past, and look only towards the future. I wait with impatience the news of your safe arrival in Cumberland, and date from it our happiness."

These words were to my soul, what the balmy breath of spring is to the frozen earth: the winds at once cease to blow, the snow sinks into her bosom, the buds put forth their verdure, and nature forgets she has suffered.

Tracey came fraught with gifts rather suited to the spirit of the donor, than that of the accepter, yet, they opened the heart of the Laird of Dornock, who listened to the avowal of Tracey's love without repugnance; and at length promised him his sister, if, at the expiration of two years, his rank in the army entitled him to claim her.---The tears of the young lovers for ever cemented those vows his will thus authorized. Joy having disposed my heart to receive the soft impressions of every gentle passion, extinguishing all that were not so, I remem-

membered, with aftonifhment, the moment
when I readily adopted the ambitious
projects of Effex.—Rank, riches, glory,
what are ye?—Gay ornaments which lend
fplendor indeed to felicity, but which only
incumber and weigh down the foul when
ftruggling with the waves of misfortune :
gladly we lighten ourfelves of fuch ad-
ventitious goods, and grafp in tranquillity
and love, the unenvied, but rich effence,
of all our fortune.

In life, as in a profpect, we can long
enjoy only a bounded view; and all
which prefents either to the mind or eye,
a multiplicity of objects, however great
or beautiful, overftrains the faculties, and
deftroys the repofe. Rejecting at once
every gaud vanity delights in, from
the diftant throne, and the mighty multitude, ready perhaps in turn to conduct
me to it, my foul called forth the beloved
individual, and feating him at my fide in
a fafe and humble folitude, afked what we
fhould lofe by the change?—lofe!   Ah!
rather what might we not gain?—How
fweet

sweet was it then to find Lord Essex himself at length cherished ideas wholly similar;
that weary of war, ambition, envy, and
all the turbulence of life, in renouncing
the court of Elizabeth, he left, with the
power, the wish of possessing it!—That
time, solitude, reflection, disappointment
itself, had rather changed than extinguished his taste, which thus regained
its true bias; seeking in the powers of
the mind, and the impulses of the heart,
a happiness not to be found on earth,
when those sources fail to supply it.

In leaving forever the dreary scene of
my exile, I could be sensible of only one
regret: but flattering myself, Tracey
would ere long restore the sweet Phœbe
to my friendship, I soon dried up the
tears due to the floods that charming
girl bestowed upon our parting. The
rapid motion of the vessel bore no pro-
portion to my impatience; whenever I
looked, that detested isle was still in view;
I thought we should never lose sight of it.

Oh!

Oh! how I anticipated the sweet repose which awaited us in the green soli-
tudes of Cumberland! I flattered myself
Essex would already be there; though
Tracey assured me, spies still followed
his steps, from which only a long confirmation of his peaceful intentions could relieve him.

At length the pleasant shore of England was descried; welcome to my heart
was the shout which proclaimed it! Our
very souls shot through our eyes once
more, to hail our native country. We
found at the port, servants, and every
accommodation that might render our
journey easy. Ah! how beautiful was
that journey!---a thousand various objects
of simple majesty united to form one
perfect whole, and a new delight stole on
every sense, as we wound through va-
rying vallies embowered by hanging
woods, reflected in many an expanse of
clear water, dim shadowed at intervals by
mountains, whose arid heights defied the
sun they seemed to swell to.

Far

Far in thefe green labyrinths we came at once upon the Caftle from whence I now write.—It is in fact only an elegant ruin, and might rather be termed the refidence of the anchorite, Solitude. In tearful gladnefs the fair owner threw her arms round my neck, and bleft the power which permited us at laft to reft here.

From this antique manfion do I date my narrative; and in arranging it, feek only to fill up thofe hours yet unbleft with the prefence of him born to fill every future one. Dear Lady Pembroke, I cannot exprefs the divine repofe which hufhes at laft my overworn faculties.—I look back with wonder on all the paft griefs, the mortal conflicts, my fhattered frame has contended with. So pure, fo perfect, is now my grateful tranquillity, that it feems proof even againft misfortune itfelf.—No more fhall my beating heart— my burning brain—but why fhould I revert to fuch difmal recollections?

Embofomed in the maternal arms of nature; fafe in the obfcure and folitary

fitu-

fituation of this ivied afylum, here my
affrighted foul, like a fcared bird, faintly
folds up its weary wings; delights to be
alone, and joys in mere fafety. I think
I can never be happy, be grateful enough,
and while my heart exhaufts itfelf in enjoyment, I ftill call on it for ebullitions to
which it is unequal. Pride, paffion, vanity, all the groffer particles of my nature are at once exhaled, and every pure,
every focial virtue, unfolds and bloffoms
to the vernal fun, forerunning even the
fnow-drop.

Oh! that radiant, glorious luminary!
how new to me feems its influence!—
Dark have been the films through which
I have hitherto viewed it. Pardon, my
darling friend, thefe flights of fancy: how
playful does the mind grow when at peace
with itfelf?

Haften, generous Tracey, haften to
my love, and inform him of our arrival.
But is not Tracey already gone? Oh!
haften then, my Effex; quit that bufy
fcene, where virtue inceffantly hovers
on the verge of a precipice a thoufand
                                    ready

ready hands would plunge her over,---
partake with me the deep repofe of thi
folitude—no longer heed Elizabeth herfelf, not even her power can reach us
here. Nature's gigantick phalanx, im-
paffable mountains prefent their formidable fummits in long array, overawing
every inferior guard; while in their vivid hollows, happinefs repofes on the bofom of her mother, Nature.—Oh! come
then, and in

   " *A life exempt from public haunt,*
" *Find tongues in trees, books in the running ftreams,*
" *Sermons in ftones, and good in every thing.*"

  * * * * * * *

A thunder-bolt falls on my brain!
avenging heaven, why does it not wholly
fplit it? Tried---fentenced---condemned
---while I, entombed in a now detefted
folitude, gaily dreamt of endlefs happinefs.—Oh! let me once more rufh madly
into the world, overwhelm my agonized
      L 4   fenfes

senses with the shouts of armies—the
groans of the dying—fountains of blood
—rivers of tears—find if possible a horror in nature may counteract that now
raging in my soul.—The wreck of the
universe alone can equal it.—But let me
give the ruin scope—wherefore, wherefore, should I wish it lessened—Oh! Lady
Pembroke!

LADY PEMBROKE WRITES,

The trembling hand of the friend last
invoked, takes up the pen to finish the
woes of a fair unfortunate, who will never more be her own historian.—Alas,
they had now reached their climax.

The eccentric turn of mind which
made the sweet Ellinor form a plan so
extraordinary as her supposed death and
burial, excited an astonishment in me,
its artful execution alone could increase.
Nevertheless, the regular pursuit of a
single idea was far from persuading her
friends, her intellects had recovered their
tone, or equality.

When-

When this heart-breaking narrative
came to my hands, I could not but ob-
ferve that the fweet miftrefs of Effex had a
very partial knowledge of his character,
or information of his actions.—Bleft
with the moft equitable and generous
heart that ever actuated a human bofom,
his virtues often took a falfe colour from
the felfifh views of thofe who once found
the way to it. Credulity was fo much
his fault, that even his enemies pro-
fited by it, whom he always ceafed to
confider as fuch, the moment they deigned to deceive him with a falfe proteftation
of regard.—In fact, the lenity of his nature continually counteracted that ambition, which was its only vice; and irradiated his character with the milder glo-
ries of humanity: a luftre, more foft, pure,
and lafting, than mere conqueft can beftow.
Neverthelefs, the early habits of power
and diftinction had feized on his affections,
and even his love co-operating with that
indulged foible, they increafed together.
The daring project he had formed, was
no

no way unfeasible, had he managed it
with address; for he possessed the hearts
of the whole kingdom, a few envious individuals excepted. But art was unknown
to Essex; and those his superiority offended, were proficients in that science:
unhappily too, they were so immediately around the Queen, that they could
convert the suspicions she sometimes entertained of his conduct, into certainty.
Yet so rooted was her love for this unfortunate favorite, that it long contended
with that she bore herself; and tears
of ill-judged fondness often absorbed the
bitterness his enemies would have wrought
to his ruin. Such a weakness alone could
induce a sovereign, wise and experienced
like Elizabeth, to delegate a power scarce
inferior to her own, into the hands of a
Nobleman, valiant, popular, and as-
piring. In consenting to Essex's command in Ireland, the Queen made an
absolute sacrifice of her own inclination
(which was only gratified when he was
near her) to his; or, perhaps, in effect,
                                    both

both unconfciously yielded to the fecret
policy which invariably fought to fepa-
rate them.—Convinced fhe had bound
him to her by every tie of gratitude,
honor, and confidence, how muft fo high
a fpirit as that of Elizabeth be fhocked,
wounded, and irritated, to fee him loiter
away his days inactively in Ireland, regardlefs alike of her admonitions, and
the cenfures of the people ?—Infenfibly
fhe imbibed the prejudices of the Cecil
family, the inflexible enemies of the
Earl ; to whom fhe fubmitted the government of the ftate, lefs from any efteem for
their talents, than the latent defire of
piquing the negligent favorite, to whom
they were equally obnoxious. Time confirmed to the Cecil faction, the influence
they at firft owed folely to refentment.
The wearifome fupinenefs of the Lord
Deputy was at once fucceeded by a
fufpicious, and myfterious conduct. His
fecret treaties with the arch rebel, Tiroen, the anonymous captive who feduced
him into thefe—all was reported with ag-
gra-

gravation to Elizabeth. The refentment occafioned by the error of his conduct, was doubled when fhe knew that of his heart: jealoufy took full poffeffion of hers, and fhe determined to make him feverely fenfible of her power: but fhe was told it was not fafe, at that period, to recall him. Obliged for the firft time in her life to controul herfelf, and meditate how to get him again into her power, her temper became abfolutely intolerable. Her Ladies perferved a melancholy filence, fave the artful few inftructed to foment, and profit by, her irritated paffions. The fate of Effex feemed wholly to depend on the event of a war, hitherto unprofperous: when to the aftonifhment alike of friends and enemies, without performing any confiderable exploit which might fecure him a welcome, the Earl pofted fuddenly home, and prefented himfelf before Elizabeth, with the dauntlefs air of unblemifhed innocence. Whether the furprize of the moment really revived that powerful paffion of which

he

he had fo long been the object, or whether fear for her life made her diffemble
the bitternefs and rage fwelling at her
heart, is a circumftance which never reached my knowledge. It is certain the Queen
received him gracioufly, and liftened to
a very imperfect and incoherent defence
of his conduct. They parted friends;
and Effex inftantly giving way to that
credulity, which fo often made every
talent art and nature could unite in his
perfon, abortive, confidered himfelf as
effectually re-eftablifhed in her heart,
and indulged all the exultation fuch a triumph over his enemies could not fail to
occafion.

What a thunder-ftroke then was his immediate difgrace! a difgrace he could not
but impute to his own imprudence; fince
in returning without advice, he had delivered himfelf voluntarily into the hands of his
enemies. To the mortification of a long
and humiliating imprifonment, was fhortly
after fuperadded a killing grief, in the
fuppofed lofs of the beauteous Ellinor.

4   Re-

Refigning himfelf to a fullen and filent
defpair, he no longer condefcended to
offer Elizabeth any further vindication of
his conduct, nor could be perfuaded to
make the leaft fubmiffion. This con-
cuffion of feelings, however, fhivered
his animal, no lefs than his mental, fyf-
tem. A fever followed, which foon rofe
to a dangerous height. Obftinately rejecting all medical advice, he declared a
thoufand times he wifhed only to die;
nor had that wifh been vain, but that the
Queen, unable wholly to fubdue the fentiments of tendernefs which had fo long
reigned in her heart, fent her own phyfician to attend him, with offers of peace
and pardon. The defperate ftate in which
he found the Earl, was faithfully reported
to Elizabeth; who, touched to the heart,
hefitated whether fhe fhould not revive
him by an immediate vifit; fo hard will
it always be to counteract by political
manœuvres the genuine impreffions of
nature. The Cecil party fuddenly found
themfelves on the brink of ruin; and
every

every argument, fear, pride, or prudence,
could suggest, was enforced to delay this
interview. Elizabeth yielded to the powerful combination of reasons in that instance, but could not deny herself the
pleasure of corresponding with Lord Ef-
sex as he grew better; and soon suffered
him to vindicate his conduct: nay, even
condescended to reproach him with the
unknown lady who had so fatally influenced it. To this perplexing hint, he
replied, his grief alone must answer;
and the melancholy tenour of his life so
exactly agreed with this declaration, that
Elizabeth pressed no farther into a secret
it was plain the grave now veiled: rather seeking by kindness to invigorate
a mind ill-fortune had borne too hard
upon.

It was now the shining time in the life
of Essex. The purple torrent of suc-
cessful war had hitherto swept away, or
sunk those sweet humanities, those social
virtues, time at length cast up in the vale
of adversity.—Endued with eloquence,

taste,

tafte, fcience, fenfe, and fenfibility, he now refigned himfelf to the charms of philofophy, poefy, and the mathematicks. Innocent and tranquil refources, to which the mind muft ever turn when difappointed, if bleft with powers capable of relifhing them. The Cecils never thought Effex more dangerous. Age and infirmity now made Elizabeth anxious for peace abroad, and tranquillity at home, and there wanted only a meeting between her, and the much altered Earl, to re-eftablifh him in her favour: but that meeting his enemies entered into a league to prevent; and began, by winning Elizabeth's phyfician to order the Earl of Effex into the country.—An artifice fo refined as his liberation was not immediately difcovered to be policy by any party; and the Queen, lulled into a belief that fhe could honorably receive him when he fhould return, fuffered him to depart without an audience.

Wearied of wars, camps, and political jealoufies, and difcuffions, the melancholy

choly Effex defired in freedom only the
folitude he found; when Tracey returned with the aftonifhing news that
the miftrefs he ftill adored yet exifted.
---Fatal news to his future repofe!---The
impoffibility of openly claiming Ellinor,
revived, with his paffion, all his dangerous
and precarious projects.---Every other
effort to obtain her was made without
fuccefs, ere he fecretly applied to the
King of Scots; who always knew his own
intereft too well to grant any favour without having fecured an adequate return.
James ardently defired to be nominated as
the fucceffor of Elizabeth by herfelf, and
had not fpared bribes, promifes, or flat-
tery, to intereft thofe around her whom
he thought likely to influence her choice.
The unhoped folicitation of the man
whofe courage and ambition James moft
feared, was a circumftance of importance.
Uninformed of the real name or characters of the prifoners Lord Effex fo eagerly
defired to recover, the King of Scots fent
the Laird of Dornock notice to guard
them more ftrictly.   The vehement tem-

per of Effex made him always refign to the prevailing object, every other intereft: but a treaty like this could not be carried on fo fecretly as to efcape the fufpicious eyes of the minifters. With what malignant joy did they filently watch its progrefs, till the moment when its publication would inflame the Queen to their wifhes!

Effex now once more thought it his intereft to be bufy, admired, and popular: he relapfed into all his old habits, and having gained the Queen's permiffion, returned to London. Far, however, from profiting by this indulgence, to obtain her pardon, he remained at home; throwing open his doors to all impoverifhed officers, and clergy, among whom a number of fpirited adventurers appeared, whofe lavifh praifes feemed to render his popularity greater than ever.

Elizabeth, with difguft, beheld him affume the favor fhe perhaps intended once more to beftow; and kept in filence a ftrict watch upon his conduct. By a
re-

refinement known only in politicks, his
enemies fcattered among his partizans
many creatures of their own, inftructed
to dive into all his intentions, and fpread
abroad feditious and treafonable projects,
as though intrufted by himfelf with fuch.
This malice was but too fuccefsful.----
Inflated with the adulation of misjudging
friends, the extravagant admiration of
the multitude, and the infidious attacks
of his enemies, the felf-deluded Effex
fprung the mine himfelf which deftroyed
him.

The mifchief commenced by a broil
between the Lords Southampton and
Grey; the laft affaulting the former in
the ftreet; and though the offender was
ceremonioufly punifhed, the fpirit of
party broke out in a thoufand little
daily quarrels. The Queen already perfuaded that Effex, ever haughty and
impetuous, fcorned her power, defpifed
her perfon, and only waited a favorable moment openly to infult both, was
irritated beyond all bearing by the artful

difcovery (at this cruel crifis) of his fecret treaty with the King of Scots.---Its real caufe was unknown to her, and the offence, though trifling in itfelf, of a nature moft likely to exafperate a Sovereign whofe eyes were ever turned from a fucceffor fhe refufed to acknowledge.——— The difcovery proved decifive---Elizabeth inftantly refolved to deliver the ungrateful favorite up to the laws of his country, and authorized a judicial enquiry into his conduct. The Cecil party defired no more; for well they knew, Effex would rather die than brook the deliberate indignity. The commiffioned Lords affembled at his houfe on a Sunday, as the time when they fhould be moft fafe from the infults of the partial populace.----They found the Earl fufficiently inflamed; who fwearing he never more would be a voluntary prifoner, fhut up the Lord Keeper, and the reft, in his own houfe, rufhing forth armed, and followed only by a few friends and

do-

domeſtics, to claim the protection of the people.

By a fatality not peculiar to himſelf, the bubble, popularity, which had ſo long ſwelled and glittered before his miſtaken eyes, burſt at once, and left to him a vacuum in nature.---The ſacred day was but too judiciouſly choſen by his enemies.----Without preparation----almoſt without a friend, the unhappy Eſſex ruſhed through the ſtreets of London, crouded only with peaceful and humble mechanics, who emerged from every cloſe lane environed by their wives and children to enjoy the weekly holiday.--- To people of this ſtamp the galiant Eſſex was almoſt unknown---certainly indifferent: with ſtupid and curious eyes, they turned to gaze on thoſe warlike ſteps none ventured to follow----ſteps which bore the noble Eſſex ſo faſt toward ruin. Diſtreſs, however, only increaſed his deſperation, and the citizens being ſpirited into making an ineffectual effort to prevent his return, a ſkirmiſh

M 3   caenfued. The amiable Tracey had the fate he defired, and fell at the fide of his Lord; who even in this cruel moment, dropt a tear on a youth fo beloved. Fame, honor, happinefs, nay, even life, were fleeting faft from Effex; and however carelefs of thefe goods, friendfhip ftill afferted her rights over his feelings.----In compaffion to the few generous adherents who muft have fallen in his caufe, had he longer refifted, the Earl at length furrendered his fword.

All was now over with this admired, and erring favorite.----Imprifoned in the Tower, he had ample leifure to re-confider the events which brought him there.----The defertion of the people had opened his eyes to the realities of life.---- He too fenfibly found, while he miniftered to their neceffities, their pride, or their pleafures, the multitude could rend the air with acclamations; but the moment a claim was in turn made on their feelings, they always become cold, torpid, and inanimate. He perceived with
vain

vain regret that he had been duped into this outrage on the laws of fociety, by the manœuvres of his enemies, no lefs than the credulity of his heart. But he was not formed to profit by thefe humiliating difcoveries; they impreffed a nature fo upright, only with the deepeft difguft.---He was, however, confoled with remembering felf-prefervation was the fole motive for his daring attack, and that no action of his life had yet violated the duty he had fworn the Queen. He refolutely prepared himfelf to meet the judgment of his peers, and only lamented the friendfhip which involed the generous Southampton in his fate; who fhared without regret the prifon of a friend fo dear.

The Queen, meanwhile, experienced every emotion fuch a painful contrariety of paffions muft neceffarily occafion.--- The imprifonment of her favorite, as ufual, feemed to cancel his offence: but he was now beyond her jurifdiction, and the victim of the laws. She had un-

M 4

hap-

happily furrendered him up to them, and robbed herself of every prerogative but that of pardoning; a prerogative she feared so high a spirit would never follicit her to exert.----She regretted, too late, having driven him to so dangerous an extreme, and while his fate was yet uncertain, fuffered more, perhaps, than he did in its completion.

The friends of the Earl, perfuaded no kind of influence would be spared to bring him to the block, were unanimous in intreating him to win over the Queen by an early repentance, and fubmiffion: but they knew not the grandeur of the heart they would have humbled.----Born to diftinguifh himfelf moft eminently when outward diftinctions were withdrawn, it was then only Effex feemed to ufe his better judgment. "Can any one call himfelf my friend, would he indignantly exclaim, and yet wifh me poorly to petition for an obfcure, an ignominious life? What! to pine away the flower of manhood in infamy aud folitude! fhunned by all, yet unftigmatized by public juftice,

and

and fhunning, in turn, the exalted characters I dare no longer emulate.----Shut
up with thofe tormenting companions,
my own thoughts, till led, perhaps, by
defperation, to inflict that fate upon myfelf, I have meanly evaded receiving
from the law.----No, my friends, I am en-
thralled here as a traitor---if proved one,
it is fit I expiate my crime; and if acquitted, I know the value of a life ventured hitherto only for my country."---
Neither arguments, or intreaties, could
fhake his refolution; and he heard with
unequalled firmnefs, that public fentence, from which, he ftill perfifted, there
was no appeal. In vain every dear and
affecting image was pourtrayed in the
ftrongeft colours before his active imagination.---From that of the woe-ftruck
Ellinor, liberated too late, and weaving in
a diftant folitude a thoufand fairy bow-
ers for love and happinefs to dwell in---
from her alone his nature fhrunk. "You
may wound my heart, would he fighing
fay, through every vein; but my reafon
is ftill inflexible, nor is even that fweet
crea-

creature an argument for my fubmitting to difgrace.----No! when I raifed my eyes to thee, dear Ellinor, my confcious foul beheld in itfelf all that could intitle me to mate with thee.---I cannot refolve to look up even to the woman I adore.--- Better fhe fhould weep me dead, than fecretly defpife me while yet exifting.--- Pure and precious will be the tears that fall upon my grave, but never could I behold one which would not fecretly re- proach me.------Leave me, my friends, to my fate; honor has hitherto been the invariable rule of my conduct, nor can I now adopt another."

From the moment the condemnation of Effex reached the Queen, peace and reft were ftrangers to her.---The chofen of her heart was now the victim of the laws, and that heart muft bleed through his, unlefs he could be induced to throw himfelf on her mercy. A thoufand emif- faries affured him of a ready pardon--- a word, a wifh, would have obtained it.--- To thefe he ever replied with the fame col- lected

lected air, " that had the Queen earlier
shewn him this indulgence, his life had
never come within the censure of the law;
but as even her utmost bounty now could
only prolong to him the liberty of breathing, he was willing, as well for her safety,
as in submission to his sentence, to resign a privilege, which became a burthen the moment it was his only one."
An answer thus calculated to touch the
most indifferent heart, stabbed that of
Elizabeth: yet as, unasked, to grant him
a pardon, would stamp her declining life
with inexcusable weakness, she under-
went every hour the most trying conflicts.

Ah! why do I say the most trying?
alas, there was a fair, and forlorn one,
buried in Cumberland, who more than
died when this cruel intelligence reached
her. As the sentence of Essex included
his friend Southampton, the relations of
the latter dispatched an express to his
wife; hoping she would arrive in London
time enough to sollicit his pardon of the
Queen.

Queen. The meſſenger found the unfortunate Ladies buoyed up with ſafety,
ſolitude, and many a gentle hope.
When the approach of horſes echoed
through the remote valley, no other emotion was excited in either, than the fond
and latent flutter ariſing from the idea
that it might be one or both of the con-
demned Earls.---How terrible was then
the tranſition in their minds, when fully
informed of their deſperate ſituation;
and bereft of every reſource expected
miſery ſupplies? The unhappy wife of
Southampton, engroſſed by her own ſhare
in the affliction, obſerved not its deep,
its deadly effect, on the intellects of her
equally ſuffering friend; till the ſtupefaction of Ellinor became intenſe, and
obvious, and the evil irremediable.

The human mind, even when moſt
elevated, is not equal to the influence of
two oppoſing paſſions---a ſacrifice muſt
be made, and friendſhip yields to love.
Lady Southampton poſted away with
unremitting diligence; intruſting her
                                    friend

friend to the care of faithful fervants, who
were directed to bring her forward more
leifurely.---The deep gloom of the fweet
Ellinor's mind, in the courfe of the journey, gave way to a vague and irregu-
lar gaiety; but as this had fometimes
forerun her recovery, fo might it then,
had fhe been furrounded with fuch perfons
as knew her difpofition.·---Thofe who
had her in charge, uninformed of her
name, fituation, and wounded fpirit, could
not reafonably be expected to guard a-
gainft events they could not poffibly fore-
fee. It happened, one day, while they
were refting, Ellinor caft her eyes upon an
extenfive building, full in fight, and her
wandering imagination called it Kenilworth.---An officious attendant informed
her it was Fotheringay Caftle.--She wildly
fhrieked, ftretched forth her arms expreffively towards the fatal manfion, then tearing thofe lovely treffes once before devoted to her calamity, and fcarce grown
to their ufual luxuriance, threw herfelf on
the ground, and relapfed into total infanity.

But

But when Lady Southampton entered the prifon of her Lord, upon whofe aching bofom fhe poured forth all her grief and paffion, his difturbed friend found every fibre of his heart wrung; and turning a fearful, eager eye toward the door, felt a horror, not to be expreffed, at finding no one followed her.---The afflicted wife wanted prefence of mind to conceal a truth which confummated the fate of Effex---a truth fo terrible, that fain would he have believed it invented by his friends to reconcile him to his fentence.---Convinced at length---" now indeed do I feel the weight of my bonds---now indeed am I a prifoner, would he exclaim.---Oh, Ellinor, matchlefs Ellinor, that I could fly to thee! recall once more that unequalled foul, which always, like a frightened bird, forfakes its home when mifery hovers over it.---Thou, thou, haft broken a fpirit equal to every other affliction---thou haft made a coward of me---to fave thee, my love, I could almoft refolve, poorly to condition for a difgraceful life, and wifh to furvive my honor."

Per-

Perfuaded his prefence would have the fame effect, it once before took at St. Vincent's Abbey, he paffionately follicited to fee her.------This fingle idea feized upon his mind---it even became his folemn requeft---his dying wifh. In the hopelefs ftate of her diforder, the effect of their meeting was dreaded only on his account; but as all intreaty and argument proved vain, his friends at length refolved to yield to his paffionate, his only follicitation. The day was now appointed for the execution of Effex, and the pardon of Southampton granted, which alone he defired: as all his friends were freely admitted to his prifon, there was no difficulty in leading thither the darling of his heart, in the habit of a youth, accompanied by Lady Southampton.-----Worlds could not have bribed *me* to witnefs fuch an interview,---Ah, deareft Ellinor! were thofe fenfes they fo eagerly defired to reftore to thee, in reality a lofs? How, had they been perfect, wouldft thou have fupported the trying fcene, expiring

piring love, and officious friendſhip,
dragged thee to witneſs?---How wouldeſt
thou have fixed thine eyes on the gloomy tower, or thoſe guarded gates through
which thy lover muſt ſo ſoon be borne,
but never more ſhould paſs?---How muſt
thy ſoul have bled to behold thoſe fine
features, a few hours were to ſeparate
from the heart which then gave them ſuch
agonized expreſſion? But that ſuperla-
tive miſery was not ordained thee.---Re-
tired beyond the reach of love itſelf,
were all the various powers of that ſuſceptible ſoul!---Thy vague eyes con-
feſſed not their everlaſting object ---thy
ear caught not his voice---nor did thy
boſom anſwer with a ſingle ſigh, the
burſts of grief which ſtruggled at that
of thy lover, ſtill exquiſitely alive to every
human affliction! To thee, his parting
ſoul yet clung; and when his eyes beheld
thee no longer, they willingly ſhut out
creation. He ſaw not, from the moment
of Ellinor's departure, friend, or relation;
but turning all his contemplations towards
the

3

the awful futurity in which he was fo foon to launch, died to this world even before his execution.

On the night which preceded that event, this billet, equally addreffed to my fifter (with whom the dear unfortunate refided) and myfelf, was delivered.

"Dear, generous guardians of the loft angel, my foul yet bleeds over, receive in this my parting bleffing; and pardon, oh, pardon, an incredulity but too feverely punifhed by conviction! a conviction fo terrible as reconciles me to the death to-morrow will beftow. Yes, thefe eyes have been blafted with beholding the pale ftatue of my love, dead while yet breathing---fpeechlefs---infenfate.----To the gathered multitude—the fatal fcaffold ---the axe which feparates foul and body, I turn for relief when this remembrance preffes upon me.

"Adieu, ye faithful fifters of the gallant Sydney----Oh! if intelligence too late fhould vifit the fair form bequeathed to your friendfhip, with fympathy foothe every aching fenfe.------Yet wake no

more to woe my worſhiped Ellinor !---
Still may thy pure ſpirit ſlumber in its
breathing tomb, till that appointed hour
which at length unites thee to thy
ESSEX."
Tower.

It ſeemed as if in this epiſtle were encloſed every lingering weakneſs of mortality : for the remaining hours of his
life were devoted ſolely to the duties of
religion.---In the flower of manhood, at
the age of three and thirty, this envied
favorite reſigned every earthly diſtinction,
and aſcended the ſcaffold with a compo-
ſure innocence and Heaven alone can
beſtow. The melting multitude too late
bewailed to ſee his glorious youth ſet thus
in blood.---His ear caught the general
murmur of ſorrow and applauſe ; he caſt
a look of corrected knowledge on the
ſpectators; then lifting his eyes to Heaven,
ſerenely ſubmitted to the executioner ;
who ſevered a head, and heart, which, had
they acted in uniſon, might have awed the
world.

Of

Of her ſo much beloved, ſo generouſly, ſo fatally faithful, little more remains to be ſaid.----Neither time, care, or medicine, ever availed toward the reſtoration of thoſe intellects which might only have proved an additional misfortune ---Yet even in this ſtate of inſanity, Heaven permitted her to become the inſtrument of a ſingular and exemplary vengeance.

A year or more had elapſed, during which her calamity took all thoſe variable and dreadful forms peculiar to itſelf.----The deſire of having every medical aſſiſtance, made me bring her with me to London; where one evening, with a degree of reflection and art often blended with inſanity, ſhe eluded the care of her attendants; and well knowing every avenue of the palace, paſſed them all with wonderful facility.

The Queen wholly ſunk in the chilling melancholy of incurable deſpair, and hopeleſs age, reſigned herſelf up to the influence of thoſe evils.----Her ladies were often employed in reading to her, which was the only amuſement her chagrin admitted.——One memorable

N 2   night

night it was my turn--Elizabeth difmiffed every other attendant, in the vain hope of finding a repofe of which fhe had for ever deprived herfelf. I purfued my tafk a long while, when the time confpired with the orders of the Queen to produce a filence fo profound, that had not her ftarts now and then recalled my fenfes, hardly could my half-clofed eyes have difcerned the pages over which they wandered.--- The door flew fuddenly open---a form fo fair---fo fragile---fo calamitous appeared there, that hardly durft my beating heart call it Ellinor. The Queen ftarted up with a feeble quicknefs, but had only power to falter out a convulfive ejaculation. I inftantly remembered Elizabeth believed her dead, and imagined this her fpectre. The beauteous phantom (for furely never mortal looked fo like an inhabitant of another world) funk on one knee, and while her long garments of black flowed gracefully over the floor, fhe lifted up her eyes toward Heaven, with that namelefs fweetnefs, that wild ineffable benignity, madnefs

nefs alone can give, then meekly bowed before Elizabeth.---The Queen, heart-struck, fell back into her feat, without voice to pronounce a fyllable.---Ellinor arofe, and approached ftill nearer; ftand-ing a few moments, choaked and filent. " I once was proud, was paffionate, in-dignant," faid the fweet unfortunate at laft, in the low and broken voice of in-expreffible anguifh," but Heaven forbids me now to be fo---Oh! you who was furely born only to chaftize my unhappy race, forgive me---I have no longer any fenfe but that of forrow."------Again fhe funk upon the floor, and gave way to fobbings fhe ftruggled in vain to fupprefs. The Queen dragged me convulfively to her, and burying her face in my bofom, ex-claimed indiftinctly,---" fave me---fave me---oh, Pembroke, fave me from this ghaftly fpectre!"---" Effex---Effex---Ef-fex!" groaned forth the proftrate Elli-nor, expreffively raifing her white hand at each touching repetition.---The vio-lent fhudderings of the Queen, marked

the

the deep effect that fatal name took on
her.—"Somebody told me, continued the
lovely wanderer, that he was in the Tower,
but I have looked there for him till I am
weary---is there a colder, safer prison,
then? But is a prison a place for your
favorite, and can you condemn him to
the grave?—Ah, gracious Heaven, strike
off his head--- his beauteous head!---Seal
up those sparkling eyes forever.----Oh,
no, I thought not, said she with an altered voice.---So you hid him *here* after
all, only to torment me.---But Effex will
not see me suffer---will you, my Lord?
So---so---so"---the slow progress of her
eyes round the room, shewed, she in
imagination followed his steps.---"Yes---
yes,---added she, with revived spirits, I
thought that voice would prevail, for
who could ever resist it?---and only I need
die then; well, I do not mind that---I will
steal into his prison and suffer in his place,
but be sure you don't tell him so, for he
loves *me*---ah! dearly does he love me,
but I alone need sigh at that, you know."

And

And figh fhe did indeed.---Oh ! what a
world of woe was drawn up in a fingle
breath!---The long filence which followed, induced the Queen once more to raife
her head---the fame fad object met her
eyes, with this difference, that the fweet
creature now ftood up again, and putting
one white hand to her forehead, fhe half
raifed the other, as earneftly demanding
ftill to be heard, though her vague eyes
fhewed her purpofe had efcaped her.---
" Oh, now I remember it, refumed fhe,
I do not mind how you have me murdered,
but let me be buried in Fotheringay ;
and be fure I have *women* to attend me ;
be fure of that---you know the reafon."
This incoherent reference to the unpre-
cedented fate of her royal mother, affected Elizabeth deeply.----" But could
not you let me once more fee him before I
die ? refumed the dear wanderer.---Oh!
what pleafure would it give me to view
him on the Throne !---Oh, I *do* fee him
there ! exclaimed fhe in the voice of furprize and tranfport. Benign, majeftic!---

Ah,

Ah, how glorious in his beauty !—Who
would not die for thee, my Effex !"——
" Alas, never, never, never, fhall *I* fee
him,!" groaned forth the agonized Elizabeth.——" Me married to him ! refumed our friend, replying to fome imaginary fpeech,—oh, no, I took warning
by my fifter!—I will have no more bloody
marriages : you fee I have no ring, wildly
difplaying her hands, except a black one ;
a *black* one indeed, if you knew all—but
I need not tell *you* that—have I, my
Lord ?—look up—here is my love—he
himfelf fhall tell you." She caught the
hand terror had caufed Elizabeth to extend, but faintly fhrieking, drew back
her own, furveying it with inexpreffible
horror. "Oh, you have dipt mine in blood!
exclaimed fhe, a mother's blood ! I am
all contaminated---it runs cold to my
very heart.---Ah, no,---it is---it is the
blood of Effex ; and have you murdered him at laft, in fpite of your dotage,
and your promifes ? murdered the moft
noble of mankind ! and all becaufe he
                                    could

could not love you. Fye on your wrin-
kles!---can one love age and uglinefs?---
Oh, how thofe artificial locks, and all
your paintings fickened him!----How
have we laughed at fuch prepofterous
folly!---But I have done with laughing
now---we will talk of graves, and fhrouds,
and church-yards.-----Methinks I fain
would know where my poor fifter lies bu-
ried---you will fay in my heart perhaps---
it has indeed entombed all I love; yet
there muft be fome little unknown corner in this world, one might call her
grave, if one could but tell where to
find it: there fhe refts at laft with her
Leicefter---he was your *favorite* too---a
bloody, bloody, diftinction."------The
Queen, who had with difficulty preferved
her fenfes till this cutting period, now
funk back in a deep fwoon.

The diftrefs of my fituation cannot be
expreffed.---Fearful left any attempt to
fummon a fingle being fhould irritate
the injured Ellinor to execute any dire
revenge; for which I knew not how fhe
was

was prepared, had not Elizabeth at this juncture loft her fenfes, I really think mine would have failed me. I recollected that the Queen by every teftimony was convinced the unhappy object thus fearfully brought before her, died in the country long fince; nor was it wife or fafe, for thofe who had impofed on her, now to acknowledge the deception. "So---fo---fo, cried Ellinor, with a ftart, would one have thought it poffible to break that hard heart, after all? and yet I have done it.---She is gone to---no, not gone to Effex."——"Let us retire, my fweet Ellen," faid I, eager to get her out of the room, left the Queen fhould fuffer for want of affiftance.---"Hufh, cried fhe, with increafing wildnefs, they will fay we have beheaded her alfo.---But who are you? fixing her hollow eyes wiftfully on me, I have feen you fomewhere ere now, but I forget all faces in gazing on his pale one.---I know not where I am, nor where you would have me go, added fhe, foftly fighing, but you look like an angel of light, and may be, you will carry

me

me with you to Heaven." I feized the
bleffed minute of compliance, and drawing her mourning hood over her face,
led her to the little court, where my fervants waited my difmiffion; when committing her to their charge, I returned to
wake the ladies in the antichamber,
through whofe inadvertent flumbers alone,
Ellinor had been enabled to pafs to the
clofet of the Queen; a circumftance,
which, combined with a variety of others,
to give this ftrange vifitation the appearance of being fupernatural.

Every common means were tried in
vain to recover the Queen, and the ap-
plications of the faculty alone could recall
her fenfes; but the terror fhe had endured has fhook them forever. Shuddering
with apprehenfions for which only I can
account, fhe often holds incomprehenfible conferences; complains of an ideal
vifitor; commands every door to be fhut;
yet ftill fancies fhe fees her, and orders
her to be kept out in vain. The fuppofed difregard of thofe in waiting, in-
cenfes a temper fo many caufes concur

to

to render peevish, and her unmerited anger produces the very difregard she complains of. Rage and fear unite thus to harrafs her feeble age, and accelerate the decay of nature. When. thefe acute fenfations fubfide, grief and defpair take poffeffion of her whole foul;--nor does she fuffer lefs from the fenfe of her decaying power. Unwilling to refign a good she is unable to enjoy, she thinks every hand that approaches, is eager to fnatch a fceptre, she will not even in dying bequeath. Oh, fweet Matilda! if yet indeed thou furvivest to witnefs this divine vengeance, thy gentle tears would embalm even thy most mortal enemy! thou couldst not without pity behold the imperial Elizabeth, lost to the common comforts of light, air, nourishment, and pleafure. That mighty mind which will be the object of future, as it has been of past, wonder, prefenting now but a breathing memento of the frailty of humanity. --Ah, that around her were affembled all those afpiring fouls whose wishes center in dominion;

minion ; were they once to behold this distinguished victim of ungoverned passion, able to rule every being but herself, how would they feel the potent example! Ah, that to them were added the many who scorning social love, confine to self the blessed affections which alone can sweeten the tears we all are born to shed !-.--Gathering round the weary couch where the emaciated Queen withers in royal solitude, they might at once learn urbanity, and correct in time, errors, which when indulged, but too severely punish themselves.

* * * * * *

Absorbed and blended in the busy and woeful scenes this heart-breaking history presented to my mind---an anxious partaker in each succeeding calamity---I seemed to live over again the melancholy years we had been separated, in the person of my sister.---My own misfortunes ---my darling daughter, the whole world vanished from before my eyes---deep-fixed

on

on objects no longer exifting, or exifting but to double my affliction : I remained almoft the ftatue of defpair;
every fenfe feeming rivetted on the manufcript I held; and buried in fo profound
a reverie, that Lady Arundell judged it
prudence to interrupt it. The confolatory
reflections her friendfhip dictated, died on
my ear, but reached not a heart which deeply purfued the fad chain of ideas thus prefented to it.---Starting as from a frightful
fleep, I, at laft, funk on my knees, and
raifing my eyes, with the manufcript, at
once toward Heaven.---" Oh, mighty author of univerfal being! fighed I, thou
who haft lent me fortitude to ftruggle
with almoft unequalled trials, fupport my
exhaufted foul againft this laft---this great-
eft.---Let not the killing idea that it is
a *human* infliction, trouble the pure
fprings of piety, whence alone the weary
fpirit can draw confolation.----Rather
ftrengthen me with the holy belief that it
is thy vifitation for fome wife end ordained ;

ed; fo fhall my enemies fleep in their graves uncurfed, and my heart remain in this agitated bofom unbroken. Alas, who knows but by thy divine appointment, I may be at laft permitted to recall the fcattered fenfes of this dear unfortunate? to foothe that deeply-wounded, that embittered fpirit! Ah, Ellen!—Ah, my fifter!, groaned I, deluged at laft with falutary tears,—changed—loft—annihilated as thou art, my unaltered affection muft ever defire thee.---I need not enquire whether fhe is here—your fympathizing, generous tears, dear Lady Arundell, inform me that the fame roof fhelters the twin heirs of misfortune.."

Although Lady Arundell acknowledged that my fifter was under her protection, fain would fhe have perfuaded me to delay a meeting fo touching, till more able to fupport it; but deaf to the voice of reafon, nature, powerful nature, afferted her rights, and my foul obeyed her impaffioned impulfe. The deep, the eternal impreffion of this agonizing meeting, recurs even now with all its firft
force.

force. I had fhuddered at the murder of
my mother—I had groaned on the coffin
of my hufband—I had wept a thoufand
times over the helplefs infant who trembled at my bofom—but all thefe terrible
fenfations were combined when my fad
eyes refted on thofe ftill fo dear to me.—
When I faw all their playful luftre
quenched, and fet in infenfibility—when
I felt that heart, once the feat of every
feminine grace and virtue, throb wild
and unconfcious againft one which I
thought every moment would efcape from
its narrow boundary.—But let me quit
a fcene too trying for recollection—too
touching for defcription. Oh, Ellinor!—
my fifter!

THE

THE

RECESS, &c.

PART VI.

TIME, which inures us to every kind
of suffering, at length strengthened my
mind against the heavy sadness impressed
on it by the fate of this dear unconscious sufferer. Slowly I ventured to pon-
der on the past; to meditate the future.
It was with true gratitude and concern
I learnt Heaven had called to itself the
amiable and accomplished sister of Lady
Arundell, who caught a cold during

her attendanee on the fick Queen, which
ended in a confumption, and carried her
off a few months after Elizabeth. Actuated to the laft by the fublimeft fympathy and friendfhip, Lady Pembroke
had added, to the moiety of the furvey-
or's treafure (which fhe had caufed to be
dug for in the fpot fpecified) a fufficient
fum to fecure the dear unfortunate every
comfort her forlorn ftate admitted; placing with her Alithea, the favorite maid
fhe had fo tenderly commemorated, and
committed both to the charge of Lady
Arundel; who with equal generofity received fo anxious a truft. A virtue thus
confummate fanctifies itfelf, and can receive neither glory or grace from the gratitude of humanity; yet furely the incenfe of the heart arifes even to Heaven!
accept it then, oh, gentleft of the Sydneys, although infphered there!

The ftrange and unaccountable difference in my fifter's opinion and my own,
refpecting Lord Leicefter, fupplied me
a fource of endlefs meditation: yet as
this difference became obvious only from
the

the time we arrived in London, I could not help imputing her blindnefs to the fame caufe fhe affigned for mine.--Certainly fhe imbibed the unreafonable prejudices of Lord Effex; whofe ambition (however fatally expiated) always inclined him to diflike a Nobleman born to fuperfede him. I faw but too plainly from the irritation and vehemence to which her temper from that period became fubject, how much a woman infenfibly adopts of the difpofition of him to whom fhe gives her heart. I had not however looked on her choice with the contemptuous afperity with which fhe regarded mine.--- Lord Effex, I will frankly own, ere yet he rofe into favor, was gifted like herfelf with every captivating advantage of nature.-----The fire and ingenuoufnefs which afterwards marked his character, then lived only in his eyes; and the cultivated underftanding he poffeffed, pointed every glance with elegance and expreffion. One muft have loved Lord Leicefter to fee Effex with indifference--- one muft have loved him to the excefs

I did

I did perhaps, not to remark the attachment my sister avowed.---Innumerable instances of it now flashed on my memory, I was astonished could at the moment escape me.   If *she* was indeed more clear sighted than myself---But why do I enter on so vain a discussion?---Alas, dear Ellinor! beloved Leicester! I have no right but to lament ye.

I had likewise gathered another painful doubt from the story of my sister. England had gained a King in the son of Mary Stuart, but her unfortunate daughters must not hope to acquire a brother. From the moment I had been informed mine had acceded to the throne, the tender mother's heart had fluttered with the idea of presenting to him that lovely girl so nearly allied to his blood. Although regardless of distinction in my own person, I could not turn my eyes on the fair daughter of Lord Leicester without coveting for her every human advantage.---Unwilling to be swayed by prejudice, I separately consulted with the
few

few friends fortune had left me; who all concurred in giving me an impreſſion of the King, degrading, if not contemptible. They repreſented him as national, vain, pedantick, credulous, and partial: wanting generoſity to beſtow a royal funeral on the body of the martyred ſaint, his unhappy mother; yet daily impoveriſhed to meanneſs by favorites and paraſites. Enſlaved by the imperious ſpirit of a Queen he neither loved nor valued, and only endeared to the people he governed through the fickleneſs of their natures, which are always gratified by change. As thoſe who ſpoke thus, could have no poſſible intereſt in villifying or depreciating him, I could not but give ſome credit to their account; and made it my firſt concern to ſee the King; anxious to read in his countenance a confutation of every charge. How unaccountably was I diſappointed when my ſenſes took part with his enemies!---I beheld with aſtoniſhment in the perſon of James, youth without freſhneſs, royalty without

O 3   gran-

grandeur, height without majesty---an
air of slyness and a secret servility, characterized features, which, though devoid
of the graces of either distinguished parent, wanted not regularity; and a stoop-
ing slouch gait gave an invincible awk-
wardness to a figure nature had endued
with symmetry. Offended and repelled,
my heart sunk again into its own little
mansion, nor claimed the least alliance
with his.---I determined to watch at lei-
sure his real character and conduct, nor
ventured to confide to his care the single treasure Heaven had permitted me to
retain, of all it once bestowed. Resolved
to educate my daughter suitably to the
fortune she was born to, I thought it wise
to bury in my own bosom, at least for a
time, the secret of her right to it ; and
the eccentric turn of mind every succeeding day rendered more obvious in the
King, made me continually applaud the
moderation and foresight which guarded
me on this interesting occasion.

I, how-

I, however, judged it neceffary to affume a title no human being envied,
or offered to difpute with me; and to
fupport it properly without encroaching
on my daughter's valuable acquifition, I
found I muft refolve to re-vifit Kenilworth Caftle, now the property of another family.---In the building were contained cabinets fo fecure and unknown,
that Lord Leicefter always depofited there,
ere he journeyed to London, fuch papers, jewels, and other valuables, as he
thought it unfafe to take with him. On
the memorable night when laft we quitted
that pleafant dwelling, I had affifted him to
place in the moft curious of thefe refervoirs
feveral cafkets, for which he feemed more
than commonly anxious; and I added to
their number, that containing Mrs. Marlow's papers, and the teftimonials of my
birth. As if actuated by fome fad pre-fenti-
ment that he fhould never more re-vifit this
fpot, my lord took great pains to familia-
rize me to the management of the fprings,
and gave into my hands duplicates of the

O 4   keys.

keys. By a fingular chance amidft all
the tranfitions of my fate, thefe keys remained, and feemed continually to re-
mind me, how important to my daughter's welfare it might one day be to recover the cafkets.---A motive ftrong as
this alone could conquer the reluctance
I felt again to behold a fpot facred to the
memory of a hufband fo beloved, You
will call this, perhaps, a childifh weak-
nefs, after all I had borne; but alas,
the mind feebler and feebler from every
conflict, fometimes finks under a trifle,
after repelling the more powerful attacks
of ill-fortune with magnanimity.

Lady Arundel, with her ufual kindnefs,
propofed accompanying me; and we for-
rowfully meafured once more thofe miles
which fo ftrongly revived in my mind the
moft interefting remembrances. At Coven-
try we refted to enquire into the character
of the prefent owner of Kenilworth Caftle.
We were told that this magnificent manfion I had left fit for the reception of
a Sovereign, had long been in the hands
of

of a miser, whose avarice had induced
him to strip it of its princely ornaments:
not less from the desire of converting
those into money, than to deprive it of
every charm that might tempt the en-
quiring traveller to knock at the inhof-
pitable gate. Yet even when this ruin
was effected, the structure itself was so
complete a piece of architecture, as to
attract a number of unwelcome visitors;
to exclude whom, he had now let it to
some manufacturers, and resided himself
in a remote apartment. The chagrin
this extraordinary revolution could not
but occasion in my mind, was increased
when I recollected how hard it would
be, perhaps, to gain admission; and even
when that was obtained, we knew not
whether the only room I wished to lodge
in was now habitable. Lady Arundell,
with her usual foresight, advised me to
seem to have no other motive for this
visit, than a desire to re-purchase the
Castle; and when shewn through it, to
appear to be struck with so severe an in-
disposition, as soon as I reached the
chamber

chamber which contained the cabinets, as
should render it impoffible to remove
me; leaving it to her to reconcile the
owner to fo troublefome an intruder, by
the moft lavifh generofity. A fineffe of
this kind alone could afcertain me any
fuccefs, and the ficklinefs of my afpect,
I was fure, would fufficiently corroborate
fuch an affertion.

We fet out immediately, that by arriving in the evening we might have a
pretence for paffing the night there.—
My foul turned from the well-known
fcene, and fickened alike at fight of the
reviving verdure, and the fplendid manfion, to me alas, only a gay maufoleum.
Humbly I follicited entrance at a gate
which once flew open whenever I appeared; but, ah, though the exterior was
the fame, how ftrange feemed the alteration within!—No more did the liveried
train of affiduous domeftics affemble to
the diftant winding of the huntfman's
horn.—No longer did I reft in gilded
galleries, whofe pictured fides delighted
one fenfe, while their coolnefs refrefhed
another.

another. No longer could I, even in
idea, behold the beloved, the noble owner, whose gracious mien endeared the
welcome it conveyed—A change which
jarred every feeling had taken place. A
numerous body of diligent mechanics
were plodding in those halls were Elizabeth had feasted, and their battered sides
hardly now informed us where the rich
tapestry used to hang. My ears were suddenly stunned with the noise of a hundred
looms; and the distant lake once covered
with gay pageants, and resounding only to
the voice of pleasure, presented us another scene of industry not less busy,
strange, and surprizing. By incidents
of this kind, one becomes painfully and
instantaneously sensible of advancing into
life. When first we find ourselves sailing
with the imperceptible current of time,
engrossed either by the danger of our situation, or enchanted with its prospects,
we glide swiftly on, scarce sensible of our
progress, till the stream revisits some favorite spot : alas, so visible is the desolation of the shortest interval, that we
grow

grow old in a moment, and submit once more to the tide, willing rather to share the ruin than review it.

Among the few servants retained by the meagre master of this desolated mansion, one appeared who immediately recalled himself to my mind by the name of Gabriel. I recollected his having been warden of the outer lodges. The title by which I was announced---the weed I still continued to wear, overcame one already bowed to the earth by age, infirmity, and penury: and when to these circumstances was superadded the remembrance of the plentiful and peaceful days he had known under a Lord ever munificent to his domestics, gratitude became agony, and the poor old man sunk in a fit at my feet. An incident like this might well have affected an indifferent spectator.---I was scarce more sensible than himself: and the alarm soon spread through the laborious mechanics, till it was conveyed to Sir Humphry Moreton.---Timorously he emerged from
his

his apartment, and as the humble croud made way for him, he meafured me afar off with his eye, and feemed loft in conjecture on the fubject of my vifit.--- My purfe was yet in my hand, and part of its contents in thofe of fome perfons who had lent a ready affiftance. Whether this, or the wan delicacy of my looks interefted him, I know not; but every care-fur-rowed feature gradually relaxed as he ap-proached me, ftriving in vain to foften into the fmile of benevolence. I rofe to return his courteous falutation, and in-formed him, that when laft I paft the walls of this Caftle, I was its miftrefs, the dear and happy wife of Lord Leicefter; but perceiving uncertain apprehenfions of fome remote claim began again to con-tract his brow, I added, that fenfible I had loft every right in a fpot yet dear to me, I came to enquire whether he was difpofed to part with it, and to refcue from po-verty fuch worthy fervants of its late noble owner as had alike outlived their labour, and him who fhould have recompenfed it.

4   What

What heart is infenfible to that virtue
in which we alone can refemble our
Maker?-----Benevolence, like religion,
awes even thofe it cannot win. The
mifer loudly applauded my liberality;
and by a greater effort on his part, allowing for the difference of our characters, invited me to fpend the night in
the Caftle. The chamber I had been
accuftomed to inhabit, he called his beft,
and thither was I conducted. I was not
unprovided with the means of enfuring
my own welcome, and my fervants having fpread the cold viands we brought,
Sir Humphry's fpirits grew light over
luxuries he was not to pay for. A temptation fo agreeable prolonged his ftay,
and I at length difcovered the only way
to fhorten his vifit, would be to compli-
ment him with all that remained: feeing my fervants in compliance with the
hint, were about to convey it out of
the room, fear left any fhould be loft
by the way, prevailed over the hilarity
of

of the moment, and he departed with the wine.

With an impatient beating heart I raised the tapeſtry, which providentially had been preſerved in this room, leſs from its beauty than antiquity; as it was ſo worn that it had long been pannelled in many places.---Behind the bed we diſcovered the ſecret ſpring of the cabinet, which I opened without any difficulty; and with the aſſiſtance of Lady Arundell took down the well-remembered caſkets, pauſing at intervals, to weep over all the tender ideas the ſight of them recalled ſo forcibly to my memory; then raiſing my eye toward Heaven, while devoutly thanking the God who thus proſpered my remaining wiſhes, I almoſt fancied I beheld the bea-tified ſpirit of him who concealed theſe treaſures.

Lady Arundell would not reſt without inſpecting their contents. The largeſt was filled with family papers, bonds, contracts, mortgages, many of which were to me unintelligible, and all uſeleſs. The

The next contained letters and little ornaments, less precious from their intrin-
fic value, than their analogy to particular events.---Under these was a gilt casket
filled with jewels of great value, and
what was of infinitely more, the authenti-
cated bonds and acknowledgments of all
the sums Lord Leicester had informed
me he had providentially deposited in
other countries; and of which I knew
not any memorandum remained. This
was so noble an addition to the bequest
which already enriched my sweet Mary,
that it seemed to me, her father even
from the grave delighted to endow her:
while the Almighty, gracious even when
we think him most severe, had thus secreted for her advantage, treasures it
would have been impossible for me to
have preserved through so many desperate
vicissitudes.

The next casket was a gift from the
fond mother to the darling of her heart:
it contained all the testimonials of the
Queen of Scots, and other parties concerned

cerned, on the fubject of my birth, with
the contract of marriage between Lord
Leicefter and myfelf. I felt rich in thefe
recovered rights; and though prudence
might never permit me to claim alliance
with King James, yet to bequeath to
my daughter the power of doing fo, at
whatever period it fhould appear ad-
vantageous, was a great confolation to
me.

Lady Arundell and I paft part of the
night in packing thefe valuables in empty
trunks brought for that purpofe; then
clofing the fecret cabinet, and leaving no
traces of our fearch for it, we retired
to reft. We departed early the next
morning, carrying with us that ancient
domeftic of Lord Leicefter, on whom memory had fo powerfully operated, and two
others, who long fince expelled from the
Caftle, fought a miferable fubfiftence in
the hamlets around it. It joyed my very
heart to fupply to thefe poor wretches a
lofs irremediable with refpect to myfelf,
and the profound attachment of their

few remaining days amply rewarded
me.

Through the intervention of the friends
I yet poſſeſſed, ſome eminent merchants
in London undertook to get the bonds,
notes, &c. duly acknowledged: and in
proceſs of time, ſuch conſiderable ſums
were of conſequence recovered, as aſcer-
tained to myſelf and child our accuſtomed
affluence. Years and misfortune had
only cemented the ancient friendſhip between me and Lady Arundell.—I added
my income and family to hers.—Her
houſe was fortunately ſo near London,
as to allow me the advantage of procur-
ing the firſt inſtructors for my daughter,
and the infirm ſtate of Lady Arundell's
health, rendering her as much a priſoner
from neceſſity, as I was from choice,
both inſenſibly found in the improve-
ment of my daughter, a mild and grow-
ing ſatisfaction, which more than made
amends for the world we ſhut out.

Ah! could I deſire a greater pleaſure?
Pardon, madam, the fond extravagance
of

of maternal love, and allow me to prefent to you the darling of my heart in her
fixteenth year. Already fomething taller
than myfelf, to a form that united the
ftricteft fymmetry with the wild and variable graces of glowing youth, my Mary
added the perfect features of her father;
exquifitely feminized by a complexion
tranfparently fair, and a bloom alike delicate and vivid; her hair, of the golden
brown I have defcribed as peculiar to
his, fell below her waift in a profufion of
artlefs ringlets, heightening her beauty
even to luxuriance.—If fhe had borrowed
any thing from me, it was the collected
modefty of her mien; and from my
fifter fhe had ftolen that penetrating, faf-
cinating fmile, thofe two alone of all I
ever faw were gifted with:—alas, it was
now wholly her own.—Although light-
nefs and elafticity characterized her figure,
every limb was rounded even to polifh-
ing, and never did I contemplate the
foft turn of her white arms when raifed
to touch the lyre, without thinking thofe

more perfect than even her face.—Her
voice was no lefs fweet in fpeaking
than finging; with this difference—in
the firft fhe foftened the foul to pleafure,
in the laft, elevated it to rapture.—Her
underftanding was ftrong and penetrating,
yet elevated and refined.—Her fenfibility
(the firft formed of all her feelings) was
rather deep than ardent. Maternal experience had moderated the enthufiafm
incident to youth, nor was it obvious in
any inftance but the love of knowledge.
Inceffant, unremitting, in her ftudies,
books were her only extravagance, and
mufick her only relaxation. To com-
penfate for the worldly pleafures I judged
it prudence to deprive her of, I was lavifh
in indulgences to which her tafte naturally led: I kept muficians on purpofe
to accompany her, and found in the years
filled up by herfelf and her employ-
ments, that fweet though faddened pleafure parents only know, and which,
perhaps, more than makes us amends
for all the more lively ones it recalls to
our

our memory.   In effect, the more lovely
she grew, the more neceſſary I found it to
hide her; and offering her daily up to
God, I left her wholly to his diſpoſal;
determined neither my pride, vanity, or
ambition, ſhould interfere with the happineſs I ſupplicated for her.

On peruſing this deſcription, I perceive at once the impoſſibility of your
crediting it; yet far from accuſing myſelf of partiality, I could call on all who
ever beheld my daughter to atteſt my
candor.—How readily would Lady Arundell have done ſo—entendered to her by
a love only inferior to my own, that faithful friend found in declining life a new
tye wound round her heart, for which ſhe
daily thanked me.

As nothing robs us of the confidence
of youth like the appearance of myſtery,
when time called reflection to being in
her tender mind, I ſlowly, and by degrees, confided to my daughter the painful events you have thus obliged me to
commemorate.   This indulgence ſecured

to me her whole heart, and I trembled only lest her deep sense of past misfortunes should affect her health; for sensibility was the leading feature in her character. Far from seeking to expound the future in her own favor, the flattering prospects her distinguished birth, and yet more distinguished endowments, might well spread before her, passed away like a shadow, and she saw only her mother. A thousand times has she bedewed my hand with a reverence the most endearing; and the tears with which she often embalmed the memory of her father, almost recompensed me for his loss. From that period her expressive eyes were fixed ever on mine with such blended sadness and admiration, as proved she thought me almost fainted by misfortune. More studious henceforward of my pleasure, more submissive to my will, more solicitous for my repose, it seemed as if in learning she was my only remaining tye on earth, she conceived the various affections and duties of all I had lost

loft devolved to, and centered in, herfelf. But fympathy was the genuine impulfe of her nature; for with equal care
fhe watched over her unhappy aunt.—
Whenever that dear creature's incurable
malady affumed the appearance of melancholy, fhe was extravagantly fond of
mufick.—At thofe intervals my lovely
Mary would lean over her lute with the
meek benignity of a defcending angel,
and extract from it fuch folemn founds
as breathed at once of peace and forrow :
infenfibly foothing the perturbed fpirit,
and melting only thofe yet undifturbed.
That fubtle effence of our natures, fenfibility, which madnefs can only unfix,
not annihilate, often paufed unconfcioufly
upon the pleafure, and foftly funk into
repofe.

A child thus eminently amiable at once
concentered my affections—commanded
my efteem—poffeffed my whole confidence—actuated, in fhort, my very being.
—Ah, how noble, how affecting is the
friendfhip grounded on the maternal and

filial

filial tye; when unconfcious of any weak-
nefs in her own heart, the mother dares
prefent it as a pure and unflattering mir-
ror to her child, and with that felf-ap-
plaufe which even Heaven approves, con-
templates the upright, the innocent foul it
reflects!—Sacred and indelible becomes
that precept which is expreffed but by
example.—Happy are thofe enabled to
form fuch an attachment as inexperience
ftrengthens on one hand, and knowledge
on the other:—Neither the gufts of
youthful paffion, nor the nipping frofts
of age, can deftroy a plant rooted thus
by mutual virtue;---it only gains vigor
from time, and by the peculiar indulgence of the Almighty, our fublimeft
merit ripens into our moft perfect pleafure.

Satisfied I had already acquired fuch
an influence in my daughter's mind as
fhould enable me to regulate her principles, I left it to time and circumftances
to call them into action.---The great
bufinefs of my life now feemed over;
and

and delivering my heart up to the flattering prefages of maternal love, a thoufand vifions of almoft forgotten grandeur and happinefs floated before my eyes,
and fometimes half-deluded them.

The fluctuating complaints of Lady
Arundell at length fettled into a confumption :—It was an hereditary diforder
of the Sydneys; nor perhaps could all
the folicitude of myfelf and my fweet
Mary have availed toward her reftoration, even if a cruel fhock in which we
were all equal fufferers, had not precipi-
tated her fate.

Among the unconfcious caprices which
by turns actuated my unfortunate fifter,
was a paffion for fitting in the open air.---
Neither times, or feafons, had any influence over her; and fhe would infift on it
alike in the fnow of December, and the
fcorching fun of July.---To this felf-will
I had no doubt greatly contributed.
From the moment of my return to England, I had vehemently oppofed the fevere controul to which fhe had hereto-

fore been fubject, and habituated her attendants to yield to her in every inftance
which did not abfolutely endanger her
fafety: fully determined not to render
an exiftence wholly wretched no human
being could now make happy. But as
uninformed minds never know a medi-
um, the people appointed to watch her,
gradually fuffered her to become fenfible
of her power, which foon grew into an
unbounded indulgence. It was now the
depth of winter, and fhe had fat in the
keen air for hours, watching the fnow,
which fell in abundance.----The moft
violent fhiverings enfued, followed by a
fever which fettled at laft on the nerves,
and brought her to the very verge of
the grave.---Neverthelefs, it appeared to
have falutary effects---her fpirits were
funk indeed to extreme lownefs, but
they became more equal; and traces of
reafon were often difcernable in her actions. If fhe did not remember, fhe yet
ftrove to know me; and fometimes ftudied my features in a manner the moft
touching.

touching.---I confidered this as the very crifis of her fate---her only chance on this fide Heaven, and fcarce dared leave her for a fingle moment. I entrufted the care of Lady Arundell (whofe fituation, though more dangerous, was not fo melancholy) to my daughter; fearful left her youthful fpirits fhould be injured by conftantly beholding an object fo affecting. But I had forgot that my own fhattered conftitution was not equal to the fatigue and anxiety of watching over my fifter. I fell one evening into a fucceffion of fainting fits; the fervants conveyed me to bed; and the fear of alarming Lady Arundell hindered them from informing my daughter of my fituation. My faintings at length gave place to a drowfinefs fo intenfe, I might call it a ftupor.--- I remained thus for fome hours, when I ftarted with an indiftinct idea of a heavy fall, and a deep groan. Terror roufed, and collected in a moment, every dormant faculty.----I rufhed through the chamber which divided mine from my fifter's, but I blamed myfelf for impetuofity

tuofity when I perceived all was pro-
foundly filent in hers. The two nurfes
were in a deep fleep, and the expiring
watchlights heavily winked, and revived,
before the cold dawn of the morning.
I gently opened the curtains of her bed---
Ah, gracious Heaven, what did I feel
when I beheld it empty !---The agonized
fhriek I gave, rouzed both her carelefs
attendants, who impreffed with but one
idea, flew towards a door I now firft
perceived to be open : it led to a gallery ornamented with fuch portraits of
our family as had furvived the wreck of
their fortunes ; among them was incau-
tioufly placed that (already fatally commemorated) of the Earl of Effex at the
ftorming of Cadiz; an unfortunate legacy bequeathed to Ellinor by Lady
Pembroke.---My foul took in at a thought
all the fearful confequences.---I tottered
into the gallery---alas, only to behold
my worft apprehenfion verified.---The
fair fpectre, which once was Ellinor, lay
proftrate before the picture---one hand
had convulfively gathered her difordered
                                  garments

garments over her thin cheſt; the other was ſtill expreſſively extended towards the inanimate image of him ſo beloved.---Impatiently I laid my hand upon her heart---it anſwered not the trembling enquirer---its wandering eſſence was exhaled, and ſhe had ceaſed forever to ſuffer. Thy parting prayer, oh Eſſex! was ſurely prophetic, for her ſoul in recovering memory, had burſt its mortal bound, and ſoared to Heaven.

Scarce were the dear remains quietly interred, ere thoſe of the amiable Lady Arundell followed them. I bore theſe loſſes with devout reſignation.-----The tears which fall when Heaven recalls the unfortunate, ſtill the wild paſſions of the ſad ſurvivor, and deeply wound only the ſoul yet new to ſuffering. It was with a quickened apprehenſion I perceived the effect of theſe firſt afflictions on the tender ſpirits of my daughter: not that I ſought totally to ſtifle the lively impreſſions of natural affection;---the tears of youth, like the genial ſhowers of

May,

May, ferve only to fave the planter's
toil, and fimply ripen the rich fruits of
the mind; but when either fall too often,
they impoverifh the foil, and wafh away
the buds yet blowing.

My own foul afforded no variety of
chearful images with which I could hope
to invigorate the gentle fpirits of my
Mary; unwilling to form new connections, I rather thought it prudent to
change my abode, and by a variety of
fcenes infenfibly amufe her; and my
fteward was fent accordingly to feek another manfion. I called back the moment
when the gloomy aifles of a ruined con-
vent, by poffeffing the fimple advantage
of novelty, diverted my mind even at the
forrowful crifis which robbed me of a
fofter mother. Alas, in yet untried youth,
the profpect that is unknown, ever adds
to its own charms thofe of imagination;
while in maturer life, the heart lingers on
all which once delighted it, hopelefs of
finding in the future, a pleafure fancy
can ever compare with thofe it reviews
in

in the paſt. To my daughter, however, the whole world was yet new, and in fixing on a ſcene habitual to my feelings, I could not fail to delight hers. I hired a manſion near the Thames ſide, in Richmond, to which we removed early in the ſpring.

Perhaps, in this choice, I was influenced almoſt without knowing it, by a latent motive: diſtinct as I had lived from the world ſince my return to England, the fame of the Prince of Wales had yet reached me.---This accompliſhed youth had at once roſe above the weakneſſes of his father, and the prejudices of his rank; devoting his heart to the virtues, his mind to the ſciences, and his perſon to thoſe manly and becoming exerciſes, which invigorating every human power, prepared him alike for the enjoyment of peace, or the purſuit of war. Delighted to underſtand a Stuart was riſing to redeem the glory of his declining race, I paſſionately longed to ſee, know, and be valued by the royal Henry.

Henry. The King, unworthy a fon fo diftinguifhed, took no pleafure in his company; but even in tender youth, refigned him to a court of his own, from the adulation of which, merit fuperior to praife alone could have guarded him. Henry had, like myfelf, a partiality for the beautiful village of Richmond; he always paffed part of the fummer in a palace near the Thames, and I took pleafure in thinking a partition of wood alone feparated his gardens from mine. With a judgment unequalled at his years, the Prince knew how to be affable without abating aught of his dignity; and, while in the circle of his own court he preferved the authority of a Sovereign, to the unfortunate who addreffed him, he had the benignity of a brother: fuch was his character in Richmond, where the people almoft adored him, and took pleafure in amplifying on the fuperior qualities he fo eminently poffeffed. The fweet hopes his merit fometimes infufed

into

into my bofom, came accompanied with an equal number of fears, yet could not my heart forbear to cherifh them.

The revolving feafon tinged this fweet retreat with every variety of verdure; the waves of the Thames were more tranflucent than ever; all nature awakened once more to perfection, when the Prince of Wales took up his abode in the adjacent palace.---This news heightened the foft red of my daughter's cheek, and even faintly colored my wan one.--- Not daring to exprefs to her the eager defire I felt to fee the Prince, and not accuftomed to venture out without her, day after day elapfed in anxious expectation. My gentle Mary, with a delicacy from which I drew the moft happy prefages, now always chofe to go abroad either fo early or fo late that it was almoft impoffible we fhould ever meet the Prince, and the veil fhe ufually wore was clofed with fo much care as to enfure her the happinefs of being overlooked, even if fortune threw him in our way.

Neverthelefs, I took notice the arrival
of the royal Henry ftrangely filled up
the void in our lives.---What he would
do, or what he would not do, conftantly
regulated our motions, and employed my
daughter's thoughts even more than my
own. His tafte afforded us a variety of
indulgencies of which he knew not we
were partakers.---Sometimes moon-light
concerts, or magnificent fireworks; at
others, parties on the Thames; where
the Prince ftill took pleafure in beholding
a variety of little veffels, built and orna‐
mented for the amufement of his early
years, and which were manned by chil‐
dren.---They were often fo near, we fan‐
cied we heard the voice of Henry, when
both mother and daughter would give
way to the fame impulfe, and haftily re‐
tire. The fummer might have elapfed
in this manner had not chance been more
favorable to our wifhes than we could re‐
folve to be.

We were returning home one morning
in an ill-contrived carriage, newly in‐
vented

vented for airings, the inconvenience of which I bore patiently from not being able to walk or ride on horfeback for any length of time fince my memorable fever.---The fervant who drove, ftopt as ufual at the brow of the enchanting hill, that we might enjoy for a few minutes its beauties, when the found of horns approaching near, informed us the Prince of Wales was returning from hunting, which at once ftartled the horfes and ourfelves. My Mary actuated only by the impreffion of the moment, made an eager fign to the man to drive on; and the horfes, already frightened, yielded impetuoufly to the flighteft touch of the rein, flying forward with the moft dangerous rapidity. The clumfinefs of the carriage, and the badnefs of the road, threatened us every moment with being overturned ---for me there was no efcape, but could my daughter be prevailed on to leap out, I was fenfible fhe would be fafe. Far from obeying my intreaties, or even commands, fhe threw her arms around

Q 2   me,

me, and protefted it was for me alone fhe
feared. The carriage funk into a deep
rut at laft, and we were thrown out at a
fmall diftance, with a violence that almoft deprived me of my fenfes :---my
darling Mary had wholly loft hers. I
perceived the train of Henry approaching, but the favorite wifh of feeing
him was forgotten in that of recovering
her.-----I was prefently environed by
the hunters without regarding them, till
their extreme follicitude obliged me to
raife my eyes from the lifelefs face of my
daughter in acknowledgment. I perceived with a furprize even that moment could not conquer, that on either
hand ftood a young man, adorned with
the order of the garter, and fo diftin-
guifhingly handfome, that I knew not
which was the Prince of Wales, but
turned from the one to the other with
an air of wildnefs and ftupor.—My looks,
however, made little impreffion on the
ftrangers, their whole attention being
fixed on the inanimate form of my daughter.---

ter.---In truth, fortune had contrived
to shew her to the utmost advantage.
I had thrown up her veil to give her air,
and bared her beautiful hands and arms,
polished and white as Parian marble; the
wild rings of her auburn hair played on
her youthful face as the yellow leaves
of Autumn curl over a later peach; whilst
every feature formed with a truth which
might bear the nicest examination, perhaps
only appeared more exquisitely regular
from the absence of expression; and even
her figure and attitude (leaning on her
mother's knees) presented a perfect model for a sculptor. The affiduities of the
strangers, together with my own, at
length recalled her scattered senses.---
She opened those eyes so dear to
me, and fixing them on the two strangers, a rosy suffusion alone proved
she saw them, with such quickness did
she turn toward her mother; when beholding me to appearance unhurt, she
lifted her soul to Heaven in a look of
gratitude, and throwing her arms round

Q 3   my

my neck, relieved her overcharged heart
by weeping on my bosom. "An an
gel in soul as well as form! exclaimed
one of the strangers; assure me, madam,
continued he, that this terror is the only ill
consequence of my sudden approach, or
I know not how I shall forgive it to myself." This address ascertaining the
Prince of Wales, he became the sole
object of my attention.----Ah, where
shall I find words to endear to you, Madam, the royal youth my heart at once
opened to adopt? Henry was yet but
in the dawn of manhood, nevertheless
his height was majestic, and his figure
finished. The beauty of his features was
their least charm---virtue herself seemed
to sublime every happy lineament, and
spare beholders the trouble of developing
his character by conveying it in a glance.
His manly voice united the firmness
of his own sex, with the sensibility of
ours. A confusion of sad remembrances
were at once presented with him to my
mind; and the admiration he excited

was

was ſtrangely blended with regret.---I forgot that he had addreſſed me, and continued to contemplate him in ſilence ; ever and anon turning my ſtreaming eyes wildly from him to Heaven, even then, my dilating heart bids me add, ſcarce changing the object. The amiable Henry, in whoſe nature ſympathy was the prevailing ſentiment, touched with a conduct ſo myſterious, almoſt forgot my daughter in turn, ſo wholly was he engroſſed by me.---Informed of my unfortunate lameneſs by my attempting to riſe, he immediately concluded it to be the conſequence of the recent accident, and ſcarce was ſatisfied by my aſſurances of the contrary. Oh! as my eyes ſurveyed the ſuperior ſoul, living irradiated in the bright orbs of his, how did they ſtream at ʾremembering that had his father been born to half his virtues,. I might now have been cheriſhed by affection---dignified by rank---unwidowed---unbroken---a ſtranger yet to ſorrow! ---My mother too.---Moſt unhappy of parents as well as ſovereigns! I had a

Q 4   tear

tear for thee at this interesting moment.

The respect due to strangers induced the Prince to conceal the curiosity my conduct could not fail to excite, but having informed himself from the attendants of my title, he addressed me by it, and insisted on conducting me home. I now understood the nobleman who had divided my first looks with the Prince, to be the Viscount Rochester: that contemptible favorite of the King, celebrated only for his beauty.---The visible coldness of my air checked a forward insolence I observed in him and obliged him to quit us on our arriving at home.

With what secret transport did my soul welcome a Stuart worthy that name, glorious for so many ages!---The Prince seemed delighted with his new acquaintances.---The soft reserve of my daughter's air---the deepening roses of her cheek, and the low accent of her harmonious voice, when politeness obliged her to answer the Prince, whose animated eyes reduced hers often to seek the ground,

ground, prefented to my elated heart
every fymptom of that paffion which
alone endears the fufferings it occafions.
A flow of happy fpirits new to my daughter,
almoft forgotten by myfelf, gave chear-
fulnefs to the hour which Henry faw
elapfe with regret.

On this chance introduction was
grounded an acquaintance a few days
ripened into intimacy.---Led to diftinguifh the Prince alike by his own merit,
and the ties of blood, which fecretly
allied me to him, it was with the ten-
dereft fatisfaction I beheld him cherifh
the inclination he had already conceived
for my daughter: yet the dignity of his
mind forbidding him to form an engagement he knew not how to fulfill,
it was through me alone he addreffed
himfelf to her. Convinced it was in
my power to prove her entitled even
to fuch a lover, I fuffered fate to take
its courfe, attending only to prudence.

Confcious that Henry had hitherto
moved in a very confined circle, I was
aware to extend it muft draw much obfervation

vation on thofe he favored. To guard
therefore againſt the malice of ſurmiſe,
I fixed on the hour of the Prince's viſit
for my daughter to ride out; and always
received him alone.   His-attendants, who
ſaw her regularly depart, were at a loſs to
imagine what could attach their royal
maſter to the infirm widow of Lord Leiceſter.   The charm was in truth ſimply
affection.----The amiable Henry had early
been accuſtomed to every kind of homage
but that of the heart, and had too much
ſenſibility not to feel the want he knew
not how to ſupply.   Deeply ſuſceptible
of the true regard I had conceived for
him, impreſſed at once by my mind, my
manners, and my mien, with the idea
of myſtery, and the deſire of obtaining
my confidence, it was only by his own
candor he ſought to gain upon mine.
Slowly and by degrees he deigned to re-
poſe with me thoſe regrets and anxieties
from which the utmoſt indulgence of nature and fortune cannot exempt a ſingle
individual.   He often lamented the
dangerous diſtinction of being the firſt-
born

born of his father's children, since it cost
him every other.---Separated almost in
infancy from his parents---surrounded
with mercenary sycophants, who sought
to make their court to the reigning King
by a partial representation or misconstruc-
tion of his actions, he had shot up un-
loved, uncherished, and seen those tender affections he was born to share, gradually center in that son from whom
his parents had nothing to fear.---Nor
were wanting insidious flatterers equally
ready to undermine his filial duty, by
pointing out the weaknesses of his father,
even where they were most likely to
wound him. He had punished himself,
he added, for yielding to these impressions by an absolute obedience to his authority, but it was with grief he remembered that was now the only tye between
them.---Nor would I wonder, he continued, it should be so, if I considered that,
born as he was to imperial power, with
an ardent passion for glory, he had hitherto been shut up in the narrow sphere
of his own court, languishing away the
                              flowe:

flower of his youth without a choice, a friend, or a pursuit:---Till the infamous Carr should deign to decide what foreign Prince's bribe he would condescend to accept, and to what bigoted Papist he should sacrifice the son of his master.

While the admired Prince of Wales, the idol of the People, the heir of Empire, the endued of Heaven, thus confided to me the simple and rational griefs which clouded a fortune so brilliant, could I fail to meditate on the equality of providence ?---Which graciously allots even to the lowest situation, some portion of happiness, and depresses the highest with the sad sense of misfortune.

It is the fatal peculiarity of youth to throw the strongest light on every secret grief, and waste away under an oppression imagination often doubles. To cure this propensity is therefore the province of experience. I sought to imbue the Prince's mind with the only principle mine had derived from all my sufferings. ---That the noblest use we can make of

un-

understanding, is to convert it into happiness; and every talent which does not conduce to that great end, ought rather to be considered as a burthen than a blessing to the possessor.----That the mind, like the eye, ever magnifies the object 'of fear or aversion, which often on a strict examination, excites no other sentiment than contempt. --Infine, that he was not at liberty to shew any other sense of his father's errors, than by presenting a faultless example in his own life; and that if he would have it without blemish, he must divert his taste from channels where it would meet with opposition, and turn it into those through which it might flow freely.----That the cultivation of the sciences would at once fill up that void in his life ever so painful at his years, and attach to his welfare all who loved them : a body whose influence was never known unless opposition called forth the powers of eloquence.

The

The Prince had too much judgment not to fee the utility of this council, and too much generofity not to value its candour: neverthelefs, it was a language yet new to his ears.----Ingenuity had been exhaufted to teach him to govern others, but to fubdue himfelf was a lefson none had ventured to inculcate. How did I lament a foul fo ductile had in childhood been injudicioufly delivered up to its own guidance, and fuffered every day to imbibe fome new prejudice, deftined perhaps to mark the character through life; and which an upright and fkilful monitor might fo eafily have eradicated!

The Prince could not be infenfible to the maternal caution which induced me to fend my daughter abroad whenever he honored me with a vifit, yet the obfervation did not for fome time appear to influence his conduct.----Satisfied with merely beholding her as he entered or departed, the defire of opening his heart to me feemed to fupercede every other impreffion.

fion. Neverthelefs, long reveries would follow the moft accidental meeting, and long paufes intervene in the moft interefting converfation; rendering it fufficiently obvious that his mind labored with fome projeét, hitherto fuppreffed either by pride or prudence.

Perhaps I fhould ever have wanted courage to open my lips on fo delicate an occafion, had not my daughter complained to me that fhe was now become the univerfal objeét of attention; and that the fuite who attended her were often rudely furrounded, and fometimes interrogated by fuch of the Prince's court as had not benefited by his example.--- By going abroad unexpectedly with her, I found fhe was not offended without reafon, and fenfible of my imprudence in thus rifquing her fafety, I came to the refolution rather to abridge myfelf of the pleafure of the Prince's fociety, than purchafe it by endangering my daughter.-----I defired her to retire for awhile when Henry fhould vifit

me

me next, and ere he could account for
the fingularity of finding her at home,
entered into the delicate explanation.
With an acknowledged attachment to
him, that I bore my child, alone could
have over-ruled, I fubmitted it to himfelf, whether I could too cautioufly guard
againſt a cenſure or inſult ſhe had no natural protector to reſent.---The generous
Henry pauſed for a few moments with ir-
refolution, when fuddenly collecting courage, he broke filence.---" Will Lady
Leiceſter pardon, faid he, thofe ob
trufive vifits ſhe has fubmitted to with
fo much complacency?—Will ſhe deign
to become the confidant of the only incident in my life I have hid from her---
will ſhe liften with indulgence?"----He
pauſed a moment, but ere I could
refolve how to anſwer, purſued the dif-
courſe.-----" Accuſtomed even from
childhood to the enſnaring glances of
the light and the lovely---led to imagine
myſelf older than my years by the con-
zinual propofals for marrying me that
                                have

have conftantly fucceeded each other, it is not wonderful that a heart naturally fufceptible, fhould mature before its time. Among the many beautiful girls, who have already fought to attract me, I foon diftinguifhed one by whom my peace, my honour, my innocence became endangered: perhaps they had been loft, had I not found her felfifh and ambitious. I need hardly inform you that this feducing fair one is the Countefs of Effex!—Vain of her influence over me, fhe took pleafure in publifhing it, and taught me early to blufh for my choice; but I could not refolve to do fo continually. I formed the bold refolution of contending with my own heart, and retired hither to recover it, or die. Lady Effex, enraged and humbled at this conduct, confirmed me in it, by attaching herfelf to Vifcount Rochefter: thus rendering it fufficiently obvious fhe had never loved me.—Befotted with her beauty, that weak favourite is governed by her caprices, and him I was born to obey yields to thofe of Rochefter. Al-

though

though I do not immediately perceive how Lady Essex means to effect her revenge, I am convinced it is only maturing; and daily expect a blow from which I know not how to guard myself. Under these circumstances how can I venture to involve your fate with mine?—How can I ask you, to permit me to offer to your lovely daughter the heart which ever hovers near her?—Speak, Madam—my happiness is in your hands—dare you risque your own to promote it?" While I listened to this sensible, this frank declaration of the Prince's error, and his attachment, my fond heart found its first wish accomplished, and adopted at once the royal youth; solemnly vowing to share, without repining, every evil that might follow an alliance so dear: nor did I fail secretly to exult in my Mary's hereditary right even to this distinction.

To cement the confidence between us, and convince the Prince his present choice was judicious, I resolved to confide to him the secret so long, so painfully preserved ; and

and related my whole hiftory.   As I re-
traced its affecting incidents, I knew them
to be fo only by his eager, his generous
fympathy; fo wholly was my own foul
engroffed by the happy profpect he had
opened before it.

The Prince of Wales acknowledged
with joy the relationfhip I claimed; to
confirm all I had advanced, I prefented to
him the long-faved teftimonials, which he
perufed with filent reverence: then fixing his eyes, ftill impreffed with that elevated fentiment, on mine, he gave utterance to the dictates of his heart.——
" Who could fuppofe, exclaimed he, a
fortitude fo unexampled could poffibly be
combined with a frame delicate even to
fragility!—May the misfortunes you have
indelibly impreffed on my memory, my
more than mother, be the laft of your
life.—May that being who directed my
foul to cherifh the admiration and efteem
infpired by your lovely daughter, and
matchlefs felf, fuffer the youth before
you to fupply to your heart, all it ought
to have inherited—all it unhappily has

R 2   loft

loft. Dear will be the moment when to the form of your angel mother my authority ſhall add the name, and that moment will hereafter, oh! moſt honoured of women, infalliibly be mine."

While I liſtened to predictions ſo flattering, I almoſt believed them accompliſhed. In thy unblown youth, oh, royal Henry, was comprized every promiſe that could dilate or fill the heart: mine centred at once in thee, and my daughter: finding in the mere hope of ſo glorious a union, a total ſuſpenſion from ſuffering and ſorrow.

I had now no reſerves with the Prince, and leading in my bluſhing Mary preſented her to her royal Couſin; who gracefully offered up his unblemiſhed ſoul on the hand he bowed over. So pure a tranſport took poſſeſſion of mine, as obliterated every other impreſſion. I ſnatched the united hands ſo dear, ſo beloved, and preſſing them to my boſom, ſickened with very extaſy, and withdrew **to recover** myſelf.—Wandering alone by the

the fide of the Thames, I raifed my full
eyes to heaven; and called the happy
fpirits of my mother, fifter, and Lord
Leicefter, to fympathize with me in an
event which promifed to end the perfecu-
tions of my family, by thus bleffedly
uniting the laft fprung branches of it. A
ferenity of the fublimeft nature fucceeded
the fweet trouble of my fpirits, and enabled me to rejoin the youthful lovers with
the dignity due to my own character.

The fituation in which we ftood endeared us ftill more to the Prince, by perpetually reminding him how intimately
our welfare was connected with his own.
Every hour feemed to unite us more and
more to each other. Henry fpoke to me
with the freedom of a fon; conjuring me
not to take any ftep that might create the
leaft fufpicion of my birth, or the fecret
tye formed between us, till he had well
weighed every confequence that might
enfue: and to elude the watchful fpies,
with whom we were alike furrounded, he
propofed paffing in the evening through
his garden to ours, if I would deign for

R 3 awhile

awhile to allow him thus to reach the
faloon. Our fituation was too delicate
not to require the ftricteft caution, yet as
I could difcover no mode of receiving
the Prince which was not equally que-
ftionable, and more dangerous, I confented to that he propofed: as well as
that he fhould render one of his gentle-
men (Sir David Murray) a confidante of
this intimacy, though not of its nature,
or extent.

An incident fo important engroffing
my every thought, my heart returned
once more eagerly into the world. It had
now an intereft in fully underftanding the
real characters of the King, the Queen,
Vifcount Rochefter, and every individual likely or intitled to interfere at this
interefting crifis.— I examined, confidered, weighed every thing. I foon difcovered the whole Royal Family were at
variance! That the imperious Queen,
unable to wreft her hufband from his fa-
vourites, or her fon from his duties,
fcorned the firft, and neglected the
latter: confining herfelf wholly to a
court

court formed of her own creatures, who
affifted her to fpoil her younger fon;
whom fhe had almoft eftranged from his
brother. Her beautiful daughter who
united in her own perfon the graces of
Mary, with the fpirit of Elizabeth, alone
allured to the court of the Queen the few
perfons of merit it afforded. Henry was
often lavifh in the praifes of his fifter,
and as fhe was the only relation he ever
voluntarily fpoke of, I naturally concluded fhe was the only one entitled by fuperior qualities to that diftinction. King
James, who had mounted the throne
under happier aufpices than almoft any
preceding fovereign of England, had already lived long enough to lofe the affections of his people. By turns a pedant
and a buffoon, his folemnity was even
more difgufting than his levity. Governed by a predilection of the moft abfurd and fingular nature, to a beautiful
favourite he always delivered up the reins
of empire; readily fubmitting to a fhameful fubjection in all important points,
provided he might enjoy a ridiculous fu-

R 4   premacy

premacy in his hours of indulgence and
retirement. From such a weak and in-
confiftent King, and his profligate Minifters, the wife, the fcientific, and the
good, had gradually retreated; and in
neglect and filence contemplated from
far the growth of that exemplary Prince,
who promifed to retrieve the fame of his
anceftors, and the glory of the kingdom
he was born to reign over. A youth of
eighteen capable of uniting the unblemifhed virtues of that age, with the difcernment of a maturer one, was a phæ-
nomenon, and of courfe either adored or
detefted.——While the body of the kingdom regarded him only with the firft
fentiment, the worthlefs favorites of his
father were actuated folely by the latter.

To marry and efcape the plans of Rochefter was the intereft of Henry; and
to marry without his father's knowledge
his unwilling choice.——Yet highly fenfible
of the flavery impofed by his rank, he
had refifted every temptation from beauties of an inferior one:——but when apprized of my ftory, he faw, or fancied he
faw

faw in my daughter, a wife alloted him by heaven---one to whom no juft objection could poffibly be made, one born to give happinefs to his heart, and honor to his name. Nor could he doubt, even if his father fhut his eyes againft the truth, but that he fhould be able to convince the people of my birth, when the publication of the marriage fhould give my ftory the whole weight of his credence.

Succefs in his judgment depended folely on the concealment of the purpofed union till it could be accomplifhed; for if the intention tranfpired ere the event, he was fatisfied the moft defperate efforts would be made to wreft us from him. Yet as at this very period a publick treaty was negociating with a foreign Prince, he could not form a tye of fuch importance without giving his father juft caufe of offence, the nation at large a contempt for his character, and the diftant Sovereign thus infulted, a mortal difguft. We therefore agreed to wait till this Minifterial project like many others fhould difappoint itfelf, and feize that moment to

celebrate

celebrate and publish a marriage, which was to end all our fears, and complete all our hopes.

During this interval I obferved with pain that the extreme timidity of my daughter's character prevailed over the enthufiafm incident to her years; and damped with vague apprehenfions thofe moments love and hope might have made fo happy. I faw this little feminine weak-nefs with extreme uneafinefs. The Prince of Wales was diftinguifhed by a manly firmnefs, which ever wifely weighed the approaching trial, then calmly dared it. For a foul fo noble, I defired to find a faultlefs bride; and looking fearfully into the future, I fometimes thought my Ma-ry's timid heart would one day throb without caufe againft that of a fovereign opprefied with innumerable cares, he perhaps fought to lofe the remembrance of, in her fociety. Neverthelefs I did not perceive my tender admonitions on this fubject, had any other confequence than that of inducing my daughter to bury in her bofom thofe fentiments and emo-

tions

tions, I had so many years delighted to participate.

It was now autumn!---The time of the King's periodical progresses.---The Prince could not avoid following his father, but he lingered in his duty; and having staid a day too long with us, hastened to overtake the King, whom he was to feast at Woodstock. He wrote to me from thence, complaining of fatigue and lassitude; but with his usual attention, informed me he was in treaty for Kenilworth Castle, where he flattered himself, I should again see golden days like those I still remembered with so much pleasure.

Alas, those he had irradiated, were quickly hastening to a period! At the first visit he paid me on his return, my soul was struck with a very apparent alteration in his person; which was grown thin and wan beyond conception, considering the shortness of the time. Not all the joy he expressed a our meeting could satisfy me, he was either well or happy, but observing he evaded my question; and fearful of alarm-

ing

ing him without reason, I strove to sup-
press that maternal anxiety all his assurances of health and chearfulness could
not dispel. I perceived my daughter was
impressed with the same idea, for though
she spoke not, it was visible to me she
wept greatly when alone.

The evenings were now too short and
damp for me to allow the evening visits
of the Prince; and I rather chose to
risque every danger by receiving him
openly, than subject him to any by an
ill-judged caution.---Alas, these cares
were vain.---The rapid decay of the
Royal Henry's health, became visible even
to indifferent spectators. An affecting
languor was the only expression of those
fine eyes once so full of fire, and the
youthful cheeks every following day
should have tinged with a deeper bloom,
grew more and more wan and hollow---
He could no longer conceal his illness.
Alas! it pierced me to the soul! I was
miserable at remembering a charge so
precious, as his welfare should be committed to servants of whatever denomi-
nation

nation.---No mother---no fister---duties
indifpenfable in every other rank of life,
were it feems incompatible with royalty.
Oh, Henry!---dear amiable youth! even
yet am I tempted to accufe myfelf for
not having better deferved the tender ap-
pellation thy filial reverence fo often be-
ftowed on me, by daring every thing for
thy fake! Slaves to imperious cuftom,
our actions are too often regulated by that
idle multitude, whofe moft lavifh ap-
plaufes would but ill confole us for one
fingle reproach, from that unerring monitor, our own confcience.

Either not convinced this fecret malady
was undermining his conftitution, or indifferent to the event, the Prince ftill continued in the purfuit of his ufual athletic
exercifes and habits, till his ftrength
was wholly unequal to them. I once
more perfuaded him to call in medical
affiftance, and he promifed to attend
to himfelf as foon as his fifter and the
elector fhould depart.---Obliged to appear
at the celebration of their marriage in
London, he came to pay us a parting vifit.

fit. Impreſſed, perhaps, with the idea it
would be the laſt, he threw himſelf into
my arms, and ſhed there the firſt tears
I had ever ſeen fall from his eyes.---Mine
readily overflowed---a grief too deep for
utterance preſſed upon my ſoul, and
Henry recovered ere I could. His heart
miſſed my daughter, who was gone
abroad.---He ſighed, ſunk into a little
reverie, and breaking it, with a faint
ſmile, ſaid, " he ought rather to congra-
tulate himſelf on her abſence." He ſighed
again, and after another pauſe, reſumed
his diſcourſe in a low and broken voice.—
" Mourn not thus, my mother (for I
will ſtill give you a title you may juſtly
claim from her who bore me; ſince who
ever loved me as you have done?) I have
youth in my favor, and this oppreſſive
malady may not be mortal : for your ſake
alone do I wiſh it to be otherwiſe, believe
me.---Already weary, diſguſted with this
world, I could retreat from it almoſt
without a pang, did I not know my loſs
would be to you an irremediable calamity.
Yet, who ſhall judge of the diſpenſations
of

of the Almighty?---I might fulfil all
your wishes without seeing you happy---
I might obtain all my own without ceasing
to be wretched. Recall this often to
your memory, whatever follows our parting; and remember your name will be
ever on these lips while they have power
to utter a sound.---For the adored of my
soul---but she is surely become a part of
it; and if not permitted to possess her
in this world, I will expect her in a better."---Perceiving his dim eye was fixed
on a picture of my daughter which hung
at my bosom, I presented it to him.---
" And do you too, beloved Henry, returned I, in a broken voice, remember
the mother who gives you this, would
have comprized in the original every
grace, every virtue, to be found through
human nature; and having done so,
would still have thought her honored in
your choice.---Ah! royal youth! resign
not a heart so noble to vapourish depression!---Your life, your happiness, are
not your own merely---a nation are born
to pray for the former, to crown you with
the

the latter.---For myself---upon the sweet hope of matching my daughter with you, of sharing the soft transports of mutual virtue and affection, I have learnt to live, but surely I could never survive its extinction."---My full soul allowed not of another syllable. The Prince fixed his suffused eyes on mine, with a mysterious melancholy, almost amounting to despair; and touching with his lips those hands his trembling ones still grasped, rushed precipitately into the court yard. The sound of his voice drew me towards the window---the graceful youth made me a last obeisance, and galloped away; while my partial eye pursued him till beyond its reach, and even then my ear seemed to distinguish the feet of his horse.

With his usual kind consideration, Henry wrote to me the next day, that he found himself better; and in the pleasure of seeing his sister happy, felt reconciled to the impolitick match made for her.--- He even assisted at the various festivals with which the nuptials of the royal Elizabeth were honored; but scarce were
they

they over, when his health and spirits failed at once, and the faculty were called in to his aid. A malady which had been so long engrafting itself on his constitution, left but little hope of his life;--- I had ceased to entertain any: yet, far from supporting the idea of losing him with fortitude, my soul mourned as if it then had first known sorrow. Not daring to give free vent to my apprehensions in the presence of my daughter, I strove with cold and watery smiles to flatter those hopes in her heart my own had long rejected, and saw with vain regret, the deep excesses of a sensibility I had laboured to excite and strengthen.

What days, what nights of sadness and suspense were ours, while the unfortunate Henry was languishing away every vital power ere yet they had reached maturity! ---Frequently delirious, our names escaped unconsciously from those lips, which at his lucid intervals, uttered only sighs and groans. Murray, his beloved attendant, gave us constant information of the progress of his fever; nor did the

ami-

amiable Henry fail at intervals to charge
him with tender remembrances.　Sir David at length acquainted me that the impaffioned delirium of the Prince, pointing
ever towards us, the King had been apprized of it,---that he had minutely
queftioned his fon's moft favored attendants, and among them himfelf, on
the origin, progrefs, and ftrength, of an
attachment thus fuddenly and ftrangely
brought to light, deeply ruminating on
all he heard.　"I could not feel acquitted to myfelf, madam, concluded the
faithful Murray, were I to conceal this,
nor dare I add a furmife on fo delicate an
occafion."

　Ah, of what importance to us are all
the late enquiries, the vague conjectures
of James! cried I, folding my daughter
to my bofom, if heaven deprives us of
his ineftimable fon, neither his love or
his hatred can greatly affect us.---Beloved
Mary---dear inheritor of misfortune!---
widowed ere yet thou art a wife, a long
obfcurity, a folitary youth is all thy por-
tion---a forrow which can never end thy
Mo-

Mother's.——But why fhould I hefitate to avow myfelf?——Wherefore fhould I not publifh claims which even tyranny can not cancel; but perhaps it will not.difpute? The timid, abject.fpirit of James knows not how to contend with one firm in virtue---immutable in truth.---Ah, had I done fo long fince, I might at this moment, dear Henry, have hovered near thy couch, and foftened the anguifh no mortal can prevent!---Perhaps the King already furmifes the fact---let him demand it.

Sir David Murray's next letter breathed the very fpirit of defpair.——" Prepare yourfelf, madam, faid he, for the worft; perhaps, ere this reaches you, England will have loft its deareft hope, the royal Henry's friends their only one. The moft defperate efforts of art have failed, and exhaufted reafon often now revifits with a languid ray the noble heart fhe is fo foon to quit forever. The Prince has juft ordered me to commit to the flames every letter and paper in which

S 2   your

your name is mentioned :—a sure proof
that he has given himself up.—Alas, he
knows not how often names so dear have
escaped him; he has called for you,
madam, and your angelic daughter, almost
the whole night, but frequently recollecting himself, has waved his feeble hand,
and sighed out no--no---no."——

Three hours after, another express arrived.——"Pardon, madam, the haste
and incoherency of scrawls penned at so
trying a moment.---Alas, the most san-
guine of us has now ceased to hope.---
Our royal master's speech entirely fails
him---his last effort was hastily and re-
peatedly to call me---I flew to his bedside,
but though my every sense seemed to resolve into ear, I found it impossible to
understand him---either I widely erred or
he named France; perhaps I commit a
second error in supposing he referred to
you, madam, but I voluntarily risque
every thing to fulfil the parting wish of a
master so adored. The King, the phy-
sicians, all have taken a long leave of
the

the almoft beatified Prince; and there is nothing left for thofe who love him beft to wifh, but that his pure fpirit may pafs away in peace."

The agony and ftupor this affecting billet occafioned, were hardly abated when another arrived.——" It is all over, madam, concluded the worthy Murray, raife your ftreaming eyes to heaven; it is there alone you can now look for the incomparable Prince of Wales.——Fatigue and anguifh difable me from faying more."

It was not till the awful moment which reftored the unfullied foul of Henry to its omnifcient Creator, that I had dared to breathe a wifh of which he was not the object, or allowed my thoughts to pafs beyond himfelf.——That exquifite fenfibility which lives through all dear to us, had made me feverely fuffer with him, and confequently pray for that releafe which alone feemed likely to give him eafe, nor did I recollect till he was gone forever, the void his lofs would leave in

S 3   my

my hopes.---The tremendous calm by
which death is ever followed, now took
its turn.---Bereft of a support on which I
had long unconsciously rested, I sunk
into a desolation which made me almost
wish to follow the lamented Prince.---
It is at these intervals, madam, we become most truly sensible of all the im-
perfections of our nature.---How often
had I flattered my own erring heart with
the vain belief it had acquired strength,
purity, and virtue, from its various trials! alas, what but pride, vanity, and
ambition, still throbbed unalterably
there! time had only altered the object,
not the passion, and centred them all in
my daughter.

We shut ourselves entirely up and deeply joined in the general mourning. The
sad pleasure of knowing him we bewailed, universally lamented, was yet ours.
I perused, I appropriated, with a mother's
fondness, the lavish eulogies, all sects,
all parties, all poets, graced the memory of the Prince with :---it was the only
mi-

mitigation my grief could know.----A
confiderable time had elapfed without our
hearing any thing from Murray, in confirmation of his conjecture concerning
Henry's laft wifh, and the imperfect accents which lingered on his dying lips.----
But though I could not refolve to become a guiltlefs fugitive even in compliance with Prince Henry's will, I had
had no other motive for remaining in
England than to fhew I was not driven
out of it. I now determined to quit a
country which had been the grave of a
hope fo dear, and found my daughter entirely of my mind. In gratitude for the
unwearied attention of Sir David Murray,
I informed him "of my intention to retire into Flanders, not doubting but that
the Hollanders would afford an honor-
able afylum to the widow and orphan of
Lord Leicefter.----I befought him to accept a ring of confiderable value in token
of my deep fenfe of the generous attachment he had fhewn alike to myfelf, and
that incomparable Prince whofe lofs was
ever prefent to my mind; and requefted

as a laft proof of his regard, the reftoration
of that picture of my daughter I had
given the royal Henry at our memorable
parting."

The anfwer of Murray ftrangely ftartled
and alarmed me.——" Your intention of
quitting England, madam, faid he, re-
lieves my mind from extreme anxiety;---
time and circumftances have united to
convince me I did not mifunderftand the
laft imperfect accents of my much-loved
mafter.----Lofe not a moment in haften-
ing to the afylum you have fixed on.---
The picture, madam, is, I fear, irretrievably gone---I cannot by either bribes
or intreaties procure any tidings of it---
power, alas, I now have not !---If ever it
comes to my hands, rely on its being reftored by him who will ever devoutly pray
for your happinefs."

This inexplicable letter roufed every
dormant faculty.---Wherefore fhould my
retiring abroad relieve the mind of a
perfon unconnected with me *from extreme anxiety?*----Why fhould he urge
thus my departure? As it was rather
pride

pride than prudence which induced me
to seek a country where I might fearlessly
assert my every right, that project was now
rejected from the very motive which first
dictated it.---A mystery my nature ever
disdained. Resolved to comprehend all
the motives on which Murray wished me
to act, I ordered every thing to be replaced, and sat down once more quietly
at home; resolved to brave the storm,
if indeed there was any gathering, rather
than ascertain my safety by a disgraceful
flight. I once more wrote to Sir David,
acquainting him with my present conduct, and its reasons, insisting on being
fully informed of those which actuated
him to offer me advice so singular and
mysterious.---How infinitely was my impatience, curiosity, and disdain, heightened by his answer!------" I hear with admiration, madam, a determination which
from a perfect knowledge of your character, I ought, perhaps, to have foreseen; nevertheless, my sentiments are not
altered, nor less urged durst I divulge the
reasons

reafons on which they are grounded : but decorum and delicacy give way to your commands, and the occafion. Neverthelefs, I find it impoffible to commit them to paper.-- Dare you give me admiffion at midnight ?---I fhall be near your gate upon the chance, but be wary in the choice of my conductor, as perhaps my life, nay, even your own, depends upon its being fuppofed you never had any private correfpondence or communication with me."

How did, my nature take fire at this incomprehenfible letter !---Me to ftoop to fecrefy !-----to be expofed to fhame !-----The unknown danger with which he reprefented me to be environed, appeared wholly indifferent; fo exquifitely fenfible was my foul of the imputation of difhonor. --At times I refolved to fhut out Murray, and leave the brooding mifchief to difclofe itfelf by its effects; but love for my daughter controling the ftrong fpirit of indignation infeparable from innocence, I yielded to the fuggef-

tions

tions of prudence, and prepared to admit
him.----Inured to every other species of
suffering, I knew not how to blush before
any human being.

My perplexed and agitated mind passed
through the infinitude of possibilities
without fixing upon one.----At times, I
imagined all the caution of the royal
Henry had been insufficient, and that
the King, by means of some lost or secreted letter, had been fully apprized of
his son's attachment to us, and the hopes
that were grounded upon it; though
even then, I knew not why my life should
be in the question; still less could I imagine it endangered, had his discoveries
reached farther, and traced out the long
buried secret of my birth. Involved in
busy, vague, and alarming conjectures,
I hardly knew how to wait with any
patience for the singular hour appointed
to ascertain them.

Sensible, by the deep effect this took
on my own mind, that it must dreadfully
shock my daughter's, and still flattering
myself

myself that this indistinct danger might
be the creation of a desponding temper in
Henry's favorite, I resolved to wait the
event of my midnight interview with him,
ere I confided more to my Mary than she
must already have learnt from the change
in my resolution respecting quitting England.---But as to see her was to explain
all, (for how could I hope to veil emotions which burnt indignantly on my
cheek?) I sent her word I was seized with
a violent headach, which I would endea-
vour to remedy by sleep ; and accompanied this message with a new book she
had an eager desire to see, and which
I sincerely prayed might wholly occupy
her attention at this interesting crisis.

Oh, world ! how false, how erroneous
are the feelings we imbibe from thee !---
Nature ordained shame the companion
of guilt, but overbearing custom has
broke that tye, and oftener bids her
follow virtue. Scarce could I resolve to
know my imputed crime, or look with
complacency on the amiable man who
had

had ventured to fuggeft the unforefeen danger.----It was the utmoft effort of my reafon to govern this unworthy impulfe.

The eftimable Murray was fenfible of an equal conftraint, and by the generous confufion with which he appeared before me, reftored my mind to its dignity and compofure. His mourning, and the tears which followed the name of his loft royal mafter, drew forth mine, and at once blended our feelings. Sir David, with infinite delicacy and addrefs, entered into the Prince of Wales's fingular illnefs, as well as the various opinions his death had given rife to :---but how did my foul freeze with horror to learn that there were many (and among them fome of his Phyficians) who believed him poifoned ! The killing grief fuch a fufpicion muft at a more tranquil moment have caufed, vanifhed, however, at once before the confufed and rapid fenfations his following difcourfe occafioned.---Oh, let me paufe here a moment to adore the in-

indulgence of the Almighty, which alone could have enabled my intellects to support so terrible a shock as the report that it was from my hands he received the deadly present!---I looked at Murray awhile in speechless astonishment!---Grief, anger, shame, and horror, divided and tore me in pieces.---I scarce heard his prayers and adjurations, but pushing him from my feet, shut up every indignant sense in my swelling heart, and only hoped it might burst with the deep convulsion.

A considerable time elapsed ere I was enough recovered to enquire into the origin of so black and malicious a calumny. I then conjured him to inform me who was supposed to be its diabolical author.---To this he answered, that when the equivocal decision of the faculty respecting the cause of the Prince's death first reached the Queen, the vehemence of her grief, as well as that of her temper, made her instantly join with those who pronounced him poisoned.--- The doubt was no sooner published than

it

it became general; every domestic of
the Prince's houshold had been by turns
the object of suspicion to his fellows, and
some of them had been weak enough to
ascertain their safety by quitting the kingdom. The rumour was by this means
corroborated and strengthened; but as
nothing transpired that could authorize
a judicial enquiry, the King became satisfied the melancholy catastrophe of his
youthful heir had been in the common
course of nature; when all at once,
by some incomprehensible means, the
vague suspicions of the multitude, which
were far from extinguished, though wholly
unfixed, revived with added force, and
centred in me. That it was now ge-
nerally believed, the Prince of Wales,
in the last visit he paid me, had tasted
some dry preserves (a little refreshment
of which he was extremely fond, though
fortunately the distraction of my mind at
that period had prevented me from offering him any) which most likely were
poisoned, as his last illness rapidly increased immediately after.----It was soon

pub-

publiſhed that I had been the conſtant
object of his delirious reveries; and every
vague or myſterious expreſſion which
had eſcaped him at thoſe intervals, had
been remembered, traced, and applied,
with diabolical ingenuity. The ſingular precaution of his ſeeing his own papers burnt, ſerved only to perſuade the
prejudiced multitude that the unfortunate Prince was unwilling to ſtigmatize
her who had deſtroyed him. By ſuch
plauſible and baſe ſuggeſtions the eyes of
an inflamed and affected nation had been
led towards the ſolitary dwelling, where,
unconſcious of danger, I remained buried
in a grief the moſt charitable imputed only
to remorſe. There wanted but little to
incite the people to anticipate the ſtroke
of juſtice, by tearing me to pieces, when
the King confirmed the general ſuſpicion
by a renewed and more minute enquiry
into the nature of his ſon's viſits to me,
their continuance, and deſign: and no
perſon being able to ſatisfy his curioſity,
he dropt harſh and ambiguous expreſſi-
ons; that ſeveral of his favorites had ſince
urged

urged the propriety of bringing me to a public trial; a meafure which had the whole weight of the Queen's intereft. Alarmed. and uncertain how to proceed, Sir David had learned at this very juncture my intention of retiring into Holland; and by fuppofing me pre-acquainted with the flanders of the publick, had unwarily reduced himfelf to the painful neceffity of repeating them.— He concluded with hinting the prudence of abiding by my former defign of immediately quitting England, as in inftances where the prejudices of a nation infected even thofe individuals entrufted with the execution of its laws, innocence itfelf was fcarce a protection.: byafed judges might eafily miftake prefumptions for proofs, nor have candour enough to vindicate the honor which had thus been queftioned.

While Sir David yet fpoke, a new world difplayed itfelf before me.—Ah! how unlike the paradife pictured by my guiltlefs mind!—Thofe countenances in

which

which I yefterday faw only the living image of their Creator, now glared upon me like fo many fiends.——A horrible gulph feemed to open beneath my feet, into which a thoufand hands fought at once to precipitate me, and my timid foul retreated in vain from the danger.---To live undiftinguifhed---to die unknown, were mortifications fufficiently grievous.— But the bare idea of being arraigned— dragged as a pre-judged criminal before a partial judge, had fomething in it fo tremendous, as made every other evil appear eafe. My blood flowed impetuoufly through my frame, and my bewildered judgment wanted ftrength to govern the torrent.---A malice fo bold, profound, and diabolical, could have only one author, but where to look for that one I knew not; nor could I recollect a human being I had injured, or a villain I had provoked.---Like a wretch awakened by affaffins in the darknefs of midnight, I knew not but the hand raifed to ward the blow, might bleed on the

pre-

prefented dagger. In this terrible conjuncture I had only virtue to befriend
me: though, alas, virtue herfelf half-
withers before the blighting breath of calumny! While Sir David enforced the
arguments he had already urged to induce me to quit the kingdom, my foul,
by one of thofe violent exertions great
occafions will fometimes produce, recovered all her powers.---Indignation fubfided at once into fortitude, and anger into
heroifm.----" You have hitherto only feen
me, Sir David, faid I,---it is now alone
you can know me;---fhuddering with
horror at the imputations you have explained, I yet dare not retreat unlefs I
can confute them---no, not even condemnation could induce me to fly, and
leave my honor behind me.---What!
fhall I blight the opening virtues of my
child by expofing her with myfelf to unmerited cenfure? The pride, the pleafure, of unfullied virtue, was all fortune permitted me to retain of the wealth
and honors which once glittered before

my

my youthful eyes---nor did I undervalue
the moft dear and facred of all poffeffions
---alas, even that is now ravished from
me, and one way alone can it be re-
trieved.---Defperate as the effort feems,
it muft be ventured---yes---I will fee the
King whatever it cofts me: furely, the
fainted fpirit of the Royal Henry would
appear to vindicate my innocence (heavens! that I fhould live to know it queftioned!) were every other means to
prove infufficient.---I will trouble you
no farther, refpected Murray, unlefs
you will deign to convey a letter to
Lord Rochefter, requefting a private audience of the King."

An idea fo fingular had transferred the
aftonifhment Murray had at firft excited
in me to his own mind; that my intellects were touched then feemed to him
very probable, but perceiving that I was
miftrefs both of my fenfes and temper,
he prefumed not to contend with a fpirit injury had nerved; and ftruck with the
filent dignity I affumed, began to believe

I had

I had indeed something important to dis-
close, though quite at a loss respecting
its nature. I wrote to Lord Rochester
(now newly created Earl of Somerset)
according to the idea I had formed; and
Murray having engaged that the letter
should be delivered early in the morning, departed with the same caution with
which he had entered, leaving me alone.
---Alone did I say?---Ah, gracious heaven, never was I less so!---The shades
of all I had ever loved seemed to gather round me on this interesting occasion, and volumes of obscure ideas rushed impetuously through my brain.---I
had unexpectedly reached the very point
of my fate.---That important moment
so often delayed, so eternally dreaded,
was at length arrived, and the long trea-
sured secret on the verge of being published.---For *myself* I had long ceased
to fear.---The fraternal acknowledgment
of the King could now add nothing to
my happiness; since, alas, that incomparable youth was gone for whose sake

T 3   alone

alone I defired it: nor could his re-
jection greatly embitter a fate which had
left me fo little to hope.---But, oh, when I
remembered his fingle breath might blight
the tender bloffom I had exhaufted my
very being to rear---precipitate my youthful Mary, ere yet her virtues were known,
into an obfcure and difhonorable grave,
where, where, could I gather ftrength to
cope with this idea?

I employed the remainder of the night
in collecting and arranging fuch plaufible
reafons as fhould amufe my daughter's
mind till the event was known; thus
fparing her all the pangs of fufpenfe.—
I gathered together likewife every paper,
and proof, which could authenticate the
rights I was compelled to avow, and on
perufing them once more, found fuch
reafon to be affured, not only of fafety,
but diftinction, that a facred calm fucceeded to all the tranfports of grief and
indignation with which I had of late been
agitated.

By

By a feigned invitation from a neighbouring lady who permitted me to render her houſe my convenience, I ſent my
daughter abroad for the day; and ſcarce
had done ſo ere an expreſs arrived, to
acquaint me the Earl of Somerſet would
wait on me in the afternoon.

What were my proud emotions when
the upſtart Somerſet littered my court
with a princely retinue !—Alas, the only
Prince who had ever entered it, with a
noble conſciouſneſs, deſpiſed ſuch idle
parade. By oppreſſive offers of ſervice,
the Earl made me ſenſible of his importance, and ſought by unbounded adulation to gain upon my heart, and dive into
its intentions: but it was not by ſuch a me-
dium I ſought diſtinction. I politely avoided referring either to the ſlander, or the
purport of the requeſted audience, and
only thanked him for having obtained me
the ear of the King; half bluſhing to
have gained it by ſo contemptible an
interceſſor. I perceived chagrin, curioſity, and diſappointment, ſtrongly ex-
preſſed in his really fine features, but I

T   could

could not prevail on myfelf to confide aught to the man Prince Henry had defpifed. The Earl took his leave with the fame profound deference, and affurances of fervice, with which he entered; having appointed the next morning for prefenting me to the King.

As the privacy of the promifed audience enabled me to difpenfe with form, I made no addition to my fervants, nor any other alteration in the weeds I ufually wore, than that of forming them to the model of my mother's drefs; which ever rendered the likenefs I bore her from my very birth ftriking and obvious. A thoufand half-forgotten occurrences preffed upon my agitated foul as I paft through each well-known apartment, till all were loft in the prefent, by my reaching the clofet of the King. The affiduous Somerfet, dreft as elegantly as though he had meant to charm me, advanced on my being announced, and politely offered me his hand-- a fudden chill came over me;----I trembled,----lingered---

drooped,---

drooped,---but refolved to conquer myfelf or perifh, I fhook off the fcalding
tear which hung upon my cheek, and
accepted the favorite's introduction.---
The fuperior air with which I affected to
enter was not neceffary towards confufing
the King, who always awkward and perplexed, feemed more than ufually fo; and
doubtful, whether he fhould not fly the
moment he faw me, or at leaft call back
Somerfet who had inftantly retired.---
Bending my knee in compliance with
cuftom, I inftantly rofe, and retaining
the hand he had prefented to me, fixed
my eyes, ftrongly animated by the occafion, on his ever-varying countenance.
" Your Majefty, faid I, doubtlefs, ex-
pects to find in me a weak fuppliant,
foliciting protection, or fuing for your
pity; but on terms like thefe I had never
bent before you---I come to claim a dear
and facred title hitherto unknown, but
never annihilated. Does your heart, oh,
Royal James! added I, melting into
tears, recognize nothing congenial to it
in thefe features? this voice? the ti-
morous

morous hand which grasps yours for the
first time, in fraternal alliance?---Oh,
sainted Mary! dear author of my being, look down from heaven, and touch
the heart of your son, in favor of the de-
solate sister who now stands before him."
The King started, receded, gave ma-
nifest tokens of doubt and displeasure,
and sought to draw away the hand I ob-
stinately retained.---I kissed, I bathed
it with impassioned tears. ".Shake me
not off, reject me not unknown, re-
sumed I in the deep tone of stifled anguish.---It is neither pride, vanity, or
ambition, which induces me now to
publish a secret so long buried in my bosom. By the ashes of our anointed mother, I conjure you to hear—nay even to
believe me.—Born in obscurity—reared
in solitude, the early victim of misfortune, long suffering had reconciled my
weary soul to every evil but disgrace:
against that she still proudly revolts.—
The same blood which flows through
your veins, burns in tumults along
mine,

mine, at the very thought of aught
unworthy—it urges me to affert my innocence by indubitable proofs—it *will*
be acquitted, before men as well as an-
gels;—nor does the claim thus avowed
reft on my declaration alone, your Majefty will fee in thefe papers the folemn
atteftations, the unqueftioned hand-
writing of your royal mother; in *thefe*
you will find the corroborating teftimo-
nies of many noble and unblemifhed
perfons.—Perufe them cautioufly, and oh,
beware how you pre-judge me!" Unable to utter another word, I almoft
funk at the feet of James, and gave way
to the oppreffive, the agonizing fenfations fuch an æra in my life could not
fail to awaken. The King ftill regarded
me with an irrefolute, uneafy air, coldly
advifing me to compofe myfelf by retiring
into the antichamber, while he perufed
the papers on which he had hitherto only
glanced his eye; though even that cur-
fory view had deeply tinged his cheek
with filent conviction. I was met there
by

by the Earl of Somerset, who, perceiving me near fainting, ordered water,
and such essences as are customary,
remaining himself by my side, as if os-
tentatiously to convince me he did not
influence in the least the determination
of his royal master.---The bitterness of
the conflict was, however, over the moment the secret was avowed, and my
spirits soon began to recover their wonted
equanimity.

The obliging efforts of Somerset to
revive me did not pass unnoticed, though
my watchful ear followed the footsteps
of the King, who still continued to walk
about with an unequal pace, stopping
at intervals. He opened the closet door at
length, and Somerset retiring out of
his sight, made signs to me to re-enter
it.—The King came forward to meet
me with affability, and seizing my hand
slightly saluted my cheek.----" Take
courage, madam, said he, for however
you may have surprized us with this
sudden declaration, and wonderful dis-
covery;

covery, reverence for our deceafed mother's rights, and juftice to thofe you derive from her, oblige us to acknowledge
you as her daughter."

And now I was indeed near fainting,
I might rather fay dying.—To be at
once acknowledged as his fifter, as the
daughter of Mary! Scarce in my happieft hours had I dared to flatter myfelf
with the promife of what was now fo incre-
dibly realized. My fufceptible foul indulged the exquifite tranfport, and one
fhort moment compenfated for ages of
anguifh.----A thoufand impaffioned, incoherent exclamations, burft from my lips ;
and giving way to the genuine impulfe
of gratitude and affection, I threw myfelf for the firft time into the arms of
a brother, nor. remembered they were
thofe of a King. Never did the moft
confummate hypocrite counterfeit a joy
fo pure, fo perfect ; and though I could
have brought no other proof of my
birth, the facred throbs of nature might
well have afcertained it.

The

The King fat down by me, and turning over the papers he ftill held, queftioned me at intervals refpecting thofe that appeared myfterious or deficient. I entreated his patience while I briefly ran through the wonderful events of my life, and thus very naturally led his attention toward the fole object of my cares, my hopes, my exiftence.———"I have already heard much of your daughter, faid James; they tell me fhe is beauty itfelf---why have you thus ftrangely concealed her?" As I could not declare my real reafon, which was fimply want of efteem for his character, I pleaded various trifling ones, that indeed had never influenced me. "Say no more, faid the King, interrupting me, I eafily perceive, Madam, you was not fo referved to every one--- I plainly difcern who was your confidant; had I earlier been entrufted with your fecret, it would have been happier for all, and I fhould then have been able to account for"——He paufed ere he came to the dear name of his fon, and fighing,

fighing, dropt the unfinifhed fentence. As
to me, entranced alike with his unexpected
candor, gracioufnefs, and generofity, I
feverely cenfured myfelf for relying on
report, and not proving the character I
ventured to decide upon.   I had a long
converfation with the King afterwards,
every word of which heightened my confidence, efteem, and affection.   I gathered from many expreffions, that he feared
oppofition on the part of the Queen,
and his favorite;   and was fearful this
late declaration of his mother's marriage
with the Duke of Norfolk would not
fully fatisfy the minds of the people, or
eftablifh my rank fufficiently.   He paufed
upon the whole, with the air of one who
is a party in what he meditates; and I
thought the leaft I could do, was to leave
the regulation of the important acknowledgment in his choice.---To be vindi-
cated in his opinion, I truly affured him,
was the firft object of my life, and I fubmitted my general vindication, in the
public acknowledgment of my birth, entirely

tirely to his better judgment. That I
had been fo many years a folitary being
in the midſt of ſociety as not to have one
friend to whoſe inclination I need yield
my own. In fine, that time had gradually robbed me of all intereſted in the
important ſecret I had juſt confided to
him, which now reſted ſolely with him,
my daughter, and myſelf. He replied
that, "this inſtance of my prudence as
well as regard, infinitely heightened the
partiality he had already conceived for
me; nor need I fear his delaying the
acknowledgment longer than was abſolutely neceſſary, ſince he could not but
look on ſuch relations as ineſtimable ac-
quiſitions: neverthelefs, as he had many
points to confider, and many perſons to
reconcile, he recommended to me to
continue the ſame circumſpeſtion I had
hitherto ſhewn; but that he could not
reſtrain his impatience to behold the fair
maid of whom he had heard ſo much,
and would come to-morrow evening to
a ſeat of my Lord Somerſet's, whither

he would fend for myfelf and my daughter, and hoped by that time he fhould be
able to afcertain the day for publifhing
my birth, with a due regard for his mother's honor; after which he could gratify himfelf by eftablifhing me in a fituation that fhould make me forget all my
misfortunes."—Thofe misfortunes were
already forgotten in the unhoped-for tran-
fition in my fate. I took my leave with
the profoundeft gratitude, burning with
impatience to impart this bleffed news
to my Mary; and as the King did not
offer to return the papers, I thought
it better to leave them in his hands,
than confirm the doubt my long filence
could not but give rife to in his mind,
viz. that I wanted confidence in his honor.

I haftened to Richmond, and communicated this furprizing, this happy event,
to my darling girl.---A thoufand times
I enfolded her to my delighted heart,
and found every tranfport doubled in her
participation. She tenderly entered into

all my feelings, and sweetly smiled at
the eagerness with which I fought to
adorn her for the next day's introduction. Yet considering the King as the
flave of exterior, it was a material point
to heighten her beauty by every adven-
titious advantage. To present her in
absolute black, was to recall the most
melancholy impressions to the mind of
James; I therefore resolved to lighten
her mourning with a fanciful elegance.
I dreft her in a vest of black velvet
thrown back at the bosom in the French
fashion, with a semicircle of rich lace
points, which shewed at once her graceful waist and chest to the greatest advantage. Her petticoat was of white
sattin, wrought in deep points round the
bottom with black velvet, and richly
fringed with silver. A fuller coat and
train of silver muslin wrought with black,
fell over the sattin one, and was looped
up to the waist at regular distances by
strings of pearl, and dragged toward the
bottom into points by the weight of
rich

rich black bugle taffels and rofes of diamonds. Full fleeves of the fame filver
muflin were braced round her arms to
the elbow by ftrings of jet, and rofes of
diamonds; and from thence they were
bare, except for fimilar bracelets circling
each wrift. The rich profufion of her
auburn hair, which fell in natural curls
below her waift, required no ornament,
but to avoid the affectation of fhewing
it, fhe wore a hat of white fattin with a
narrow fringe of black bugles, and a
waving plume of feathers. This fplendid
drefs, on which the legacies of both her
father and Anana were difplayed, by
fome peculiar happinefs, either in its
make or mixture, became my Mary beyond any I had ever feen her wear.
The fond mother's heart anticipated the
impreffion fhe would infallibly make on
her uncle, and drew from her heightened
beauty the happieft prefages.

   Ah, who could have conjectured that
this brilliance and paràde were only deftined to forerun one of the moft difmal

mo-

moments of my life!---That an inhuman tyrant had delighted to employ the trembling hand of misfortune in decking a gaudy pageant, for herself eternally to mourn over!

At the appointed hour, a close carriage came for us with due attendants, and as the King had desired me not to bring any of my own, I rigidly obeyed, nor even hinted whither I was going. They drove us a long way, while engrossed by meditations on the approaching interview, as well as concerning the dear creature by me, I hardly knew how the time passed. My daughter at length observed it was farther than she expected.—I looked out, but it was too dark for me to distinguish any object, and all I could discern was an increase of attendants. I called out aloud, and one drew near, who to my enquiries respectfully replied, that the King had been detained in London, whither they were hastening by his orders. This information quieted us again; and I strove to recall my fluttered spirits

into

into their ufual channel, by turning the
converfation on our future profpects.
Neverthelefs, we went at fo great a rate,
that I thought it impoffible we fhould
not be near London, when all at once
I found we were driving through an unknown village. The furprize this occafioned, was doubled by my daughter's throwing herfelf into my arms.----It
was not immediately I could comprehend her, when fhe told me that a light
which gleamed from the window of a
cottage, had fhewn her that we were environed with armed foldiers. From this
alarm we were not yet recovered, when
by a fudden rife, and hollow found, we
perceived we had paffed over a draw-
bridge; immediately after which we
ftopped. As we alighted, I caft my eyes
round a large and dreary court-yard,
where a few ftraggling centinels were
planted, but neither lights, fplendor, or
attendants, indicated a royal gueft, or a
favorite's refidence. The gloomy paf-
fages through which we were ufhered,

U 3   feemed

feemed rather to lead to a prifon than a
palace.---Arrived at an empty apartment,
I gave way at once to the dire, the obvious truth ; and arraigning in filence my
own egregious credulity, felt, feverely felt,
its every confequence.

An officer, who had preceded us, now
offered me a packet, which I received as
the fentence of my fate, but made no
effort to open it.---Hope, fear, curiofity, every dear and powerful emotion
were annihilated by inftantaneous conviction, and a ftupor fucceeded more
dangerous and dreadful than the moft
violent operations of the paffions.---My
daughter, more terrified by this ftill agony
than even the cruel and unexpected event
of the evening, threw herfelf at my
feet.----" Oh, fpeak to me, my mother!
exclaimed the dear one ; do not indulge
the defperation your countenance ex-
preffes! do not confummate to your
poor Mary the horrors of the moment!"
I gazed at her with a vacant air, but nature refumed her rights, and fondly
plucking at my heart, the tears I refufed

fused to my own fate, flowed lavishly for
hers.---So young, so fair, so innocent,
so noble,---how could I but bewail her?
Surely those maternal tears alone preserved my senses at a juncture when every
thing conspired to unsettle them. My
Mary, by an expressive glance, requested
leave to open the packet, and starting at
sight of the paper it contained, put it
eagerly into my hand; a glance informed me it was that defamatory declaration
the crafty Burleigh had deceived my sister into signing while a prisoner in St.
Vincent's Abbey. The King, in sending
this, only added insult to injury, since
the testimonials I had delivered to him
might have invalidated a thousand such
vague and artificial falshoods; yet had
it a fortunate effect, for nothing less
could have roused my spirits from the
cold and sullen torpor which every passing moment seemed to increase ---" Inso-
lent Barbarian! exclaimed I, not con-
tent to imprison the unhappy offspring of
the Queen who had the misfortune of
giving thee being, dost thou delight in

vil-

villifying and debasing even her ashes!---
Oh, paper! dictated and preserved surely for
my ruin; by what singular chance hast
thou survived the very views thou wert
invented to serve?---Treasured, as it appears, only to effect a ruin your execrable
contriver could not foresee.---Yet of what
consequence is this single attestation towards annihilating claims all those I delivered had not power to establish in the
judgment of a cruel, insidious tyrant,
who voluntarily shut his heart alike to
reason, virtue, and nature?---Devoted
to self-interest, vain of a petty talent at
deceiving, contemptible in every rank,
but infamous in the highest, he meanly
watched the generous impulses of my
heart, and wrought out of them my
ruin.---Yet why do I name myself?---
Alas, of what importance is it to her
who no longer wishes to live where heaven or its arbitrary delegate shall have appointed her to die?---It is for thee, my
daughter! for thee alone my soul thus
overflows with inexpressible anguish.---
Rescued, in yet unconscious childhood,
from

from flavery, neglect, and obfcurity, fortune at one moment feemed willing to
reftore all the rights of your birth, when
a weak, credulous, unfortunate, mother
affifted the cruel wretch who was pre-de-
termined to entomb you, and annihilate
every trace, every memorial, of our dear
and honored progenitors.---Namelefs---
difhonored—your blooming youth mull
wither in an unknown prifon—blighted by
the tears of a parent who can never pardon
herfelf the extravagant error produced by
over-fondnefs.---I knew the King to be
mean, bafe, fubtle, yet I madly delivered into his treacherous hands every
thing on which our hopes, nay, even
our vindication, mufl be grounded."——
" Hear me, in turn, my dear, my honored mother, cried my fweet girl, bath-
ing my hands with tears of veneration and
fondnefs. Alas, the order of nature is
inverted, and I am obliged to become
the monitor.---Recollect the maxim you
have fo deeply imprefled upon my mind
---that the malice of man would in vain
ftrive to make us wretched, did not our
own

own ungovernable paffions aid his artful machinations. Oh, let us refpect even error when it has its fource in virtue --- To have diftrufted the King were to deferve to be rejected---leave him then to the contemptible fatisfaction of having wrefted from the widow and the orphan the laft treafure of their lives, and let us examine what he has been compelled to leave us. Have we not yet the power of looking down on his throne, and all its fpecious advantages, even from that obfcure prifon where his authority confines us?---Have we not the pride of reviewing our own hearts without finding aught in either unworthy of our Creator or ourfelves?---For the vain grandeur of that name of which he has unfairly deprived us, can it be worth regretting while he lives to difhonor it?--- Fortunately no favorite view depended on its attainment, confequently no hope is blighted by the deprivation. Have I not often heard you fay, a noble mind can become every thing to itfelf?---Let us then rife fuperior to our fortune; time

will

will foon calm our fpirits---reafon will reconcile us to the inconveniencies of our fate, and religion elevate us above them. ---Mourn not then for me, my much-loved mother," concluded the dear one, fweetly fmiling through her tears, " fince I fhall never think that place a prifon which contains you, nor that fate a mif-fortune I owe to your fondnefs."

Oh, virtue, how awful doft thou ap-pear, fublimed thus by generofity! When I faw this half-blown human bloffom fupport the ftorm without fhrinking, I blufhed to have bowed my head before it.---When I heard her with Spartan cou-rage apply to her own fituation the no-ble tenets I had fought, not vainly, to imbue her mind with, could I fail to profit by the principles I had taught? --From the admiration fhe excited in my foul, fprung that pure and elevated heroifm which calms in one moment every human weaknefs, and turbulent paffion; difpofing us to turn upon that fate it enables us to judge of.

I now

I now recollected that by a fond vanity in decking my daughter in all her valuable diamonds, I had inadvertently provided ample means to buy the fidelity of our keepers; nor were they aware of our treasure, as the severity of the weather had made me wrap her in a long cloak lined with fur. I hastily stripped her costly dress of its richest embellishments, and secreted them. Ah, with what difficulty did I stifle the tears and anguish which struggled at my heart when I remembered the different views with which I adorned her!

Scarce had we executed this prudent resolve, ere the man I have mentioned presented himself once more;---he was young---not unpleasing---had an air of integrity, and profound respect, that a little prepossessed me in his favour, even under all the disadvantages attending our meeting. Our countenances were now calmed, and our resolutions taken.---He appeared surprized alike with this transition, and the beauty of my daughter,

whose

whofe magnificent but difordered drefs
had a fhare of his attention.---He was
flattered with our civility, and affured
us " every accommodation confiftent
with the ftrict orders of the King, he
fhould take pleafure in fupplying us with;
and would, with our permiffion, make
us acquainted with our new home." He
then produced fome keys which opened
double doors at the farther end of the
large room we were in, and conducted
us into a chamber neat and commo-
dious enough.---The keys, he informed
us, were committed folely to his charge;
and that whenever inclination or convenience induced us to change our
apartment, we had only to touch a fpring
he pointed out, when he would attend,
and unlock the intermediate doors.---
The purport of this extreme caution was
very obvious; it excluded every poffibility
of winning over a female fervant, as all the
domeftic offices would now of courfe be
performed in either room while we occupied the other; nor was he fuffered to
supply

supply us pen, ink, or paper. As the conveniences of thefe apartments, and the air of refpect in our guard, fhewed fome attention had been paid to our welfare, as well as the moft judicious precautions taken to prevent our enlargement, I neither imputed the one or the other to the King, but rather both to his cunning favorite. Our enquiries were interrupted by the entrance of two fervants, who fet out an elegant fupper, of which neither my daughter or myfelf had fpirits to partake. Refolved however to gather all I could from my attendant, ere another fhould be put in his place, or fufpicion make him dumb, I afked the name of the Caftle, and its owner; but to thefe queftions he declared himfelf enjoined to refufe replying; neverthelefs, I conjectured from his looks that I did not err in fuppofing Somerfet directed him. The refined artifice of offering to introduce me to the King, and even remaining by my fide, while perhaps my ruin was effecting by his will,

seemed

feemed entirely confiftent with the character Prince Henry had given me of that worthlefs favorite; though I could find no crime in my own conduct could poffibly irritate him to bury us thus alive, unlefs indeed our attachment to that lamented royal youth appeared a fufficient one.

In the gallery leading to our apartment, I obferved a centinel planted, from whom we were fhut by double doors fafely locked: perceiving we were thus effectually excluded from every hope, and chance of freedom, I defired to pafs at once into a chamber, where I did not flatter myfelf I fhould find reft.

My firft employment on rifing was to examine the windows, as well as the view from them; they were fo clofely grated as to convince me however comfortable our refidence, it was ftill a prifon. The apartments we occupied, formed one fide of a quadrangle of old buildings, moft probably barracks, but now entirely deferted. On making the fignal,

Dunlop (for fo was our guard called) readily attended, and we paffed into the
other room where we found breakfaft
ready. Trunks containing all kinds of
apparel had been placed there, and Dunlop recommended to us to form our minds
to paffing the remainder of our days
in confinement. I did not fubmit to
hear this without demanding the authority by which he acted? He produced an
order, figned by the King, ftrictly en-
joining him to keep us in fafety, and beware we neither wrote or received a let-
ler, or indeed held any kind of communication with the world.—While he fpoke
I examined every lineament of his countenance, but fidelity was written there in
fuch legible characters, that I dared not
make any effort to bribe him, left if it
failed he fhould publifh that I had the
means, which might in a moment utterly
impoverifh me.

A few wearifome uniform days only
had elapfed when every hope decayed,
and my fpirits flagged at once.—Alas,

4   my

my mind had no longer the vivifying ar-
dor, the inexhauſtible reſources of unbroken youth----its bloom had paſſed
away like a ſhadow, and all its fire evaporated.—The woful realities of life had
diſſipated the bright illuſions of imagination.—Every human good was in my eſ-
timation ſhrunk into ſo ſmall a compaſs,
that freedom conſtituted a very eſſential
part of my little poſſeſſions.----I was no
longer able to rely upon contingencies, and
ſunk at once under all the ſadneſs of knowledge.—Not denied the relief of books,
I pored over them in vain ; every idea
was ſtill purſuing an abſent good, and
my ſenſes would reject the ſublimeſt author, to follow the careleſs ſteps of a
weary centinel, or liſten to his whiſtling.

Whether my daughter had really more
reſolution than myſelf, or only aſſumed
the appearance of it to ſave me from
deſpair, was a point I could not aſcertain ; but the complacency of her mind
and manners was invariable. By a thouſand little affectionate artifices ſhe engaged me to work while ſhe read, or

read while she worked, nor would perceive thofe melancholy reveries it was
impoffible to overlook.   I was not, however, thanklefs for the bleffing left me.
That my eyes opened on her every morning, ftill made me blefs it; and in com-
pofing myfelf to fleep, I nightly praifed
the God who yet fuffered her to reft by
me.

Two tedious months elapfed in unde-
cifive projects.---Dunlop ever prefent, vi-
gilant, and refpectful, precluded alike
complaint and temptation;   but as if to
guard himfelf againft the latter, I took
notice he now never remained one moment
alone with us.

The impoffibility of forming any judgment of our centinels while divided from
them by double doors, and the danger
of a fruitlefs effort to feduce one, had
at intervals engroffed my attention; but
the mind cannot dwell forever on a fingle
idea, or a remote and uncertain project.
Wearied out with this, another fuddenly
came to my relief. Though yet early
in the fpring, the weather was uncom-
monly

monly beautifnl, and the lenity with
which we were treated, left me not without hopes of being allowed, under rigid
limitations, the liberty of walking in
whatever gardens the caftle-walls enclofed. By this means I could examine
the countenances of our centinels, and
if I faw one in whom humanity was not
quite extinct, I thought I might find
fome means to fhew him a jewel; thus
proving I could largely recompenfe him
fhould he have the courage to affift us.
Nor did my lamenefs wholly deprive me of
the power of walking, though it prevented my enjoying the liberty.----After
confidering this plan in every poffible
light, I faw nothing to forbid the attempt, and ventured the requeft.----A
few anxious days elapfed ere I had the
fatisfaction of finding it was granted, on
as good terms as I could hope. Dunlop
acquainted me we muft walk feparately,
that the perfon confined might be a check
upon her that was liberated; who fhould
not remain in the garden more than an

hour, nor quit his fight one moment.
Thefe reftrictions were as moderate as I
could expect, and I eagerly prepared to
profit by the granted permiffion, ere I
ventured my daughter: certain I fhould
at leaft difcover the ftrength, heighth,
and fituation, of the Caftle.---Dunlop,
followed by two other men, attended
upon me. I caft an eager eye on the
centinel on the gallery, but faw in him
no trace of fenfe, feeling, or curiofity. I found the little garden in fo antique a ftile, and ruinous a condition,
as plainly proved this difmantled building was now only a prifon, whatever its
former diftinction. The wall around it
appeared decayed, and not very high---
it looked down on a moat, apparently
dry.---From one part of the terrace I
caught the corner of a tower I fancied
belonged to Windfor Caftle, but dared
not venture a word which might imply
defign, and returned without afking a
fingle queftion. My daughter now took
her turn, and as we continued to claim
this

this relief whenever the weather favored,
I fancied it improved her health as well as
my own.

It chanced, at length, I one day found
a centinel on guard whofe eye expreffed
both pity and curiofity.---Mine addreffed
itfelf to him in a moft pointed manner.
Without altering the pofition of my
hand (in which I always carried a diamond for that purpofe) I opened it,
and the foldier, as I wifhed, furveyed
the jewel.---I turned my head at the
inftant Dunlop was unlocking the door,
and the centinel fhook his emphatically.
Yet only to have been underftood revived
at once my fpirits, and my hopes; for to
efcape did not appear fo impracticable to
me, as to gain an affiftant. I faw him
no more for a week, but foon found that
day was the periodical one for his attendance.---Involved in a thoufand plots,
the want of pen and ink feemed to condemn them all to inhabit only my brain,
when at once I difcovered a fubftitute for
thofe ufeful articles. From the middle

X 3

of

of a large book, which we had unmo-
lefted poffeffion of, I took fome of the
printed leaves, and from the conclufion
a blank one; out of the firft I cut fuch
words as fimply conveyed my meaning,
and fewed them on the laft.---"Affift
us to efcape, and we will make your
fortune," was the fubftance of this fingular but important billet. To afcertain my ability to realize this promife,
I wrapt in it a diamond of fome value,
and carried both ever in my hand, ftill
hoping fortune would enable me for one
moment to miflead the attention of my
guards : but, alas, Dunlop, far from re-
laxing his vigilance, continually increafed it. The two men who followed him
in the garden, now attended to my door;
remaining as fpies on me while Dunlop
opened it.---Thus circumftanced, I could
not make the flighteft overture without
being liable to detection, and I dreaded
awakening the moft diftant doubt, left it
fhould condemn us to a more rigorous
confinement.---One favorable omen alone
oc·

occurred.---The foldier I had felected
clearly underftood me.---I faw his eye
ever anxioufly fixed on my hand, as if
eager to transfer its contents to his own;
nor had I ceafed to flatter myfelf I fhould
yet do fo, when an unforefeen incident
at once annihilated every hope and project, and plunged me in the deepeft forrow.

I had always counted the moments of
my daughter's abfence, and nothing but
the conviction that the air and exercife
were neceffary towards her health, could
have enabled me to fupport it. What
then became of me when one day I
found her walk unufually lengthened!---
I endeavoured to perfuade myfelf that
my fears foreran the danger.---But more
than twice the ufual time had certainly
elapfed; nor dared I venture an enquiry, left I fhould fuggeft a hint to
my perfecutors which hitherto had efcaped
them. The hours thus paffed on, but
Mary returned not.---Ah, me! while my
weak hand repeats this, I almoft expire

X 4   under

under the recollection.----Every evil my
untoward fate had yet teemed with, became peace, nay pleasure, on a comparison with this.----Though the turbulence
of each succeeding storm had swept away
invaluable treasures, something yet remained my weary soul might cling to.----
This single gem, this solitary relique
of all my fortunes, more dear, more
precious from becoming so, a dreadful,
a deceitful calm had at length swallowed
up even while I was fearless of the danger.----Heartstruck----incapable at once
either of distinguishing, or complaining,
my respiration became perturbed, and
deep.----A still agony, more dreadful than
the wildest tumults of the passions, numbed
my very soul; every hair seemed to start
from, and pierce my too-sensible brain;
while drops cold as those of death chased
one another down my scarcely throbbing
temples.----When Dunlop presented himself, I rose not from the earth, I uttered
not a syllable; but lifting an eye to him
which would have melted a savage, he
turned

turned away, unable to fupport the fhock, and offered me fome order from the King bewailing at the fame moment the painful duty impofed on him. This roufed my torpid fpirits---I tore it indignantly into a thoufand atoms ;—refentment reftored my fpeech.—I called for my Mary in the moft piercing accents—nothing could fufpend, or mitigate my anguifh. I bitterly reproached Dunlop with tearing the beauteous innocent from her mother's bofom, only to deliver her up to affaffins.—In vain he declared himfelf incapable of fuch villainy, and acting under the orders of the King—in vain he affured me fhe was only removed to another apartment, fafe, and unhurt.—My foul rejected all his affertions.—Mary—Mary—Mary!—was all my convulfed lips could utter, or my difconfolate foul dictate.

Ah, God! the folitude that fucceeded! Food, light, air, nay even life itfelf, became naufeous and infupportable.---- Stretched on the cold ground---drenched in my own tears, I gave way to the deep mi-

mifery, the tremendous void this barba-
rous feparation could not but plunge me
in.---How long was it fince fhe had been
the very effence of my exiftence! From
the forrowful moment which gave her
into my arms, to that which tore her
from them, fhe, fhe alone, had occupied
my every fenfe, and enabled me to fupport every affliction.---Never, though I
had led her myfelf through an admiring
nation to the altar, and joined her hand
with that of the incomparable Henry,
never could even that advantage have
compenfated to my yearning heart for
the lofs of her fociety. What then muft
it fuffer to recollect a favage had wrefted
her, for unknown purpofes, from my
arms!---Nor could I, amid all the horrors this idea teemed with, fix on any
diftinct one.

Oh, that melodious voice!---Still it
feemed to vibrate on my ear, but no
longer could I hear it.---That unmatched
form gliftered through every tear, but
evaporated with it. The moft deadly
glooms came over me---a thoufand times
I raifed

I raifed my rafh hand to precipitate---the unfortunate Rofe Cecil alone withheld me.----I often thought I heard her aerial voice, and defpair flowly fubfided into refignation.

I now exerted every effort to gain upon Dunlop; but, too faithful to his execrable employers, I never won more from him than that my daughter was ftill in the Caftle, not only unhurt, but treated with diftinction and indulgence.---Yet, how could I credit fuch improbable affurances? or even if they were true, ought not an indulgence fo partial to alarm more ftrongly a mother's feelings? To every folicitation once more to behold her, I received a pofitive denial, nor was even the liberty of walking now allowed me. I often enquired why I was thus reftrained, if no injury was meditated to my unfortunate child? To queftions of this kind he never anfwered, but left me to my own fluctuating conjectures: They were fo numerous and frightful that conviction could hardly aggravate the evil. Neverthelefs, as Dunlop feemed

ever

ever anxious to compose my mind by re-
iterated assurances of my poor girl's
safety, and as there was an air of candor
in all he uttered, I began at length to
conclude that the contemptible Somerset
had aspired to the niece of his master,
but from being already married to the
divorced Countess of Essex, had not
dared to avow his passion. I recollected too
late the singularity of his being with
Prince Henry when first we beheld that
amiable youth;---the assiduous respect he
had shewn in waiting on me at Richmond;
---the affected offer of his interest with a
tyrant whose will he so well knew how to
make subservient to his own;---the com-
bination of refined arts by which we had
been led to throw ourselves into the prison selected for us;---and, finally, that
the prison was probably a house of his
own.---Through the whole of this, as
well as the manner we were guarded,
there was a policy too minute for a
King to plan, and too watchful to be
the work of an indifferent person.—When
by a just turn of thought we insensibly
un-

unravel any hitherto inexplicable event,
how does the mind difdain its former
blindnefs? I now confidered with wonder my long want of perfpicacity, and
found fomething every moment to corroborate, and ftrengthen the idea I had
adopted.

To fix on any thing certain appears to
the exhaufted foul a degree of relief; and
though at fome momens I dreaded art
and violence might be employed, if
gentle methods failed to undermine the
virtue of my fweet girl, yet I much oftener flattered myfelf fhe could not in-
fpire a paffion fo grofs and unworthy;
and knew her foul fuperior to every other
feduction. From the inftant I ventured
once more to hope, all my plans for efcap-
ing revived; I had no longer, it is true,
the privilege of paffing beyond my apartment, but mifery is ever ingenious, and
I was pre-informed of the days when the
compaffionate centinel guarded the door;
nay, I fancied I often heard him draw
near, attracted by my fighs and groans.---
The note I had formerly prepared was

yet

yet in being; I sewed it to a long thin
slip of whalebone, and on the day when
he used to be attending, worked it gently
under both doors, at a time when I judged no other person near, and softly rapped
at the inner one. A sweet hope rekindled
in my heart as I felt it drawn out of my
hand. I watched in vain the whole tedious day. for a reply, and often fancied
my effort had been betrayed to Dunlop;
but as I did not perceive any alteration
in his countenance, I became reassured;
and concluded that the soldier could not
write, nor perhaps even read; and if so,
a whole week must necessarily elapse ere
I could learn his resolutions. The expiration of that time verified my last conjecture. With unspeakable satisfaction I
at last saw a billet introduced into my solitude, by the same means I had suc-
cessfully ventured. I was a long time decy-
phering the almost unintelligible scrawl:
" I pity you, lady, from my heart, but I
know not how to help you; it is true,
you are rich, and I am very poor, but
then it is impossible to get at you; if
                                you

you can think of any way, I am ready
to affift." Ah, God! how did I lift up
my eyes to thee, who hadft thus ftrangely
opened once more to me a communication with that fociety from which I had
been fo unfairly wrefted! In moments
like this every thing appears poffible; already I feemed to fee my prifon gates
open, my daughter in my arms, and our
honeft affiftant rich at once in our wealth
and our bleffings. Having had the fore-
fight to prepare another billet, I conveyed it in the fame manner. " Worthy
foldier, is my daughter fafe, and yet in
this Caftle ? if fo, tear away all but the
word, yes, and my foul fhall for ever
blefs you." How pure was the joy with
which I received the precious monofyl-
lable !

To prepare another billet, comprehend-
ing my plan, was a work of time;---with
what perturbation did I undertake it! To
condenfe my meaning to a few words,
and yet leave it obvious to a common
capacity, was not an eafy tafk.---I thus

at

at laſt effected it: " generous friend, win
over him who guards my daughter's door,
while you are at mine, and I will ſhare with
both of you the rich jewels I poſſeſs, of
which you ſaw only the ſmalleſt.   Ob-
ſerve the form of the keys Dunlop brings
----buy many as near them as poſſible,
and ſo various that ſome may certainly
fit.----Procure likewiſe two regimental
ſuits, that we may paſs the gate un-
queſtioned; if you can raiſe the little
money neceſſary for this, fear not to ſpend
it; I will make your fortune in the moment our doors are opened.----Reſtore me
to my daughter---conduct us to the gate,
and we will both beſeech the Almighty
to bleſs the riches we will joyfully leave
in your hands."

Having diſpatched this, I waited the
deciding hour with the moſt anxious impatience; and ſcarce dared to raiſe my
eyes from the ground, leſt Dunlop ſhould
read in them aught that might alarm his
ſuſpicions.

4   How

How to difpofe of myfelf, and daughter, when out of the Caftle, was a queftion I could not decide upon; but I flattered myfelf that as we fhould have fome hours ftart of our perfecutors, we might reach London; where it would not be eafy to apprehend perfons who had been imprifoned without any judicial enquiry or fentence.---A greater fear however than that occurred.---How if thefe foldiers fhould not be honeft---the reward we muft beftow would prove what we poffeffed, and our lives might be the forfeit. Yet fuch was my defperate ftate, that even this reafonable apprehenfion did not induce me one moment to hefitate.

The appointed time revolved, and I received another billet. "Be ready when all is quiet---every thing is prepared if any of the keys fit. My comrade and felf muft go with you to fecure our own fafety, but it will likewife fecure yours." Oh, how did my heart bound at this happy intelligence;---my languor, my lamenefs, all was forgotten.. Maternal love, and ha-

bitual

bitual fear, feemed to wing me with fupernatural powers.

As the important moment approached,
I knelt and devoutly invoked the affiftance of heaven. Ah! not in vain; for the
firft effort of the foldiers was fuccefsful. I
reached out a rich and ready hand to
each.---They received the contents with
extreme fatisfaction, and conjuring me to
preferve the moft profound filence, locked the doors, and led me to the further fide
of the Caftle. At the threfhold of my
daughter's apartment they gave into my
hand the difguifes I had defired, and a-
greed to wait till we were ready. The
tender meltings Mothers only know thrill-
ed thro' my heart, and fweetened every apprehenfion, as I gently made my way
thro' a dark room towards one where I
faw lights ftill burning: but fearful of
alarming my fweet girl, I hefitated at the
door. What was my aftonifhment to perceive that the apartment was gay, magni-
ficient, and illuminated!---I thought at firft
that anxiety had bewildered my faculties,

but

but their truth became evident when they
centred at once on my daughter; who,
elegantly habited, had funk on a couch
afleep. A writing table covered with
due implements ftood before her, on
which lay a letter, it appeared to me fhe
had been anfwering. The deadly cold-
nefs, the namelefs fenfations this extraordinary fcene could not but occafion, at
once fufpended even the moft powerful
emotions of nature. A repulfion fo terrible obliged me to reft my head againft
the pillar of the door, and ftruggle fome
time with the ficknefs and confufion of
my foul, ere I could gather ftrength to
penetrate into the fact. She ftill continued to enjoy a repofe, it feemed to me I
never fhould know again, and I had now
loft the wifh of awakening her; of efcap-
ing---alas, even of exifting! Slowly at
length I tottered toward the table, and
catching at the two letters I mentioned,
appeared to grafp in them my very fate.
The fignature of the firft made its contents

Y 2   almoft

almoſt needleſs. "A few days, a very few
days more, moſt charming of women, and
I ſhall be able to indulge your every wiſh
---every thing is now in train :---pain me
not therefore in thus preſſing an impoſſibility. The heart of your Mother is inexor-
able to me---it has ever been ſo, and I neither dare truſt her with the truth, or you
with one ſo prejudiced, till the law ſhall have
annulled my deteſted marriage, and the
King agree to my union with yourſelf.--
I live but in that hope ; it ſupports me
under all theſe long and tedious abſences.
Why will you call the ſafe home in which
you are encloſed, a priſon ?---The whole
world appears ſo to him who beholds with
pleaſure only that ſpot where you dwell.
To-morrow I ſhall ſteal an hour to paſs
with you---ſmile for that hour, my beloved, and bleſs wiih a welcome, your devoted Somerſet."

Of what various, what manifold miſe-
ries is the human heart ſuſceptible?
none of all the exquiſite variety I had
hitherto known, ever ſurpaſſed this new
one.

one. My difdainful foul recoiled from
even the dear object of its affections---
hypocrify, that effence of all vices, had
ftolen into her heart under the name of
love, and blighted the virtues yet bloffom-
ing---fearfully I perufed her letter, to
end every doubt.

"What ages of folitude, of fuffering
does your love, my lord, impofe on me!
In vain you would fill up that place in
my heart, a parent fo juftly revered muft
ever hold. But you ftill talk of to-morrow, and to-morrow---alas, it is a day
that may perhaps never come---you think
me vapourifh, but you know not how
ftrangely my illnefs increafes---it is acute
and violent---Oh that I could lay my
burning head one moment on my mother's
bofom!---Catherine gave me fome whey
yefterday; I don't know,---perhaps I wrong
her, but I have not been myfelf fince.
A thoufand gloomy images have taken
poffeffion of my mind; my eager ear is
filled with imaginary knells; I could fancy myfelf dying: you will laugh perhaps

at this weakneſs, but I cannot conquer it---if I ſhould indeed judge right, releaſe my mother, I conjure you, and conceal forever from her————"

Ah, what? exclaimed I in the moſt terrible agony, for at this unfiniſhed ſentence the letter broke off.---Diſdain, ſuſpenſe, anguiſh, contended within me, and ſhook my frame like the laſt ſtruggle of nature.---Of all the horrors that bewildered my mind, one, one alone, could my ſenſes aſcertain.---My hapleſs girl was indeed dying---wan and ſunken were thoſe cheeks late ſo florid---the icy fingers of death were impreſſed upon her temples, and the eyes ſhe heavily opened, as her woe-ſtruck mother dropt upon earth, had no longer either life, beauty, or luſtre.---Oh, that my ſoul had eſcaped in the groan which followed this horrible conviction!---She faintly ſhrieked, and remained in a kind of ſtupor; tenderneſs, however, ſoon predominated over every other ſenſation.---I threw my arms round her in ſilence, and the tears which deluged her cheeks, alone declared what
passed

paſſed in my ſoul.---Still ſhe uttered not a word, but griped my hands as though the pangs of death were indeed upon her.   I in vain conjured, intreated her to ſpeak; it was long ere ſhe had courage to enter into a detail which ſhe had neither breath or voice to go through.   " Condemn me not wholly, my mother, at length cried the dear one, however appearances may incenſe you.   I aſk for only life enough to acquit myſelf, and will to my laſt moment thank the God who reſtores me to your arms, though only to bluſh away my being in them.   Yet have I no other crime to avow than that re·ſerve unconquerably interwoven in my nature.---Alas, yeſterday I thought it a virtue.---Heaven will, perhaps, give me ſtrength to go through the ſtory, at leaſt, I ought to make the effort.---Oh, deign to pardon my compelled abruptneſs, and hear me with patience !

" At the moment which firſt preſented Prince Henry to our knowledge, he was accompanied by the Earl of Somerſet.---How my eyes conceived the partiality my

reaſon

reafon could never erafe I know not,
but they decided at once in his favor.---
Whether the Earl perceived the involun-
tary diftinction, or was led by an equal
one on his own part, is alike unknown
to me; but I underftood the reluctance
with which he gave way to the Prince,
whom he left with us---the contempt
with which you mentioned Lord Somerfet, ftrangely fhocked and alarmed me;
yet (may I own it) I fecretly accufed the
moft upright heart exifting of pride and
prejudice; and found a thoufand reafons
for fuddenly difputing a judgment which
had hitherto been the rule of my own.——
During the frequent vifits Prince Henry
paid you, when prudence induced you
to fend me abroad; alas, to what a
temptation did you unconfcioufly expofe
me! Somerfet availed himfelf of thofe
opportunities, and by diftant homage
confirmed the prepoffeffion I had already
conceived.---What fhame, what forrow,
what humiliation, has it coft me!---Can
you ever know a more exquifite mifery
than to beftow your heart unworthily?

to

o be humbled without guilt----com-
pelled to blush hourly for errors not your
own----and reduced to a perpetual conflict with thofe powerful and natural
emotions which form under more fortunate circumftances the felicity of youth!
Senfible by the curious attention of
others, how injurious that of the Earl
might in time become, I requefted leave
to remain at home; and awed, in fpite
of myfelf, by your fentiments, boldly
refolved to facrifice the erroneous inclination of my heart, and received the vows
of Prince Henry. To fee you happy,
to flatter him with the hope of being fo,
for a time elevated and amufed my mind;
but folitude foon reftored it to its favorite
object: Somerfet ftill prefented himfelf,
and I took pleafure in the tears in which
I drowned his admired image. By fome
means or other I found letters from him
frequently in my chamber.----I dared not
enquire how, left I fhould awaken your
fufpicions; alas, perhaps that was one
of the fine-fpun webs with which love
ever

ever veils its errors! I found him regularly informed of all our defigns;---I
knew it was in his power to crofs them
by a word; and I began to efteem him
for daring to be filent. During the laft
progrefs of the King, Somerfet refolved
to profit by the abfence of Henry, and,
apprized of the interviews we granted
the Prince in the pavilion in the garden,
as well as of my habit of fitting there,
determined to take the chance of plead-
ing his caufe. My ftay was by the rifing
of the moon unufually prolonged on the
evening he had felected to prefent himfelf
before me. The pale light ferved only to
fhadow out his form---any human one muft
at fuch a moment have appalled me.---I
fhrieked, and was half fainting when the
found of his voice diffipated my terror.
Surprize, perhaps joy, that inftantaneous
confidence we ever repofe in the object
beloved, doubtlefs reaffured him. I was
fcarce confcious I had granted the audience he demanded, till he fell at my
feet to thank me. The manner in which
he

he avowed his paffion, made me fenfible too late that I had ill-difguifed my
own; I know not whether I fhould have
had refolution to attempt doing fo much
longer, had not our converfation been
fuddenly interrupted by Henry. The
Prince, to my inexpreffible difmay, entered the pavillion.----My voice had drawn
him thither, but the found of Somerfet's
made him retreat in contemptuous filence.
The Earl would have followed, but I
caught his arm and obftinately withheld
him :----then conjuring him to haften to
his boat, I flew after the Prince. Henry
had thrown himfelf on the feat near the
terrace; but fenfible of the neceffity of
feparating him and the Earl at fuch a
crifis, I intreated the Prince to accompany me to the houfe. The light of the
moon enabled me judge from his bewildered air of the diftraction of his mind.
I had not courage to break a filence he
voluntarily maintained: yet to part under appearances fo equivocal was impoffible. I hefitated at length a faint explanation.

nation. "Could you contradict the evidence of my senses, madam, sighed the Prince in a low and tender tone, I might wish to hear you: as it is, spare me, I conjure you, on a subject so hateful. I have nothing to reproach you with but a reserve which led me to deceive myself.----Adieu, I promise you inviolable silence.----He who once hoped to constitute your felicity, disdains to interfere with it. Yet one truth I ought perhaps to apprize you of: your happy, your favored lover, is married; think not I wish to reap any advantage from this information---never more shall I breathe a vow at your feet —Oh, Mary! you have undone me!" He wrung my hands in an agony of passion, and rushed through the garden to conceal the sobs which continued to pierce my heart through my ear. What a night did I pass!—sad prelude to so many miserable ones. I readily absented myself the next day at the Prince's usual hour of visiting us. I never saw him afterwards without pain, humiliation, and

and conftraint; though he omitted nothing likely to reconcile me to himfelf.
During the fatal illnefs into which he fell,
how continually did my heart reproach
me with increafing, if not caufing it?
and how deeply was my injuftice to his
merit punifhed, in the mortifying conviction that Somerfet had dared to deceive me?—What prayers did I offer up
for Henry's recovery —What vows to
atone for my error, by a life devoted to
him! Alas, I was not worthy a lover fo
noble; and heaven recalled his purer
effence, while yet unfullied. The fenfe
of a hopelefs and unworthy paffion mingled with the deep grief I could not but
feel for his lofs. A ficklinefs and difguft
fucceeded---rank, royalty, diftinction,
every worldly advantage combined, could
not have diffipated the gloom of my
mind, or reconciled me for a moment
to fociety. I took no pleafure in the
hopes, you, my dear, my generous mother, cherifhed for me; but I would not
be ungrateful, and therefore concealed
my

my ideas. Thus impreſſed, what merit was there in that philoſophy which enabled me to become your comforter under a reverſe I ſcarcely felt?—Oh, that my errors, my misfortunes, had ended here—that I had breathed my laſt on your revered boſom while yet unconſcious of wounding it! When the vain hope of freedom made you ſolicit for a limited portion of air and exerciſe, how could you foreſee the fatal conſequences of that periodical indulgence! In the firſt of theſe ſolitary walks, Somerſet preſented himſelf before me; not the creſted, aſpiring favorite; but the ſelf-accuſing, the pale, the humble lover.---My eyes reſiſted the impulſe of my heart, and turned haughtily from him; but he hung on my robe, he intreated he conjured,---he *would* be heard.---I feel I ſhall not have time to enter into the long explanation of his conduct which won from me an unwilling pardon ſuffice it to ſay, that he knew every, the moſt ſecret, tranſaction in our houſe, nor ventured to marry till convinced I was be-

4

betrothed to Prince Henry. But, oh!
the wretch he espoused!—Never may
you know the crimes of which she has
too probably been guilty.! It was to
Somerset's interposition we owed the prolongation of those lives, the pride and
rage of the King had devoted from the
moment he read the papers he took a
malicious pleasure in destroying.---Still
anxious for me, the Earl owned he had
persuaded James to imprison us in this
Castle, as well to secure our safety, as to
provide us those comforts and conveni-
encies our ·royal relation would have deprived us of.

I could not be insensible to services like
these; and finding my wrath began to
abate, he awakened my pity, by de-
scribing the domestic miseries an unhappy marriage had imposed on him.
The tears with which my wounded soul
blotted this picture, induced him still
farther to explain himself. His hopes
of a divorce seemed rationally grounded,
and I could not but enter into his views

on

on that head.---I was not however able to perſuade him you would ever think as I did, and weakly promiſed a ſecreſy I ought to have ſeen the danger of.---Yet, the prejudice which induced you to impute even our impriſonment to him, ſeemed ſo fixed, ſo unalterable, that though a thouſand times the integrity of my nature tempted me to unfold to you the only ſecret my boſom ever teemed with, I ſhrunk before a mind ſo diſguſted, nor dared to utter one ſyllable might pain you. The delays of Somerſet, however neceſſary, alarmed and diſtreſſed me.---I became cold and melancholy; and too delicate to confide to him the true cauſes of this alteration, he ſoon aſſigned a falſe one. Peeviſhneſs and altercation now robbed our interviews of all their ſweetneſs.---He often reproached me with having opened my heart to you, who alone could thus ſhut it againſt him.---Diſdain urged me one day to aſſure him I would do ſo, the firſt moment I again beheld you.---He left me in a tranſport of rage. Alas, my heart
became

became fenfible of one every way equal to it, when I found I was not permitted to return to your prifon.----I refufed to admit him to that allotted for me, and gave vent to every extravagance fo unforefeen an injury muft excite.----His anfwer convinced me that this ftep had long been meditated. He affured me " he would fooner die than reftore me to a mother who had ever hated, detefted, and defpifed him without any reafon, till his claim took place of hers, and he could call me his wife." The cruel remembrance of what you muft fuffer, foon reduced me to intreaties, and folemn promifes of continued fecrefy. " They were now, he replied, too late;----that he could not fuppofe it poffible I fhould be able to conceal from you the caufe of my abfence; and this, juftly ftrengthening the unreafonable difguft and hatred you already felt towards him, would make you go any lengths to prevent a union you muft naturally abhor."——To this he added all he thought likely to foothe my

em-

embittered spirit, and solemnly assured me
your mind was relieved, by a conviction
that this separation was only in consequence of a new order from court.——
Although I saw in this mode of conduct a
chicanery and little art, my nature disdained, I was yet glad to imagine it
lightened to you the heavy affliction our
separation could not but cause. I felt
too late the error of mental reservation,
and had sufficient reason to think every
evil might branch out from that little
root. Having in vain contended with
the man, no less master of my life than
fate, I at length was wearied into for-
giving him. The divorce was now in great
forwardness, and the manifold iniquities
of the fiend in human shape he had married, such as could not but shock, and interest, a heart disposed to love him. A
thousand busy projects passed daily from
his brain to mine, and often intervened
between myself and a mother so revered.
Every hour that went over my head made
it more impossible for me to appear before
you

you but as his wife, and I became as eager
as himfelf for a day which heaven had
pre-ordained I fhould never fee. One
who purfued her point more effectually,
has feverely punifhed all my youthful er-
rors---Oh may my premature death be received by him who made me, as an ex-
piation!---How fhall I tell you---and yet
I muft----I have often thought my food
tinctured with poifon—yefterday—Alas,
my mother, where is now your fortitude?
—where is that fublime refignation I
have feen you exert?---forget the vain
hopes you once formed for me---forget
that I am your daughter; oh think the
erring wretch this awful moment recalls,
was born to embitter the days that yet
remain to you, and adore, even in this
painful moment, the mercy of the Almighty.---If have not finned beyond forgivenefs, gracioufly extend yours to me
while yet I am fenfible of the bleffing."

As fhe threw herfelf into my arms, every
feature feemed fhrunk, and moulded by
the fingers of death---Alas! what became

Z 2   of

of me at this crisis! her paroxysms
were scarce more dreadful than those that
seized upon my soul—every emotion of
love, friendship, and kindred, appeared
tranquillity, when compared with the wild,
uncontroulable anguish of the robbed, the
ruined mother. Perpetually ready to
give vent to the tumultuous execrations
my heart pronounced against the artful,
insidious traitor, who had alienated her affections, and warped the rectitude of her
mind, an intuitive conviction that such
a transport would vainly embitter the
little time remaining to her, obliged me to
confine to sighs and groans all the miseries
of the moment. I drew her fondly to my
bosom, and poured over her pale con-
vulsed cheeks, a heart-broken mother's
solemn absolution.

One horror only could be added to a
scene like this, nor was it wanting. The
centinels, weary of waiting, and startled
by our groans, now abruptly entered the
chamber.—Scared at the sight of my
daughter expiring in my arms, the sense
of

of their own danger foon over-ruled
every other; they urged, they conjured
me to leave my Mary, now apparently
lifelefs; but they urged, they conjured
in vain.---On her, I was fo foon to refign
to her Creator, my whole foul was now
fixed.---The dear one faintly revived, but
ftruck with inconceivable horror at fight
of the foldiers, fhe relapfed into con-
vulfions, griping me ftill clofer. Ah,
God, the cold chill that followed!
when I found her hold relax at once---
the world vanifhed from before my eyes
---they beheld only the fair form, which
fought a grave on the bofom where it
firft found a being.---Infpired with the
fiercenefs of a favage, I grafped her yet
clofer, fhrieking tremendoufly, and with
a ftrength furely fupernatural. The confufed and incenfed foldiers having ufed
every perfuafion in vain, made the moft
violent efforts to fever me from the laft,
the deareft, the only object of my love.
Threats, intreaties, art, and force, however, were alike vain----nothing could

Z 3   win,

could tear her from me.   They prefented
at length their bayonets to my bofom,
and beheld me with furprize dare the
blow.----Perhaps they had really pierced
., but that fome women, attendant on
my daughter, now rufhed into the room.
Fears for their own fafety obliged the
foldiers to forbear urging or enforcing
me further.   They feized the intruders,
left any of them fhould efcape, and having bound them, fought fafety in flight.
A terrible calm fucceeded my intenfe
defperation----the blood which had tu-
multuoufly burnt along every vein, now
returned in torrents, to choak up, and
drown my heart.----The black fumes
mounted thence to my brain.----With a
grief-glazed eye, I contemplated the pale
and precious cheek from whofe rich color-
ing I of late drew life, till ignorant that I
either fuffered, or exifted.

*   *   *   *   *   *   *

Seldom

Seldom enough myfelf to diftinguifh
the fhadowy forms that flitted round my
bed, and always too indifferent to utter
a fingle queftion, I opened not the curtain, nor cared who was beyond it.—
Vague and ftifled exclamations alone informed me of the danger of that fatal
fire which raged within my veins:---
danger did I fay?---I ought rather to have
called it relief. During the fhort intervals of my delirium, I voluntarily funk
in filence under the gloom and debi-
lity it left. Suddenly I was feized with
fuch flutters, and gafpings, as feemed to
indicate an immediate termination of
every human infliction.---My weary foul
hovered at the gate of its prifon, and I
felt as if a fingle word would releafe it;
but I had neither ability or inclination to
pronounce that word; and though I perceived every curtain was undrawn to give
me air, I raifed not my quivering eyelids to diftinguifh the two perfons who
anxioufly held each hand, as watching for

Z 4   the

the laſt beat of the faint and hurried pulſe.

While thus in the very ſtruggle and fluctuation incident to parting nature, a voice ſuddenly reached my receding ſenſes---a voice ſo mellow, calm, and holy, that life yet lingered on it. I diſtinguiſhed theſe words : " oh, Almighty God! with whom do live the ſpirits of the juſt made perfect, when they are delivered from their earthly priſons; we humbly commend the ſoul of this thy ſervant, our dear ſiſter, into thy hands, as into thoſe of a faithful Creator, and moſt merciful Saviour!" A faint effort I made to releaſe my hands, with the deſign of raiſing them towards heaven, cauſed the prayer to ceaſe. An emotion I could not reſiſt, made me lift my dim eyes to behold, if not abſolutely an angel, the human being that moſt reſembled one. At a table near my bed knelt a Clergyman, whoſe reverend locks time had entirely bleached, but it had taken nothing from his fine eyes, which ſeemed

to

to reflect the divinity he served---care
and experience had worn traces in every
perfect feature; and the pale purity of
virtue, chastened alike by sorrow and
resignation, had succeeded to the vivid
hues of youth, hope, and health. I uttered a sigh, and faint exclamation.---
A sweet, yet sad, pleasure, wandered
through my exhausted frame, thus to be
assured I had reached the very point of
my being. Some women decently ar-
rayed in black having assisted my infirm
and venerable comforter to rise, conducted him to the side of my bed, and
retired. With a graciousness peculiar to
himself, he adjured me, since the mercy
of the Almighty had unexpectedly restored my intellects, to profit by the
indulgence in preparing my soul to appear before him. An impulse of gratitude made me raise my hand to take his,
that sympathetically trembled over me,
but even this trifling motion made me
sensible I had on many blisters, which
wrung my feeble sense even to fainting.

The

The women, as is usual in desperate ca-
ses, gave me some vivifying cordials,
and again retired. The reverend stranger
once more addressed me, praising the Almighty for the restoration of my intel-
lects---they were indeed restored, for, oh!
the recollection of that dismal event which
rendered their loss a blessing, returned upon my mind, and made me loath
the succors I could owe only to the detested hand that had consummated my
woes! "Oh, you, cried I, in a broken
voice, who thus seek to comfort the miserable, inform me first to whom I owe
the benefit?" He paused a moment---
his gracious eyes glanced upward, and
having thus consulted with his Creator,
he answered me with firmness; "that
his name was De Vere; the houshold
Chaplain of the Earl of Somerset."---
At that abhorred title I shut my eyes as
though I could have shut out retrospecti-
on, and waved to him to leave me.---
"Rash, unfortunate woman, returned he
in a solemn and yet tender tone, religion
                                    does

does not permit me to obey you---would
you bear into a better world, the pride,
the paſſions, the prejudices, which have
certainly embittered, perhaps, ſhortened
your days, in this?---Dare you preſent to
the pure ſource of good, your great, your
glorious Creator, a ſoul yet ſullied with
voluntary frailties and human imperfection?—Are you not on the point of ceaſing
to ſuffer, wherefore then ſhould you not
ceaſe to reſent? Religion enjoins you to
forget the faults of others, and contemplate only your own.—Attend to truth,
and I will impart it to you---reſolve to
be patient, and I will pour balm into the
deep wounds of human calamity---con-
troul your paſſions, and I will elevate
them, even under the ſtruggles of parting nature, by hopes which ſhall ſurely
be realized, becauſe they centre in im-
mortality."—The author of univerſal being ſeemed to ſpeak to me through his
Miniſter—the gathering tumult ſtood ſuſ-
pended. " You addreſs not an ingrate,
returned I feebly; I have walked in peace
through

life with my God, and fain would I die
fo: though furely to remember the wretch,
who precipitates me into eternity by a
grief too pungent for endurance, with
charity, or compofure, exceeds my ability. If you have aught to reveal that
may allay this irritation, be truly generous in unfolding it---if otherwife, prefent fuch images only to my mind as may
drive from it that of a villain, whofe
offences you cannot extenuate; nor double the agonies even you cannot relieve."
" It is my only intention, madam, replied he.—Alas, I would not probe your
wounds even to heal them!---If it is neceffary to fuffer ere we can feel, believe
me, I want not even that power of fympathizing with you; yet, muft I reconcile my divine and human character, by
vindicating the innocent, while I foothe
the unfortunate; though even the wealth
of nations could not tempt me for one
moment to palliate guilt. Have you
courage to hear a letter, given me in
hopes of the prefent opportunity?" I
con-

controuled myfelf, and figned to him to
read.

"In what words, moft injured, moft
unfortunate of women, fhall the wretch
who has unconfcioufly deftroyed your
peace, and his own, deprecate the wrath
his very idea muft occafion?----Alas,
overwhelmed with grief, horror, defpair,
every killing fenfation, (guilt alone excepted) his punifhmeent is as acute as
even malice could wifh it.

"To fill up the meafure of my afflictions, I am informed that the blow which
has robbed my foul of its deareft hope,
ftruck at·your life---that even in the
wildnefs of delirium your curfes purfue
me, and you are ready to fink into the
grave with unabated hatred.---If returning recollection fhould ever enable you
to read, or hear, thefe genuine dictates of
a breaking heart, do it, madam, I conjure you, the late juftice of an acquittal.
By the fpotlefs fpirit of the dear loft angel my fatal love deprived you of, hear,
pity---if poffible, forgive me.---Can you
for

for a moment believe I would have touched a life, dear, precious, to me, even as
to yourfelf?

The abandoned woman, to whom heaven as a punifhment for all my fins united
me, difcovered by fome unknown means
thofe views I thought impenetrable; and
forefeeing in their completion her own
difgrace, and ruin, fhe took a deadly
means to fave herfelf from both.---Alrea-
dy but too familiar with poifon, and with
death, fhe found among the maids attending on my dear loft love, one bafe
enough to aid her in tranflating an angel
too early to the fkies. To fay, that I
hate, deteft, and fhun the execrable mon-
fter, is furely needlefs---I even refign
her to your juftice, nor do I wifh to
fhelter myfelf from it, if you ftill think
me guilty.

" The laft words of an expiring faint
are not more ardent, more fincere than
thofe I now utter.---Oh, ftrive then to
live, madam, nor let my agonized foul
have the additional misfortune of fhort-
ening

ening your days, and lingering under your curfe!"

Alas, of what importance are thefe late convictions?---When a ball has gone through the heart, we are incapable of heeding the quarter it comes from.——

I could not however refuse credence to this letter, and accufing myfelf of having hitherto perhaps wanted candor towards the author, I acquitted myfelf to him, by affording him my forgivenefs.

Nature, ever fhrinking from diffolution, is eafily recalled to a lingering fufferance; but the exhaufted foul no more can recover its powers. The activity which once fupported me was gone forever.——

The venerable divine I have mentioned ftill watched over me, and by the holieft confolations contended with the apathy into which I was finking.—But who could heal a heart broken by fo many forrows?—That it *was* broken alone could confole me. Deftined to turn my dim eyes around this vaft globe without

4

finding

findidg one object on which they could
rest, De Vere led them towards heaven;
he bade me remember that my treasure
was only removed, not taken wholly from
me; and that every passing day brought
me nearer to recovering it.

For the execrable woman who had,
to the ruin of her own soul, murdered
the only hope of mine, I ventured not
to imagine a punishment.----I dared not
trust myself with so dangerous a wish.——
No, I consigned her to the God she had
offended, and he has, even in this world,
fearfully avenged me.

The pious De Vere shewed, by preserving and restoring my jewels, the equi-
ty of his nature, and I made him such
acknowledgments as must flatter his
heart, and establish his fortune. As soon
as I thought myself equal to the journey,
I resolved to retire to France, that I
might at least expire in peace, and be-
sought him to accompany me.——Not able
without ingratitude immediately to quit
his patron, he comforted me with the
hopes

hopes of foon partaking my voluntary exile.

How unworthy the man who won the innocent heart of my tranflated angel ever was of it, I had foon another convincing proof.---Becaufe I refifted the impulfes of defpair---becaufe I liftened to the dictates of virtue and religion, and deigned to live out the days appointed by the Almighty, his narrow foul began to believe mine fufceptible of human confolation: he dared to intrude upon me in the name of the King, late offers of acknowledgment, diftinction, fortune.----Heavens! how could either imagine I would owe aught to thofe I muft alike look down upon?---The very idea had well nigh difarranged my feeble faculties, and deftroyed the religious compofure of my grief. It however convinced me that no oppofition would be made to my quitting that prifon in which I left, alas, all worth enclofing.——I launched once more into the immenfe world, unknown---unindeared, and willing to be fo.

My fever returned on my landing in
France with the moſt mortal ſymptoms.
—Ah! can I fail here to commemorate
the ſecond angel heaven ſent to my aſſiſtance? The arrival of the Embaſſador in his way toward England, though
at firſt an inconvenience, in ſo narrow
an aſylum as an inn, eventually prolonged
my days. His dear and lovely daughter was informed of my ſtate---ſhe indulged the ſublime impulſe of humanity,
which led her towards the bed, where
lay a forlorn wretch who appeared ready
to draw her laſt breath in ſilent affliction.
She ſummoned her noble father's phyſician, whoſe ſkill relieved one it could
not ſave.---She even deigned to outſtay
the Embaſſador; and, by a glorious
principle known only to ſuperior natures,
began to love the wretch ſhe ſuccored.
A virtue ſo exemplary almoſt reconciled
me to the world I am ſhortly to quit.—
Sweet Adelaide, when in this faint por-
trait you ſurvey yourſelf, ſigh for thoſe
decaying powers which cannot render it
more ſtriking.

That

That my decline has been prolonged till this narrative is concluded, I do not regret; and by compliance, I have evinced my sense of your friendship:---I have now only to die.---Yet, alas, it is with regret I present to your youthful eyes so melancholy a chart of my voyage through life.---Suffer it not to damp your hopes, but rather let it blunt your sense of misfortune: for have I not said already, that consummate misery has a moral use, in teaching the repiner at little evils to be juster to his God and himself?----Glorious though inscrutable are all his ways, and short as my time now is, he has suffered me to see his righteous retribution. Condemnation, infamy, and solitude, are henceforth the portion of Somerset, and his execrable Countess.----A similar crime, long buried in oblivion, has been proved upon them, without my having once disturbed the sacred ashes of my Mary. An act so atrocious has broke the tye which bound De Vere to the Earl, and I every day expect him. I struggle to retain my last breath till I can give it up in his presence, assured

that

that his superior soul will prepare my
frail one for a long hereafter, and decently
dispose of the mortal frame I soon must
leave behind me.

Dear and lovely friend, you are now
in England.----Already perhaps your feet
have trod lightly over those spots where
my happiness withered.—Ah! if sensibility should lead you more thought-
fully to retrace them, check every painful emotion, by recollecting I shall then
be past the power of suffering.—Yet,
when your noble father reconducts you
to the home you was born to embellish,
grant a little to the weakness of mortality,
and linger once more on the spot where
we met: the pious De Vere will there
attend your coming.------Accept from
his hand the casket I bequeath, and
suffer him to lead you to the nameless
grave where he shall have interred my
ashes: drop on it a few of those holy
tears with which virtue consecrates misfortune; then raise your eyes with those
of your venerable conductor, and in a
better world look for   MATILDA.

F I N I S.

GOTHIC NOVELS

ARNO PRESS

in cooperation with

McGRATH PUBLISHING COMPANY